CRAZY PA

(John) Beverley Nichols was born
at Marlborough College and Balliol
first of his more than sixty books, a n̴...̴ ̴a̴l̴l̴e̴d̴ *Prelude*, in 1920. While a
student, Nichols became known for his outspokenness on political topics
and issues like women's rights; he continued to espouse strong views
throughout life, becoming a pacifist and advocate for disarmament after
the First World War and later, as an openly gay man, an advocate for
sexual tolerance.

Nichols wrote several novels in the 1920s and 1930s, including *Crazy
Pavements* (1927), a satire inspired by Nichols's own experiences among
the 'Bright Young People', which became a bestseller and was reprinted
frequently throughout the following decade. He published a volume of
autobiography covering his first twenty-five years, appropriately entitled
Twenty-Five, in 1926, and in 1932 published his first work on gardening,
Down the Garden Path, which has remained continuously in print. Best
known today for his gardening volumes, Nichols was a versatile writer in
many genres, publishing poetry, plays, nonfiction, children's books, and a
number of well-regarded mystery novels.

Beverley Nichols met the actor Cyril Butcher in the early 1930s, and
the two became lifelong partners. Nichols died in 1983.

David Deutsch earned his Ph.D. from Ohio State University and joined
the English Department at the University of Alabama in 2011. He teaches
courses in modern American and British drama, poetry, and prose.

CRAZY PAVEMENTS

by

BEVERLEY NICHOLS

With a new introduction by

DAVID DEUTSCH

𝔎𝔞𝔫𝔰𝔞𝔰 𝔠𝔦𝔱𝔶:

VALANCOURT BOOKS

2013

Crazy Pavements by Beverley Nichols
First published London: Jonathan Cape, 1927
First Valancourt Books edition 2013

Published by Valancourt Books, Kansas City, Missouri
Publisher & Editor: JAMES D. JENKINS
20*th Century Series Editor*: SIMON STERN, University of Toronto
http://www.valancourtbooks.com

Library of Congress Cataloging-in-Publication Data

Nichols, Beverley, 1898-1983.
Crazy pavements / by Beverley Nichols ; with a new introduction
by David Deutsch. – First Valancourt Books edition.
pages cm
ISBN 978-1-939140-35-7 (alk. paper)
1. Gossip columnists–England–London–Fiction. 2. Socialites–England–
London–Fiction. 3. Self-realization–Fiction. 4. Bildungsromans. I. Title.
PR6027.I22C73 2013
823'.912–dc23
2013008778

All Valancourt Books publications are printed on acid free paper
that meets all ANSI standards for archival quality paper.

Cover art by Ben Bailey
Set in Dante MT 11/13.5

10 9 8 7 6 5 4 3 2 1

INTRODUCTION

Crazy Pavements (1927) is a *bildungsroman* of debauchery. Reminiscent of Aldous Huxley's *Crome Yellow* (1921) and *Antic Hay* (1923), and anticipating Evelyn Waugh's *Vile Bodies* (1930) and *Put Out More Flags* (1942), Nichols's novel both celebrates and satirizes the decadence of post-War British society. Nichols's hero, Brian Elme, first appears as an unsophisticated young man who has graduated from some anonymous "School," probably a third-rate public school, and been "thrown penniless upon London," where he now works as a gossip columnist (7). Through this job, Brian meets a series of depraved individuals, the broken stones who pave the path to his depravity, i.e. the "crazy pavement" referenced by Nichols's title. Lady Julia, for instance, is rich, beautiful, and intensely manipulative. Lord William Motley over-eats, over-drinks, and takes cocaine. The Hon. Maurice Cheyne is a malevolent sponger, while Lady Anne Hardcastle is a "nymphomaniac" who looks like "an animated intaglio," having undergone no less than seven face lifts (118). This is a fantastic cast and Nichols delights in sketching its scandalous eccentricities.

Seeking some sort of freshness, these sophisticates introduce Brian, and indirectly the reader, into the fascinating, yet poisonous world of the 1920s Bright Young People. For them, life is a "game" to be "played at top speed," with "perpetually high tension," while fighting off fears of "being alone," "of being poor," and "of growing old," a battle that they lose all the faster with their constant rounds of cocktails, dope, and late-night bacchanalias (27). Nichols highlights the degradation of this life through several brilliantly bizarre scenes. One afternoon, Lord William invites Brian to his luxurious home in Queen Anne's Gate where he reveals his hall of masks, each of which he has fashioned to suggest the grotesque psyches of his outwardly refined friends. On another night, while kept waiting in Maurice's flat, Brian discovers slips of paper in a cigarette box and a tantalus reading "THIEF!" and "YOU THINK

I DON'T KNOW, DO YOU?" (111) Maurice has three thousand pounds a year, but fears someone stealing a cigarette or a drink. These characters display a monstrous, egotistical self-indulgence, which Nichols emphasizes through Tanagra Guest's party where "[e]verybody was to be dressed" and "to act as a child" (110). Nichols likely cribbed this scene from an actual 1926 Bright Young People's party, to which guests came as they were "twenty years ago," a curious reversion for party-goers not yet thirty.[1] In Nichols's portrayal, this regression to "infantility" increases disquietingly as socialites converse in baby-talk, scream, and drink champagne scarcely a year after the 1926 General Strike (115).

Huxley and Waugh, too, castigate Britain's dissipated socialites; Nichols, however, rarely satirizes his subjects as mercilessly as his more famous contemporaries. Nichols's depiction of Maurice, for instance, illustrates his sympathy. Maurice seems to epitomize stereotypes linking effeminate, queer men to aristocratic decadence, ridiculousness, and self-loathing. Effeminate men similar to Maurice exist in Rose Macaulay's *The Lee Shore* (1912), in E. F. Benson's *Freaks of Mayfair* (1916), even in Nichols's first novel *Prelude* (1920), where he observes of his hero's preference for singing, dancing and dressing up, "all this may be looked upon as effeminate. What of it?"[2] These characters, however, are fairly docile and any defense of their effeminacy is presented through authorial commentary. Nichols allows Maurice, however, to offer an insistent, even aggressive self-defense. In one particularly chilling scene, Maurice insists to the more masculine Brian, "I'm as natural as you are. . . . I can't help how I'm made." Outlining his agony, he admits to being

> [h]ideously frightened of life. . . . Sometimes I come back from a party and I turn on all the lights and I play the gramophone, and I stand in the middle of the room, just waiting, till I could scream. The room is bright and noisy, but I feel it's full of people, looking at me, condemning me. They crowd round me, out of every door, they climb in at the window, they grin down from the ceiling, and oh, God! . . . they all accuse me. (175-176)

[1] D. J. Taylor, *Bright Young People: The Lost Generation of London's Jazz Age.* New York: Farrar, Straus, and Giroux, 2007. 67.

[2] Beverley Nichols, *Prelude.* London: Chatto and Windus, 1920. 15.

Maurice's psychological trauma, his intense paranoia, is palpable
and these late-night delusions evoke an expressionist nightmare;
or perhaps they recall contemporary courtrooms where same-sex-
desiring men were judged from on high. Still, despite his torment,
Maurice talks back, demanding, "Why should I be accused? Tell
me that" (176). Moreover, if Maurice turns to drugs and alcohol
to escape from his misery, Nichols suggests, society must share
the blame for hounding him. In an age where E. M. Forster felt
he could only publish his *Maurice* (written 1913-14) posthumously,
Nichols's sympathy with the effeminate Maurice is worthy of note.

Equally worthy of note is Nichols's sympathetic portrayal of
Brian's relationship with Walter Moore. Walter is Brian's best
friend, his roommate, and, almost certainly, his lover. Bryan
Connon, Nichols's biographer, reports that "Beverley went to
some lengths to stress the idealistic and sexless nature of [this]
relationship," understandably, as homosexuality was not legal-
ized in Britain until 1967. Yet, Nichols infuses such romance into
the pair's interactions that his later admission that "[o]f course
Brian and Walter were lovers, and Lady Julia was based on one
of those predatory young queens," seems hardly surprising.[1] Julia
tempts Brian, temporarily, from the "jealous" Walter, but Brian
consistently remembers Walter to preserve his sanity (32). When
out of his depth at Lord William's country house, Brian recalls
"how he and Walter had once saved up to go to Cambridge for
a week-end" and "had slept all night in a punt at Grantchester"
(77). Brian's memory of this trip, with its frugal, Rupert Brooke-
like pleasures, comforts him. Similarly, after Tanagra's party, Brian
"wanted to slip his hand through Walter's arm, and lie back on
[their] shabby sofa, and say nothing. And then sleep" (122). Later,
after rejecting Julia's circle, Brian stumbles drunkenly into a bar
and collapses onto Walter's knee. Recognizing Walter, Brian cries
"Don't go . . . I want you – awfully" (218). Walter forgives Brian's
betrayal and the novel concludes with Brian waking and planning a
day swimming in Hyde Park with Walter, who lies sleeping across
the room. In the 1920s, as Nichols once observed, many people

---

[1] Bryan Connon, *Beverley Nichols: A Life*. Portland: Timber Press, 2000. 126-127.

"instinctively shut their eyes" to homosexuality and homosexuality nonetheless persisted, with varying degrees of visibility.[1] For discerning early twentieth-century readers, the homoeroticism of Brian and Walter's relationship would have been fairly obvious. It is notable, then, that the *Times Literary Supplement* applauds Nichols's extrication of Brian from a "bog of sensuality" by returning him to Walter and all that their relationship implies.[2]

Nichols expands British literary conventions considerably here by depicting two healthy, relatively lower-middle-class men in a nurturing romantic relationship. Brian is "strong, slim, arduous" and makes six pounds a week, while Walter Moore is "an ex-naval officer," who maintains a "healthy flush" and is content with "a few shillings in his pocket" (13). Together, they share a cozy but small and shabby flat near the Marble Arch. They are, in many ways, a happier, cohabiting, urban variation on D. H. Lawrence's Cyril Beardsall and the farmer George Saxton in *The White Peacock* (1911), or of the vital but self-tortured middle-class men in Reginald Underwood's *Bachelor's Hall* (1934) or *Flame of Freedom* (1936). Brian and Walter's simple domesticity, moreover, provides a happy alternative to upper-class excesses, cross-class inequalities, and even the delayed happiness between men envisioned in otherwise optimistic novels, such as Rose Allatini's *Despised and Rejected* (1918). Nichols champions, then, for perhaps the first time in British literary history, a fairly physical, if not overtly sexual, homoeroticism between two men with modest incomes as a successful ideal.

This happy conclusion likewise signals Nichols's desire for renewed stability in post-war Britain. Many canonical novels published contemporaneously with *Crazy Pavements* – Ford Madox Ford's *Parade's End* (1924-28), Virginia Woolf's *To the Lighthouse* (1927), and Aldous Huxley's *Point Counter Point* (1928), for instance – evoke both wartime losses scarcely a decade old and the fragility of hope for the future. Nichols evokes these post-war themes throughout *Crazy Pavements*, but is more insistent in his optimism. Brian reconnects with Walter late on "August 4th," the anniver-

---

[1] Beverley Nichols, *Sweet and Twenties*. London: The Quality Book Club, 1958. 103.

[2] "Crazy Pavements." *Times Literary Supplement*. 10 Feb. 1927: 90.

sary of "[t]he war. The *great* war" (215). These italics are carefully ironic, as what was primarily *"great"* about the war, the increasingly pacifist Nichols implies, was the great destruction it caused. Nonetheless, Walter, who as a twenty-six-year-old "ex-naval officer" would have either served or just missed serving, and many others his age are lucky to be alive and this luck is worth celebrating. As such, while Brian considers that "anniversaries" are "vulgar," this evening he "wanted vulgarity" and so he celebrates among the cheap markets near Blackfriars and the bars favored by Walter (215). Walking along, he thinks "[t]his was England. This would go on, triumphant, coarse, obscene, vital, long after Lord William, Maurice, Julia and the rest of them had retired to their futile tombs" (218). It is the British middle and working classes, Brian thinks, who keep the nation, even the Empire strong, and he exults in their continuity.

This is not to say that Nichols endorses unreservedly Brian's optimism. Brian finds "a sort of peace" here, but he does so among people who worry about how "to afford a Sunday dinner, or to pay for their next week's rent" (216). These struggles to acquire hearty food, such as a Sunday roast, and housing are depressing when compared to the abundant, unearned luxuries of Lady Julia and Lord William. Brian's "peace," even if it is a relief from the "smug brilliance" of West End society, is naïve (217). Also naïve is Brian's admiration of a "map" for sale that has "the British Empire splashed so generously in red that Canada, for example, almost infringed upon Mexico," which troubles the "absurd nationalism that made him sing out loud" (218). Troublingly, Brian forgets the violence of imperial expansion on the anniversary of a war between empires.

Nonetheless, throughout this market scene Nichols infuses an expectation that the best elements of British life will continue. Imperialism is violent but Britain's international trade provides "wagons of fruit and vegetables, with pomegranates at a half penny" and "sound Spanish" onions, which are affordable for all (218). Also, there is a *hint* of humor in Canada infringing on Mexico, essentially eliding the United States, Britain's growing rival. Brian, moreover, is "a little drunk. More than a little," having visited several bars, the sort which to Walter symbolize "the England of Chaucer and Johnson and Dickens" (90). This drunkenness, then, differs from that of the Bright Young People. It is part of the "vulgar" vitality of English existence, with its mistakes and its pleasures. Brian, true, overindulges in this vitality, but this brief break from twentieth-century morality leads him to stumble upon Walter. This is not particularly refined, but it is "coarse[ly]" pleasant and by the following morning he has recovered from his excess with no plans to repeat it. Britain, unfortunately, would not recover from the war this quickly and, as we know now, Nazi Germany would lead Europe to repeat its violent excesses all too soon. In 1927, however, Nichols maintained hope for the future and on the final morning of the novel, on August 5th, Brian has matured past his desire for decadence and plans to "scamper with Walter over" London's "clean-swept streets, into the mists of Hyde Park, and splash with a whirl of white and silver into the Serpentine" (219). The world is not perfect and Hyde Park is not Eden. But, swimming in the Serpentine is a new beginning in an experienced world and provides an ardent if imperfect hope for a modern pastoral paradise.

DAVID DEUTSCH
University of Alabama

February 2013

CRAZY PAVEMENTS

To D——

CHAPTER ONE

'SOCIETY *is marvelling at the latest example of the Dowager Lady Macrael's versatility. She is making a collection of the old Scottish ballads and turning them into jazz tunes, employing bagpipes to give the effect of a saxophone. No doubt there will soon be some very jolly parties at Macrael Castle, when the old and the new will be happily blended.'*

Brian Elme stared a little dubiously at the above paragraph, which, after great effort, he had concocted for *The Lady's Mail*, one of the papers with which the womanhood of England appeases its voracious appetite for Society gossip. Was it too obviously a fake? Was it libellous?

No. It certainly wasn't libellous. Even to the most modern mind there could be nothing actually indecent about the bagpipes. Why he had affixed this particular legend to the Dowager Lady Macrael, of all people, he would have found it hard to explain. Perhaps there was something in her photograph, which lay before him, that gave an extra piquancy to the theory. Her face was like a Scottish promontory – rocky and irregular.

Rather wearily, he laid down his pencil and stared out of the window. His 'Gossip' page was almost written, and through his mind floated a grisly procession of coroneted peeresses. He wished that he might never see another Burke's 'Peerage.' He wished there would be a revolution that would sweep all these silly women into the sea. No, he didn't. He would lose his job if that happened. Two more paragraphs to write. He glanced at *The Times* to see who had just left England.

He felt something almost akin to affection for any peeress who departed on a long sea-voyage. She was far out of the reach of the newspapers, and by the time she returned, anything he had written about her would long ago have been forgotten. Ah! Here was one.

'Lady Monk is sailing to-day from Liverpool to visit her son Patrick, who is an undergraduate at Yale.'

That was perfect. The paragraph was already forming in his mind. He looked up Lady Monk in *Debrett*. God had made her the wife of the first Baron Monk, chairman of the well-known firm of Monk and Cartney Ltd., manufacturers of paper bags. Before her marriage she had been Mrs. Elihu James of Chicago, and she was *née* Studenmayer. He therefore sat down and wrote with a sigh:

'Quite a little romance, isn't it, the sailing of the vivacious Lady Monk to her native land? I learn that there was a very long struggle before his lordship (who is doing so much to rebuild our staple industries) would consent to her scheme for Patrick's education at Yale, instead of Cambridge. However, she won the day. And already, I hear, Patrick is one of the most popular students at Yale, largely owing to the uncanny knack with which he has picked up the national sport of baseball.'

There. Nobody could object to that. He had put in a sop to Lord Monk by calling his beastly paper bags 'a staple industry.' He had called Lady Monk vivacious, and if she wasn't vivacious with all that money she deserved to be hung in crepe. As for Patrick . . .

He found himself dreaming about Patrick, wondering what manner of youth he was. Patrick had certainly never had to make a living by writing 'Gossip' paragraphs about people he didn't know, at the rate of six guineas a week. Patrick had never had to rub talcum powder on his only dress-shirt to make it 'do' another time. Patrick had never had to go into a shop and buy rubber solution with which to mend the soles of his shoes. . . . Patrick had never . . .

Brian swallowed, cleared his throat, frowned, and told himself not to be a fool.

One more paragraph. He wanted something with a touch of sentiment. He looked at the clock. It was nearly five o'clock. The columns of *The Times* informed him that no other peeresses were going abroad. Perhaps they were grimly remaining in England in order to read *The Lady's Mail*. About whom should he write? Lady Schooner, and her latest party? No. He had run her to death already. Lady Melluish, the Diana of the Cotswolds? No. She died of delirium tremens last Tuesday, and one couldn't be sentimental with such material. It would have to be his old favourite – Lady Julia.

He had written more about Lady Julia than about any other celebrity because, in spite of the intimate nature of his weekly revelations, she was the only member of his 'Gossip' circle whom he had ever seen. He had been the first to chronicle the fact that she had shingled her blue-black hair. He had attributed to her a passion for white cherries (one of the few passions of which she was really innocent), he had endeavoured, with boyish eloquence, to describe her dresses, and one day in the Park he had followed her, with heart beating high, from the Marble Arch to Kensington Gardens. In that issue of *The Lady's Mail* there had appeared the following paragraph:

'One of the keenest walkers of Society is the exquisite Lady Julia Cressey. She may be observed almost every morning in Hyde Park accompanied by her little white Sealyham, to which she has whimsically given the name of "Bubbles."'

The 'Bubbles' touch was an invention, but the white Sealyham was not. Nor, to tell the truth, was it a Sealyham. But Brian did not know that. Nor did he know that the Lady Julia, when she arrived at her destination had 'whimsically' given a vicious kick to the stray dog which, in the manner of many other stray dogs, both animal and human, had followed her home.

He took up his pencil. If only he had been a poet in the court of a former Lady Julia, that he might write her Silver Sonnets to be sung beneath a medieval moon! But he was not a poet. He was a modern 'Gossip' writer. He would never meet his Lady Julia. She had too many lovers already. The very last time he had seen her she had been coming out of a first night, leaning in all her loveliness on the noble arm of Lord William Motley. He swallowed his love. He swallowed his pride. And, quite carelessly, he wrote the following paragraph, which was to change his whole life . . .

'Curious, isn't it, the way that we are always giving away the secrets of our friends' engagements? Quite a little crop of rumours has been sown in the West End lately, linking together the names of many famous personages. Most of these rumours (as you probably know) are without any foundation whatever. But there is perhaps a teeny little bit of justification for the way in which we are all linking together the names of Lady Julia Cressey and Lord William Motley. . . .'

He laid his head on his hands. He felt tired and sick at heart. Consider him – the hero of this story – and you may for a moment feel troubled that modern civilization should twist the souls of men to such ignoble purposes.

He is twenty. His hair is of that truly golden colour which so often produces high blood-pressure when brought to the notice of old women. He is strong, slim, arduous. In a properly organized Society he would have been something both intelligent and decorative. But in Modern England, where we know exactly how human beings are made and not at all what they are made for, he was a 'Gossip' writer.

To you, perhaps, the 'Gossip' writer is something mean, and slightly comic. To me, he is one of the world's great tragedies. I am sick at heart for these lingerers in the outer courts of Society, with their brave gentility, their ears pricked for some wearisome trifle about some wearisome woman. There are exceptions, of course – the lordly ones who stroll into a night club, drink wine with a Cabinet Minister, and syndicate their secrets throughout the world on the morrow, for a consideration. But they are the exceptions. The majority consist of young men like Brian, with a single dress-shirt, and a crying hunger to get out of the whole thing.

Why, then, did Brian adopt this ignoble profession? For the same reason as any other mental or physical prostitute. He had to live. His parents had died in his infancy, and he had never known what it was to possess a home. Of his father he knew nothing. Of his mother he recalled only a dim, simple figure who, on her death, had left him with a few broken tags of wisdom, which had obstinately refused to be forgotten throughout the years. They were strange tenets on which to base a philosophy, such as:

1. Patent leather 'draws' the feet.
2. Eating flies makes cats thin.
3. October is the prettiest time of the year.
4. Cauliflower is good for growing bones.
5. Work at a table with the sun shining over your right shoulder.
6. Eat a little bread before going to church to stop rumbling during the sermon.
7. Finger-nails should be cut round, and toe-nails square.

He clung to these memories, because they had a vaguely comforting influence on him, at his school, and during his holidays at the house of a dreary aunt. But they were poor weapons with which to fight the world when he had been thrown penniless upon London. He had a dream of writing. By chance he had drifted into *The Lady's Mail*. They learnt there that an acquaintance of his, a certain speckly faced peer whom he had frequently kicked at school, had just made a secret marriage. In other words, he had provided *The Lady's Mail* with a 'scoop,' and on the strength of this he was engaged as a 'Gossip' writer. They imagined him to possess an extensive aristocratic connection. Alas! The speckly faced one was his sole acquaintance in the peerage. But hunger had prompted him to lie, and to invent, as we have already observed. He had been inventing for nearly two years.

Such was Brian's past.

He gathered together his copy, and walked across to a door marked 'Editress.' He knocked.

'*Come* in.'

These two words were uttered in a descending third. That was a good sign. It was only when the 'come' was uttered on the note C and the 'in' was pitched on a rather acrid 'E' that Mrs. Gossett was going to be really tiresome.

He entered. A thin, bunched-up woman of about thirty-eight, with very tousled hair, large horn-rimmed glasses and bare arms, held out a skittish hand for his copy.

'Naughty,' she said. 'You're ten whole minutes late.'

'I'm awfully sorry. But I think the stuff's all right.'

Instead of answering, she bent her head almost on to her shoulder, and leered at him sideways, showing a great deal of white of eye. The look was of that alarming suggestiveness which only a thoroughly innocent woman can attain.

Mrs. Gossett was a thoroughly innocent woman. Her married life had lasted exactly eight hours. A bride at two o'clock, she had been a widow at ten, her husband having fallen after dinner, from the top-story window of the hotel in which they were to pass their first night. One often wondered if there was something suspicious in the insistence of the late Mr. Gossett upon a top-story room.

'I'm sure the copy is all wight,' said Mrs. Gossett.

Brian sighed. When Mrs. Gossett left her r's behind her it meant that spring was rising in her heart. It meant more eye-rolling, more giggling, and more sudden bitings of the underlip, followed by 'I haven't said anything *I shouldn't*, have I?' He therefore prepared for the worst.

'How's the competition going?' He glanced at a vast pile of dusty sheets of paper.

'The ideal love letters?' She lowered her eyes coquettishly. 'Of course, I don't know anything about the *quality* of them . . .' She paused, and looked up suddenly. 'I haven't said anything *dweadful*, have I?' She giggled. 'What do you *mean*?'

Brian assured her that having said nothing, he had meant nothing either.

Slightly disappointed, she pouted, and informed him that the competition was due to finish in a week's time. Then, spring once more welled up inside her.

'I *must* have your opinion of my new competition. It came to me in the night. I think it's wather a duck.'

With tremendous girlishness she hopped up on to her desk, and sat on it, swinging her legs. She arched her eyebrows and pursed her lips to such an extent, that a stranger might have imagined her to be making a 'rude face.' Brian, however, knew the symptoms, and by judiciously avoiding both legs and eyes, kept his gaze firmly fixed upon her brooch. It was one of those brilliant blue brooches fashioned from the wings of South American butterflies, which are worn for the apparent purpose of reminding us how many natural horrors we are spared by reason of our temperate climate. Mrs. Gossett fingered the necklace, then, with a little giggle, she said:

'It's going to be called the "Peeresses Puzzle Picture."'

'Good God!'

Upon hearing this masculine exclamation a sound came from Mrs. Gossett's throat not unlike a horse's neigh. It seemed to have an aphrodisiac effect upon her, and her eyes opened very wide. She continued breathlessly, forgetting all about her r's:

'You see – we should get all the photographs of all the peeresses and cut them up into three pieces, and arrange them in separate piles. One pile – (don't laugh! You *are* howid) – one pile would be all foreheads and eyes, one pile would be all noses and mouths, and the other pile would be all chins.' She achieved a real blush. 'What have I said *now*? I can't say anything without you looking like that.' She tossed her head, hoping that she had indeed hit unwittingly upon some lurking impropriety.

Brian pondered the idea. The prospect of young ladies in the suburbs gravely affixing the nose of the Countess of Oxford and Asquith to the chin of Lady Ancaster, crowning it with the forehead of the Duchess of Rutland, and calling the composite result 'Lady Astor,' seemed to him one of those indoor sports which deserved the warmest encouragement. He did not, however, betray his irreverence to Mrs. Gossett. She would have resented an attack upon the peerage as strongly as she would have resented an attack upon her own virginity. Quite as strongly, he thought, as he observed the quivering mass of inhibitions before him.

'It's a marvellous idea,' he said. 'Did you think of that all by yourself?'

Mrs. Gossett, who had just 'lifted' the idea from an American magazine, nodded innocently. 'Yes. It came to me in the night. Everything comes to me in the night. Oh! – what have I said *now*?'

Brian giggled. 'Nothing.'

'I think men's *minds* . . .'

'Honestly, I wasn't laughing . . .' The end of the sentence was a gurgle which belied his words.

She pursed her lips with appalling ingenuousness. Then, with what she imagined to be a happy laugh, she dismissed the subject, wagging an ink-stained finger at him.

'Well – I'll forgive you this once. But I think you're a terrible young man. Good night.'

The last words were again pitched on a descending third. Mrs. Gossett always indulged in these abrupt adieux. They gave her a feeling of power, as though she were a haughty courtesan summarily dismissing a too-ardent swain. Brian took advantage of it, murmured 'good night,' and left the room.

The scene switches to the top of a bus. Forgive the democratic element of these early pages. Soon the last bus will have wound its way out of our story and we shall be breathing that atmosphere of rich limousines in which we all feel so at home.

But even the top of a bus can be exciting, especially when one possesses an uncomfortable inside seat, and is filled with a fierce determination to obtain a seat next to the railing. Brian, as he clambered to the top of this particular bus, which was whirling past Temple Bar, rounding the corner by the old church of St. Mary-le-Strand and snorting down the broad expanse that fronts Australia House, was filled with such a determination. He therefore took a quick glance at the occupants, saw two women holding penny tickets in their hands, and a single empty seat in front of them. Realizing that the penny tickets implied descent at Trafalgar Square, he occupied the empty seat, preparing to spring into the place behind as soon as the occasion demanded.

On the other side of the gangway sat a young man with a hungry look. He, too, was perched on the inside edge of his seat, and he appeared to be exceedingly uncomfortable, for his partner was a woman with a quite Chaucerian behind. In his hand was a fivepenny ticket (pink), in the woman's hand was a sixpenny ticket (green). So that, unless he changed his place, he would have a depressing journey.

The bus was roaring down the Strand. In a moment Nelson would appear against the sky. Past the tall pile of the Savoy Hotel, past the Vaudeville Theatre – here was Charing Cross. Brian rose to his feet. So did the young man with the hungry look. So did the women with the penny tickets. Brian advanced his arm. The women, slightly indignantly, brushed past him, and tottered down the steps. With a look of studied innocence (very difficult in view of the fact that his rival was standing on his foot) Brian propelled himself into the outside seat. He sank into it with a sigh. The young man sank, too, with a sharp dig of the elbow, which Brian ignored. He could now enjoy his journey in peace.

Really, it was a lovely evening. A sky of red, white and blue was being painted by unseen hands behind Nelson. The sky above the National Gallery was bruised with the browns and golds of a tired, wintry sun. As the bus swept up the Haymarket, Brian looked over the edge at the crowds that were whirling down from Piccadilly. Like masses of insects. Like – oh Lord, like anything on earth! He was too tired to search for similes.

The bus careered across Piccadilly, and growled along up Regent Street. Brian wondered what Nelson would have said could he have seen the destruction that was taking place here. Only a few of Nash's exquisite buildings remained, like gentlemen jostled by a crowd of vulgarians. The modern English taste – consisting of an artless blend of Gothic, Byzantine and ancient Egyptian – reigned supreme. Vulgar, vulgar, vulgar. Still, he was vulgar himself. A gossip writer. He made a grimace, which the young man with the hungry look took as a personal affront, indicating as much by a dig of the elbow.

As they capered down Oxford Street, Brian reviewed his position. Six pounds a week. Three suits. Thirty-eight pounds in the Bank. A rather cracked piano. An absurdly healthy constitution.

Here was the Marble Arch. He got off. '*Good* evening,' he whispered sweetly to the hungry young man.

He paused outside the door of his flat. A very odd noise made itself heard from the interior. He frowned, puzzled, and put his head against the door.

> '*Ho! to be in England*
> *Now that Hapril's there,*
> *And 'ooever wikes in England*
> *Sees, some mornin', hunaware,*
> *That the lowest boughs and the . . .*'

The voice, which was slightly beery, paused.

'What's this bit, Mr. Moore?'

Brian opened the door.

'Brian, old thing.'

A young man, as dark as Brian was fair, sprang out of his chair. He put his pipe on the mantelpiece and held out his hand.

'Hullo, Walter. What *is* Mrs. Pleat doing?'

Mrs. Pleat closed *The Oxford Book of English Verse* indignantly. 'It's Mr. Moore's idea, Mr. Elme,' she said. 'It's a waste of time, I call it. Makin' me read stuff like that.'

The two young men looked at each other. In Brian's eyes there was an expression of amused amazement. One never knew what Walter was going to do next. In Walter's eyes was a look merely of affectionate inquiry. One never knew how Brian was going to take things.

'She's going to be a wonderful elocutionist,' he said, with a note of apology in his voice. 'Aren't you, Mrs. Pleat?'

'*'E's crazy, Mr. Elme.'

'What's that bit you did so beautifully?' Walter began to chant . . .

> '*And after April, when May follows*
> *And the white throat builds, and all the swallows . . .*'

'I don't know anythink about white throats, Mr. Moore, nor anythink about swallows, but I do know that Mr. Elme looks tired out, and with your leave, I shall go 'ome while he 'as 'is tea, which will be cold if 'e waits any longer.'

She poured out a cup of tea and placed it before Brian, who had sat down in the only spare chair. Then, after sundry bustlings, Mrs. Pleat left the room.

But before she leaves our story, there is one thing that you must learn about her. Mrs. Pleat had a husband. That husband was a bigamist. How, why, or where he was a bigamist, one does not know. The important fact is that Mrs. Pleat only saw him on Tuesdays when he called for his midday dinner. The rest of his week was consecrated to the unhallowed woman who had stolen him away.

Mrs. Pleat lived for her Tuesdays. And so, every Tuesday morning, Brian and Walter were bustled out of bed with a deadly punctuality, breakfast was thrust under their noses, shoes were cleaned, and the flat was dusted, while an air of apprehension hung over the world. If by any chance they should forget, or delay, Mrs. Pleat would hang about, looking at them with a watery and reproachful eye, reiterating the obvious fact that 'It's Toosday.' Sometimes out of sheer irritation, Brian would be half inclined to dawdle over his dressing, as a protest against these methods, but the sight of that watery eye, the memory that Mrs. Pleat was longing to go back to prepare an undeservedly succulent dinner for her ex-husband, and, perhaps, the reflection that he might one day be a bigamist himself, caused him to relent. And so he always gobbled his breakfast, shaving hurriedly, digging Walter in the ribs from time to time, reminding him of the day of the week.

You have met the hero, the hero's employer, and his employee. It now remains only to say a few words about the hero's friend and the drama may proceed.

Walter Moore was an ex-naval officer, with two passions in the world – the first a passion for freedom. The second an almost absurd hero-worship of Brian.

The passion for freedom had caused him to leave the navy, swearing that never again should anybody tell him that he 'must' do anything. He did not care what happened to him, provided that he had a few shillings in his pocket, and provided that the open world was before him. In spirit he was curiously like a bird, unstable, reckless, lovable, singing a song on occasions when other men would have been cursing fate.

The second influence in his life, his hero-worship of Brian, dated from about two years before, when the two had casually come across each other, and had struck up an acquaintance which had ripened into one of those rare friendships which are among the few things which make one feel that life is not an uncommonly feeble joke by a vulgar and untidy spirit.

Brian—not only for Walter, but for everybody else, had a quite exceptional charm. It is a facile word, largely applied by obsequious journalists to those foreign royalties who cannot be described as either handsome, useful, or intelligent. One cannot analyse charm, one can only describe its symptoms upon other people. As far as Brian was concerned, it meant that the old flower-women at Piccadilly put in an extra carnation for him on those rare occasions when he was able to buy them, that the notoriously dishonest greengrocer at the corner of the street always picked out the reddest and juiciest strawberries for him when he bought sixpennyworth on hot August evenings, and that Mrs. Pleat, when the pressure of life allowed her to be sentimental, mournfully lamented the fact that her own sons were not of the same entrancing qualities.

All these things Walter noted and loved. But most of all he loved Brian's courage – the courage which kept his dreams alive in the most sordid occupation known to man.

Enough of these analyses of character. They bore me as much as they bore you. We will leave the young men together – Walter smoking his pipe, Brian trying to play Debussy on a piano designed only for the simpler marches of Sousa, while the gas-fire filled the room with fumes so potent that less healthy lungs would soon have shown signs of asphyxiation.

CHAPTER TWO

TEN days later the singular proclivities of the English peerage, as proclaimed in Brian's column of *The Lady's Mail*, were made public to the world. In all corners of the British Isles, tired housewives were sitting in corners of semi-detached residences, learning of the Dowager Lady Macrael's bagpipes, following the adventures of the son of the 'vivacious' Lady Monk. For Brian, the day of publication was always a trial. Each time that the telephone rang he visualized some outraged dowager ringing up to contradict the legend he had affixed to her. However, experience had convinced him that, even if the dowagers read *The Lady's Mail*, which was improbable, they never troubled to deny its assertions.

He therefore sat down at his desk in the office with a fairly light heart, to concoct further revelations. The next number of the paper would be a 'baby' number. That meant that the usual picture of a half-witted infant's face would beam from the cover in three colours, and numberless 'hints' to mothers, ranging from diet to layettes, would fill the paper. (Why, by the way, do mothers need so many 'hints'?) Brian himself would be expected to narrate the doings of the proudest babies in the kingdom, a task which he found comparatively easy. No baby would be likely to resent any talents he attributed to it, and, provided that he made all the babies models of wisdom, brightness, and beauty, not even the most exalted mother would say him nay.

The first baby he chose was the offspring of a certain Lady Porthaven, who had recently presented her husband with a son. Brian was unaware that the presentation had been something of a shock to Lord Porthaven, who had, indeed, been inclined to regard the child with grave suspicion. He therefore proceeded to weave a delicate romance round the innocent's head.

'Amazing, isn't it, how cute the modern child is becoming? Little Edward (whose coming was recently the signal for such wonderful rejoicing in the Porthaven family; in fact, they tell me that Lord Porthaven brought out three bottles of the famous Porthaven brandy) has already . . .'

But the activities of little Edward will have to remain for ever wrapt in mystery. For at this moment Mrs. Gossett's bell rang – three crisp, commanding rings, and Brian rose to his feet to obey the summons.

He knocked at the door.

'Come in.'

The voice was no longer pitched on a descending third. Instead it ascended sharply. Brian sighed. Mrs. Gossett was worried.

He entered.

'Good morning, Mr. Elme.'

Brian looked at her in surprise. There was an icy chill in her voice. She was sitting up very straight in her chair, glaring straight in front of her. Perhaps she wasn't feeling well.

'Good morning. How are you?' he asked sympathetically.

'I am very well, thank you. As well as can be expected.' She delivered herself of a theatrical sigh.

'Why? Is anything wrong?'

'Wrong? Oh *no!*' – She lowered her eyelids, keeping her neck still very erect. She had the appearance of smelling something unpleasant. Then the eyelids swooped up again, the nostrils curved in disdain, and looking him straight in the face, she pushed a letter across the desk towards him.

Brian took the letter, but for a moment he did not read it. He was so puzzled by Mrs. Gossett. She had suddenly assumed a fierce cheerfulness, and, in the pretence of ignoring his existence, was busying herself with a pile of papers. She hummed, with a voice trembling either from anger or some other emotion, snatches from her favourite tune, Annie Laurie.

All at once the humming ceased. She became once more a human refrigerator. Putting her hand under her chin, she turned to gaze out of the window. 'Perhaps,' she said, in tones of ironic courtesy, 'you would be good enough to read that letter?'

'Of course. I'm awfully sorry.'

Hurriedly he lifted it from the desk, and read:

'DEAR MADAM, –

Lady Julia Cressey's attention has been drawn to a paragraph in the last issue of *The Lady's Mail*, suggesting that she is engaged to be married to Lord William Motley. Since this is an unfounded, and presumably malicious invention, her ladyship demands a public and unconditional apology at the earliest moment. Her ladyship also wishes me to state that she is making a personal complaint to Lord Southpoint, to whom, she understands, *The Lady's Mail* belongs.

I am, Yours faithfully,

P. SMITH,

Secretary.'

I-am-yours-faithfully-P-S-Smith. I-am-yours-faithfully-P-Smith. Brian closed his eyes. God! Oh, God! What had he done?

'I'm afraid,' she said, 'I shall have no alternative but to terminate your engagement here.'

'I see.'

He was not looking at Mrs. Gossett. She seemed, somehow, nothing. He was thinking of the hurrying streets. Already, in imagination, he was tramping them in search of a job.

Mrs. Gossett cleared her throat. She was about to deliver a crushing rebuke. Brian turned to her in a sudden fury.

'Oh – it's all right. I know I'm wrong. I know I'm sacked. Let's leave it at that.'

He turned away and walked to the fireplace. Irritably he kicked a piece of coal.

'Really, Mr. Elme. I think you're being a little unreasonable.'

'Do you?' He looked at her with all the cruelty of youth for middle-age. For a moment he forgot that he was a sacked journalist, and that he was speaking to somebody whom at all costs he must conciliate. He merely saw a tousled, worn, ridiculous, inky woman.

And, instinctively, she understood. Something in her quailed before that cruel glance. She felt naked and forlorn. Yet she said:

'We *might* avoid it, you see.'

The remark brought them both back to the normal. Brian was again the reporter, she was again the editress.

'Might we?'

She played with her pencil. 'You see' – she bit her lip – 'you get on very well here, don't you, Mr. Elme?'

He looked away. This was dreadful.

'And it isn't as if this had ever happened before.'

'No. That's true.' *Why* it had never happened before, Brian could not at the moment understand. All the peeresses about whom he had written such astonishing fictions during the past two years seemed to rise before him in a hissing, accusing crowd.

'Of course if Lord Southpoint did get to hear of it . . . I mean . . . You see I can't help myself.'

'No. I understand. I'm sorry I was so rude just now.'

Her eyelids fluttered at him in a return to coquetry.

'You *thought* it was true, didn't you?'

'Yes,' he lied.

'Well, listen.' She leant forward with the breathless air of a con-spirator. 'I think you ought to go and see Lady Julia yourself, and . . . and apol – '

She was going to say 'apologize,' but seeing the look on Brian's face she turned it to 'explain.'

'Oh I couldn't possibly do that.'

'But you must.'

'I should feel such a cad.'

'It's your only chance. We can't publish such an abject denial. You might be able to persuade her.'

'I? She'd kick me out of the house.'

Mrs. Gossett's eyes rolled the complete circle. 'Oh no, she wouldn't. You see, you might appeal to her.'

Brian smiled a little grimly.

'Oh – what *have* I said?'

He smiled openly now. This was like the old Mrs. Gossett.

'Even at a moment like this you . . . Really. I mean . . .' She was all artificial confusion. But there were real tears in her eyes. Brian said to himself that she was not such a bad sort after all.

'Do let me help you,' she continued. 'I've been in this business much longer than you. And I know how much the personal touch counts.' She paused, undecided whether she should again be timo-rous at having said something she ought not to have said. Then, slowly, 'I was too hasty just now. It was just the shock. Now please will you do what I say?'

He had been walking round Berkeley Square for nearly half an hour. His wrist-watch told him that it now needed only five min-utes to twelve, the hour at which Lady Julia had consented to see him. He moistened his lips, and blew his nose. Then, with a final tug to his tie, he crossed the road and rang the bell.

The door was flung wide.

'I believe Lady Julia is expecting me,' he said. 'Mr. Elme.'

The butler looked at him in disdain.

'Is it *The Lady's Mail*?'

Is '*it*' *The Lady's Mail*? At any other moment Brian would have damned the man for his impertinence. 'It!' However, he only gulped and said 'Yes.'

'Have you a card?'

Brian produced one – a hideous thing in Gothic letters, that looked as though it belonged to a romantic piano-tuner. It seemed almost to bark at him. The butler took it, glanced at it, and said:

'If you'll wait here, I'll ask if her ladyship can see you.'

Brian sat down, wondering why everybody was so nasty to reporters. Why didn't they show him to the tradesmen's entrance, and have done with it? Perhaps, after the interview was over, they would. He told himself he deserved nothing better.

Then the butler reappeared. 'Her ladyship will see you. This way, please.'

He scrambled to his feet, and followed upstairs.

A door was thrown open, and instantly on Brian's mind a picture was indelibly stamped – one of those pictures which no hand can ever tear from the galleries of memory. He saw a green room with sunlight streaming through it, and a mass of yellow roses. It seemed to him a very superb and lovely room, typical of the splendour of the ancient house which it represented. As a matter of fact, it was nothing more nor less than a shop, for Julia's mother, the excellent Countess of Thane, in common with many equally distinguished Englishwomen, had learnt that there was a great deal of money to be made out of the antique business. This business she conducted by asking defenceless Americans to lunch, filling them with old brandy, leading them artlessly up to a piece of Chippendale (?) purchased the week before, and telling the first 'family' story about it that came into her mind. The next day the Chippendale would be removed by hairy men who smelt of beer, and another piece would take its place. Julia slightly resented these proceedings, because she never knew what her room would look like from one day to another. But she put up with it all on account of the extra pocket-money that it provided.

Brian, however, had no eyes for the room. He was looking at a figure which seemed to be wrought of light, so tenuous as to be a mere spangle, a floating bead. A trick of the imagination, of course. Lady Julia was merely standing by the window. As soon as she moved to meet him, she became a living being. She was endowed with a white skin and lips so scarlet that they glistened. She was seen to possess blue-black hair and eyebrows with a Beardsley twist. And – though Brian was unaware of this – she was dressed in a frock that proclaimed its maker a genius – so delicately did it underline her personality.

They drifted together, these two, in this sunlit room – she, bored, entirely self-confident, a little aggressive – he, humble, frightened, yet inclined to worship.

'Have you come about that ridiculous paragraph?'

'Yes.' He was blushing tragically. 'I'm afraid I have.'

'Don't you think it's monstrous, yourself?'

'Yes. I do.'

'I suppose some silly woman sent it in. Anyway, I'm sick of being engaged without my knowledge. They've got to apologize. Listen . . .'

She went to a little writing-desk. While she was turning over a bunch of papers she said, 'Do help yourself to a cigarette.' Brian did so. A fat cigarette with a big woolly end. He lit it as though he were incarcerating a caterpillar. His fingers were shaking.

She stood with her hand on her hip – gold-rimmed against the window.

'I've written this, and they've got to put it in.'

'The paragraph appearing in our last week's issue concerning the rumoured engagement of Lady Julia Cressey and Lord William Motley is without any foundation whatever. We deeply apologize for this unwarranted assumption. At Lady Julia's express wish, "The Lady's Mail" will, in its future issues, refrain from any mention of Lady Julia's activities.'

She handed him the paper. 'There. What d'you think of that?'

'I think it's quite right. Absolutely right.'

Now, there the matter might have ended. This history might never have been written. The colours might have faded from that room, and Julia have dissolved into the mists from which she came – to which we shall all eventually depart. But as Brian stepped forward, the sunlight shone on him. And, in the sunlight, Lady Julia suddenly saw him for the first time. She saw that his hair was flaming gold, that he was young, that he had a hunted look in his eyes, and that his hand was trembling. For a fraction of a second she looked him up and down. He saw the look and read into it the contempt of a lovely woman for a blundering fool. He said:

'I'll take this back to the office now.'

'Don't go for a moment.' Her voice was softer now. 'Sit down and have a cocktail. You look rather fagged.' She rang the bell.

'I'm not keeping you?'

'No, of course not.'

A footman entered.

'Bring two sidecars, please.'

She glided to the window. 'Do they work you terribly hard at your office?'

'Well – it's not that. It's . . .' Brian felt the room going round him. Oh, God! He must tell her. 'Lady Julia. You don't understand. I wrote that paragraph myself.'

'You wrote it?'

He nodded.

'But – I don't understand. I thought you were the sub-editor or something.'

'No such luck.'

'I see.' She screwed up her eyes and looked at him. This was really intriguing. To have a very decorative young man sitting before one in a state of abject servility is an emotion which would appeal to any woman – even to women who were not as versed as Lady Julia in the works of the late Marquis de Sade.

'Why did you write it?'

'I don't know. I thought it might be true.'

'Why did you think that?'

'Well – I'd seen you together – lots of times.'

'That doesn't constitute an engagement, does it?'

Brian could bear it no longer. He suddenly rose to his feet. 'I oughtn't to be here at all. I'm sorry. But I can't' – he became heroic – 'I can't drink your wine after this.'

'A cocktail isn't wine.'

Her voice was again cool and soft, for the footman was advancing across the room with a tray containing two green glasses and a little bowl of olives.

Silently they took their glasses. The footman withdrew. And Lady Julia leant against the mantelpiece and laughed. Laughed again and again. Brian was silent.

'Oh, dear! You look the very last sort of young man who would ever do anything like that.'

He still said nothing.

'Now listen. Let's talk this out. Sit down.'

He sat down.

'Do you make a living out of this job?'

'Yes.'

'What do you have to do?'

He turned his glass slowly. 'I have to – to write interesting stuff about well-known people.'

She suppressed a smile. 'It sounds awfully rude – but – you look so young. Do you know many well-known people?'

'No. I don't know any.'

'Then how do you write about them?'

Brian paused before he answered. 'I have to – to use my imagination.'

'I see. Do explain.'

'You'll think me such a brute.'

'I shall never forgive you unless you explain.'

He was suffering the tortures of the damned. Still, he told himself, he deserved it.

'Well,' he said, 'I read the newspapers and I see if anybody is going abroad.'

'That seems innocent enough.'

'Then, if they are well known, I look them up in the cuttings.'

'What cuttings?'

'Oh – we have a whole stock of them in the office.'

'I see.'

'And if there is anything interesting I – well, I rewrite it.'

'And if there isn't?'

'I make it up.'

Her eyes were glistening with delight. 'Do tell me who you've made up things about. Have you said anything about mother?'

'Lady Thane?'

'Yes.'

'This is delicious. What did you say?'

Brian cleared his throat. 'Well . . .'

'Come on. The truth.'

'Well, I gave her a parrot.'

'*What?*'

'A parrot,' repeated Brian gravely.

'Go on. Go *on*. It's too superb.'

Brian began to be infected by her own enthusiasm.

'I made it sing hymns,' said Brian, 'but Mrs. Gossett cut that out.'

'Who is Mrs. Gossett?'

'My editress.'

'Why did she cut out the hymns?'

'She thought it would offend the Nonconformists.'

Lady Julia fluttered her hands above her head. 'This is the *most* fascinating thing,' she cried. 'Go on. So what did you make the parrot do?'

Brian was now crimson in the face. 'I killed it,' he said.

'You *killed* it?'

'Yes. Or rather, Lady Porthaven's cat killed it.'

'Mary Porthaven! She hates cats more than anything on earth. Oh, you're the most thrilling young man that I've ever met. . . .' She lay back on the sofa, and dabbed her eyes with a handkerchief. 'Please, go on. Have you ever said anything about Anne – about Lady Hardcastle? She's a *great* friend of mine.'

'I'm afraid I have,' said Brian.

'What did you do to *her?*'

'I gave her a bath.'

Lady Julia beat a tattoo with her heels on the carpet. 'Go *on*. Giving Anne Hardcastle a bath. My God!'

'I mean,' continued Brian, 'I said she had a very exotic bathroom.'

'She has. Dozens. How did you guess that?'

'She looked the sort of woman who would.'

'You're a genius. What sort of bath did you give her?'

He told her. He told her that, and a great deal more. Tired, over-wrought, feeling that after all he might have saved his job, feeling, above everything, a strange exhilaration in the presence of the most beautiful woman whom he had ever seen, Brian made a soul-confession to Lady Julia.

And the result was forgiveness. She did not in the least care about the paragraph. She did not want any sort of apology. She had been quite terribly amused. And a little – just a little fascinated.

As she dismissed him, she looked at him closely. His clothes were quite presentable. He was almost too good-looking. He had the most delicious hair. He appeared to be absurdly innocent. A sudden whim took her.

'I forgive you absolutely,' she said, 'on one condition.'

Brian gulped. If she had asked him to jump out of the window, he would have done so.

'But anything . . .' he said.

'You must take me out to dinner the day after to-morrow.'

'Lady Julia!'

He went slightly pale. If she had asked him to undress in Berkeley Square he could not have been more alarmed. To him she had always been Lady Julia Cressey, a thing to be worshipped at a distance, to be glimpsed through a window, or humbly followed in the street. The suggestion that he should take her out to dinner filled him with unmitigated terror. He could have told her a great many reasons, that he could not afford it (although he would spend his last penny on the thing), that his dress-clothes were shabby, that she would be bored. . . . But these reflections were cut short.

'You're not engaged for that day are you? Because there's a first night of a new play I want to see.'

'Oh no.'

'Well, then. A quarter-past seven. You might call for me here. I've got tickets.'

He felt the room reeling round him. 'Thank you very much indeed.' He cleared his throat. 'Where would you like to dine?'

'Oh – anywhere. We'll see how we feel, shall we?'

Brian was quite certain how *he* would feel. He would feel a lump of stolid, hopeless misery, shot through with fires of terror and exaltation. However, he merely said:

'That's right. Thank you awfully. Good morning.' And he left the room backwards, as though departing from the presence of royalty.

Lady Julia, with a smile on her lips, tiptoed to the window, and looked out on the square below. In a moment, she heard a door slam, and saw a figure stepping quickly across the square. The figure, though young and alert, was walking somewhat unsteadily.

'What a divine young man!' she said to herself. She lay back on the sofa, closing her eyes, and thinking how amusing it would be to have his untutored lips pressed close to her own (which had been trained in the best European schools).

CHAPTER THREE

ONCE that the Society reporters, professional and amateur, had applied to Lady Julia that nauseating phrase a 'modern girl,' they considered that their duty was done. They put a cigarette in one hand, a cocktail in the other, a smart platitude on her lips, and they cried, 'Here she is!'

It was, in fact, in this precise attitude that Mr. Ivor Isaacs, the famous artist, who gave up painting sheep in order to paint Society (wisely retaining his former technique), had represented her at the Royal Academy. But we – we cannot dismiss any living, breathing woman with such facility. We must begin a little nearer the beginning.

One night, when she was but ten years old, her mother had dressed her in a frock of silver, put a sheaf of lilies in her arms, and stood her at the top of a long, winding staircase. Slowly she had walked down to the great hall, wondering a little what it was all about, yet not displeased by the sensation she was evidently creating. For the chatter in the hall was hushed, and they were saying that never had they seen a lovelier sight. And then they crowded round her, old men with strange ribbons across their shirt-fronts, old women with bare bosoms, in the crevices of whose wrinkled

necks the powder lay like snow in a creek, young men with laughing eyes and medals tinkling on their breasts, girls with red lips,
smelling of sweet, faded carnations. . . .

They had crowded round this silver child, with flutter and fan-
fare, telling her that she was beautiful, kissing her hands. And one
young man with a flushed face had kissed her lips. But he had
left the party in a hurry, and they say it was the last time he ever
entered Thane House. However, he was soon forgotten, for the
Ambassador of a great and friendly country (slightly *too* friendly,
some had thought) had led her to his table, and had given her a
glass of something which was cold, and sweet, and ran through
the veins like fire, turning the lily to a rose. (The phrase is the
Ambassador's, not mine.)

The memory of that evening – that ten-years-old evening – had
never left her. For, in a sense, the whole of the rest of her life had
been merely a series of repetitions of it. She seemed always to have
been walking down staircases, in some way or another. In fact, life
itself was like a staircase that wound on and on – to where? She
did not ask herself that question. The chief thing had been that
there was always a crowd to applaud her, always a sensation to
be experienced, and later on, always a lover to reject. Or if not to
reject . . . Anyway, the whole game had been played at top speed. If
life was a staircase, then she had slid down the banisters.

And she was still wondering what it was all about. There were,
of course, a great many people to tell her, but they none of them
seemed to provide the right answer. The psycho-analysts had
discovered in her mind strange and unnatural passions for her relations, male and female, but as she hated all her relations, that did
not get one much further. The lovers had told her that life was
meant only for sighs, and passions, and the linked sweetness of
long-drawn-out embraces. But frankly, although she loved being
loved, craved for adoration as a child craves for sugar, she had never
experienced the grand passion herself. The spiritualists had merely
made her laugh, because she could not see the point of sitting in a
dark room while somebody played a record of Clara Butt singing
'Abide with me.' It had never been one of her favourite tunes, and

the idea of abiding with Clara Butt held no fascination for her. As for the scientists, she did not understand them, and their fingers were usually dirty. It was all very puzzling.

Yet she was still hungry for the glittering colours of life. Her taste in colours was typical of her whole mentality. She loved colour indiscriminately, with a blunted sense. The splash of a pink coat against the grey fields of – let us call it Glebeshire – the vermilion of a cherry in a cocktail glass, the lazy drip of purple from bougainvillæa over a Venetian wall, the tenuous, ghostly blue of cigarette smoke as it drifted in front of a lighted window, the cruel whites of snow, the greeny-black of her own hair, the multitudinous soft tints of a pearl, the coarse, stringy yellow of limelight. It was a form of fever, a nervous reaction caused by a life at perpetually high tension.

What does that sort of life do for you? Well, it had done at least one thing for Lady Julia. It had given her, beneath the cold, polished surface of her mind, a series of minor phobias which had in them all the germs of immense Fears. It is an unpleasantly medical way of describing the mind, but we cannot help that. She had:

A fear of being alone, that made her see a single gap in her engagement-book, a single unoccupied week-end as something sinister and horrible.

A fear of being poor (a ridiculous fear, one would have thought) that made her cling feverishly to acquaintances she disliked, merely because they were richer than she, and even, in wild moments, gave her nightmares of Revolution, when she and her class would be tramping the streets, cold and starved.

A fear, above all, of growing old (common, one supposes, to all women, but morbidly developed in herself).

All these fears, if you analyse them, were ridiculous, except the fear of growing old. (Yet, were the young women of 1827 haunted in their so early youth by the phantoms of this still-distant spectre?) For it was obvious that she *would* grow old. It was equally obvious that it would alter everything, deprive her of conquests, shift the life-giving limelight to others. And that, she had to face.

Well, she was facing it already. It was the day of her dinner with Brian, and she was making up. In front of her was a jar of cold cream, a dead white powder, a rose-coloured powder, a powder of palest mauve, a bottle of astringent, two lip-sticks, crimson and vermilion, and an eyebrow pencil. She sat down before a triple mirror, and began.

Cold cream all over – forehead, eyes, nose, cheeks, chin, neck. How cool it felt! Delicious. Then she took a towel and wiped it off, carefully and methodically.

God! how awful she looked. Hardly a touch of colour. She stretched out her hand for the astringent, dabbed some on a piece of cotton wool, and patted her face with it. That was better. One could feel the skin tightening. It had an effect that exhilarated mentally as well as physically. And so it should, at three guineas a bottle.

The groundwork was now prepared. She took the vermilion lip-stick and turned her right cheek to the glass. (If a male reader imagines that lip-sticks are only made for lips he is much mistaken.) She then drew a series of tiny lines, thick near the cheek-bone, very faint lower down. When it was finished, her face looked like a human chess board. Putting down the lip-stick, she proceeded to smooth these lines, gently and imperceptibly, into each other. When they were all merged her right cheek had an appearance of glowing health. The same process was repeated with the left.

She stretched out her hand for the pale mauve powder, covering with it her eyelids, and the space immediately beneath her eyes, removing all traces from the lashes with an eyebrow pencil. For her cheeks and her chin the rose-coloured powder was employed. For her forehead, nose, neck and shoulders, she used the dead white. And when her mouth had been carved out in crimson, she dabbed her whole face with a clean puff, tapping it afterwards with her finger-tips.

If that reads like an advertisement of a beauty specialist, it cannot be helped. For if Julia is late for dinner in subsequent chapters, or is irritable, or fails to look her best, you may know the reason why.

Just before she switched out the light, she caught sight of her untasted cocktail gleaming on the mantelpiece. She hurried over, and before she drank it, held it up to the light. Here, she thought, is an obvious emotion. The-tired-little-rich-girl-destroying-her-digestion-but-stimulating-her-conversation-by-drinking-martini's. She gulped it down. And in a moment she ceased to be the prey of obvious emotions. She became eager, uncaring – she felt an inward sparkle. •

    She swept out of the room, humming a song. To-night would be *such* fun. That delicious boy. . . .

> 'Then come kiss me, sweet and twenty,
>   Youth's a stuff will not endure,
>   Not endure . . .'

The notes faded away, echoing in the darkness of the hall. There was the sound of a closing door.

And Grist, her maid, came in, surveying the debris with tired eyes. She noticed with regret that the cocktail, which she had placed on the mantelpiece in the hopes that it would be forgotten, had been drunk. For Grist felt the need of a cocktail, now and then.

Meanwhile, Brian, in his way, was also making up. The process, if of a different nature, was equally complicated.

He stared somewhat disconsolately at the array of objects on his bed. Taken as a whole, they certainly constituted an evening-dress. But if each object were viewed coldly and with calculation, the result was depressing. However, they were all he had, and he must make the best of them. He took up the 'patent' shoes. Their patent had evidently long ago expired, but they were not quite beyond redemption. A new pair of laces gave them an almost challenging appearance, especially when the laces were fluffed out slightly at the ends in the manner of a bow. And after he had spat on each toe-cap, and polished and polished, a dreary sparkle appeared which slightly heartened him.

He paused, thinking of Lord William. *He* did not have to spit on his toe-caps to make them shine. To put it quite vulgarly, he would not have the guts to do so. This cheerful thought carried Brian on the socks.

They were quite all right. They were not silk, but if he let down his braces a little nobody would notice their humble material. The trousers were another matter.

He held up the trousers at arm's length. The light shone piti-lessly on the well-worn seat, which was so burnished that Brian could almost see his face in it. How could he possibly get rid of that shine? A wild idea came to him. Perhaps he could *shave* the trousers, thereby roughening the surface? Impetuously he darted to the cupboard, and produced his safety-razor.

As he laid the trousers on the bed, preparatory to submitting them to this strange rite, he again thought of Lord William. *He* certainly did not have to shave his trousers. Of that there could be no possible doubt. Damn Lord William. He gripped the razor. Scrape, scrape, scrape. Examining the blade, he saw that a little fluff had come off. He held up the trousers once more.

Distinctly better. The shine had gone from the places where he had shaved. Scrape, scrape, scrape. Most of it was done now. Another scrape, *scrape* . . .

What was that? Had he . . . don't say that. . . . The razor dropped from his hand, and his underlip trembled. He had cut the cloth.

He sat down on the bed. What was the use of it all? What was the use of life? He wouldn't go. He didn't belong among such people. He was poor and shabby and dull. He ran his hands through his hair and tried to smile. It was damned funny. Oh, damned funny. He thought of other occasions when poverty had stung him – that awful time when he had visited his old school, and had been dis-covered wearing a shirt of which the sleeves were cut short at the elbow because the cuffs had long ago been worn out. He thought, too, of one of his first days in Fleet Street when, with lordly pride, he had invited three of his fellow-journalists to have a drink, and since they all chose double-whiskies and soda, he had been forced to humiliate himself by borrowing the money from them. But those occasions, and many others, were nothing to this. Here he was, standing before the gateway of Romance. And the door was barred by a pair of trousers. It was enough to make a chap give up.

The door opened. It was Walter.

'Hullo! B.'

'Hullo!'

'What are you looking so mouldy about?'

'Am I?' He glanced at Walter. He hardly saw him.

'I say.' Walter had observed the preparations for the festive occasion. 'Dressing up already?'

'I'm not going.'

'What?'

'I'm not going.' Brian knew perfectly well that he was going, but he had to allow himself this little moment of self-pity.

'Why the devil not?'

For answer Brian held up the ravished trousers, putting his finger through the cut, and wagging it about.

'That looks so awfully aristocratic, doesn't it?'

'How d'you do it?'

'I was shaving the beastly things.'

'Oh, B.'

They looked at each other. And then they laughed. Loud and long.

'Give me a cigarette.'

Walter gave him one.

'I'll fix that,' said Walter. 'It only wants half a dozen stitches.'

'Could you honestly?' The furrows on Brian's forehead were slightly smoothed.

'Of course. I wasn't in the navy for nothing.'

'Thank God we've got a navy!'

The rest of the preparations, now that this great difficulty was met, went without a hitch. His bow, after a certain amount of coaxing, was induced to remain straight, and his two nine-carat gold studs, which had been polished in the morning by Mrs. Pleat, looked bright, if not exactly rich. His white waistcoat was spotless, and his white shirt, having been rubbed with bread by Walter, to remove a shady patch, would 'look all right in the light.' He had been inclined to darken some of the faded threads of his coat with Indian ink, but Walter had advised against this.

'You may have to dance,' he said, 'and if Lady Julia leant on your coat, she'd have a face like a nigger.'

'Shut up,' Brian had replied. Thinking of Lady Julia looking like a nigger! However, he had taken Walter's advice.

There now remained nothing but the question of funds. However, it was a very urgent question indeed.

'You see,' said Brian, sitting on the end of the bed, holding himself very still because of his waistcoat, 'we'll have to go to the Savoy or somewhere, shan't we?'

'Why not take her to Lockhart's and give her a cut off the joint?'

'I wish you'd stop talking rot.'

'It isn't rot. She'd probably much rather. It'd be a new sensation.'

'It certainly would,' said Brian grimly.

'Besides it isn't as if she were after you for your money, is it? She doesn't want *that*. Whatever else she does want,' he added. (It may be guessed that Walter was slightly jealous.)

'Why do you hate her so?' said Brian, with a sudden flash of intuition.

Walter flushed and put his hand on Brian's knee. 'Don't be an ass. I don't hate her. But I think it's rather hard luck on you to have to spend a week's wages on taking a woman like that . . .'

'Lord!' Brian rose to his feet. 'A week's wages! That's six pounds. I've only got four.'

Walter leant back and laughed. 'Oh, you are the world's prize kid. Four's tons.'

'Is it?'

'Of course.'

'Honestly though?'

'Well, you can't eat more than a pound each. And if you drink more than a pound's worth of wine you'll be so tight that it won't matter.'

'It'll *have* to be champagne, I suppose.'

'You'll have to ask her, at any rate.'

'Suppose she wanted a magnum?'

'Well, you'd give her a clap over the head and say she could have a small beer.'

'Ass.'

'Ass?'

'Good Lord! It's nearly seven. I shall go. If I walk, that's half a crown saved.'

He stood in front of the glass and surveyed himself. Really, it wasn't so bad. Perhaps a carnation might have added to the effect? No. One mustn't overdo it.

He sighed and turned round, caught Walter's eye, and laughed, gurgling for no reason at all.

As Brian approached No. 140 Berkeley Square the shame of not having taken a taxi increased. Perhaps he might wait till somebody else's taxi passed, and then ring the bell very quickly? If the butler opened the door at once, the servants might think that the passing taxi had been his own. But he rejected this as impracticable. He decided to look very haughty, to frown at all menials who came his way, quelling them. He paused, still two houses away from his destination. A cold wind shook a cluster of yellow leaves from the trees in the square, reminding him that October was almost past. 'October is the prettiest time of the year.' This strange sentence from the faded philosophy of his mother floated through his head. What would his mother have thought had she known that he was going to take so superb a creature as Lady Julia Cressey out to dinner? Would not she have burst with pride? Still, she could not have mended his trousers any better than Walter. He fingered tentatively his hind-quarters. One could hardly even feel where the patch had been sewn. And unless anybody asked him to stand on his head, he need have no qualms at all.

Taking a deep breath, and giving a final tug to his tie, he walked up the steps, and rang the bell. Instantly the door was flung open. He saw the same butler who had been so contemptuous on his previous visit. But this time there were also two footmen. This was ghastly. To whom should he give his coat? To the butler, or the tall footman, or the short one? However, he found his coat taken from his shoulders without any choice on his part.

'Mr. Elme?' whispered the butler.

'Yes,' said Brian in a loud voice. There was no question about his being an 'it' now.

'This way, sir.'

With remarkable agility the butler sprinted up the stairs. Brian was about to sprint also, but remembering that he had to be haughty, he walked slowly, even pausing for effect, to examine a very dull and large-busted Venus who glared at him from a niche in the wall. He would have liked to stroke the lady's chest, but he felt that this would be carrying *sang-froid* a little too far. Trembling in every limb he completed the ascent.

Ah! She was there.

'Good evening.'

'Good evening.'

He looked at her shyly. She had on something green that glittered. She smelt of violets.

'I say. You do look lovely.'

'I – or the dress?'

'Everything.'

She smiled. 'It's made by a man in Paris who can only work well when he's drunk.'

'He must have had D.T. when he designed that.'

Fool, fool! Why had he said such an appalling thing? She would despise him. However, she only said:

'Have a cocktail.'

'I'd love one.'

'I've had three already, so I'll just watch.'

He started slightly. Three already? Did that mean he'd have to do the same? If so, he would be entirely *hors de combat*. Perhaps . . . then she put all other thoughts out of his mind by saying:

'I hope you won't be bored. But I've asked two other people to come. We've got a box, you see.'

Brian went very pale. He put down his glass. He tried to smile. He said: 'No. I'm delighted.'

His mind was a whirl of conflicting thoughts. Four pounds for four people. Four pounds for four people. What could he do? Could he – oh, God! . . .

'Only too delighted,' he repeated.

'And as I've turned it into my dinner, of course you must dine with me.'

Dine with *her*?

'So,' she went on, 'would you be an angel and act as host? I think this ought to be enough.'

This? She was holding out three five-pound notes. Was she trying to insult him?

He put his hands behind his back, and moved uneasily from one foot to the other.

'Please,' he said. 'I'd much rather you dined with me.'

'Don't be absurd.'

'But I *asked* you to dinner,' he said doggedly.

'Quite.' There was a touch of impatience in her voice. 'And you didn't ask two other people as well. Therefore it ceases to be your dinner at all. Come along.' She still held out the notes. Then she stepped forward and stuffed them into his pocket. 'I'll dine with you another night.'

Brian felt miserable. There were tears in his eyes. Not only was he faced with an entirely new set of complications, but the honour which he had been about to taste was taken from him. Instead of feeling an equal he now felt more than ever subservient. Yet – what was the alternative? A vast bill that he would not be able to pay? Public ignominy? No. It was no use. He must keep the money. But already the evening seemed to him to be darkened.

'Whom else have you asked?' he said, as casually as possible.

'Only William Motley and Maurice Cheyne.'

And as soon as she had said it, the door opened, and Brian heard the voice of the butler, this time very loud:

'Lord William Motley. Mr. Cheyne.'

It seemed instantly as though the room were filled with a series of hurricanes.

'Darling.'

'*Covered* with Molyneux.'

'Ooh – my *favourite* cocktail!'

'We both feel like seven sorts of death.'

And a dozen other exclamations.

He took in the details of Lord William's appearance. He appeared to be about forty-five. On the top of an immense, large-hipped body, a pale head, fitted with eyes of remarkable intelligence, rolled from side to side. The mouth, loose and sensual, was always opening and closing, either in speech, or in the preparation for speech. The small moustache seemed quite out of place. On the first finger of his left hand was a small scarab ring.

He wore a dinner-jacket of the double-breasted variety – (a type rather rare in London in those days) – which he was constantly smoothing down over his hips.

His companion, Maurice, was a pale, good-looking young man, with a dark, Italian face, longish hair, and a clover-red carnation in his button-hole. He seemed very tired, but that, as Brian later discovered, was the effect he always desired to give. Unlike Motley, he wore tails.

Ridiculously, in the maze of introductions, paragraphs flitted through Brian's head. For example:

'*Smart men don't seem to have decided yet whether to don full or semi evening-dress, do they, dear? Lord William Motley never wears anything but a dinner-jacket – one of those cute double-breasted sorts – while the Honourable Maurice Cheyne – the good-looking heir of Lord Pedersfield* . . .

The concoction of these titbits was interrupted by Maurice himself.

'Julia is impossible,' he said. 'She never introduces anybody. I am the one who is *not* Lord William.'

He held out his hand with an engaging smile.

Julia detached herself.

'I'm terribly sorry. Mr. Elme. Mr. Cheyne. Lord William Motley.'

Three 'how-d'you-do's.' And as they went downstairs, Brian heard Lord William saying, 'What a deliciously *new* young man.' Which embarrassed him acutely.

The car slid away from the door, curved through the shadows of the lamplit square, took Carlos Place in a majestic sweep, and sighed itself to rest outside Claridge's. Nobody had spoken during this brief transit, except Maurice who had said:

'Does my face look terribly pre-war to-night?' and had been answered by a languid affirmative from both Julia and Lord William.

Short as the drive was, it had been enough to raise several new problems in Brian's brain. They were:

1. What was the exact position of the restaurant in the hotel? It would be terrible to lead his guests carelessly to the gentlemen's cloak-room.

2. Did he have to pretend that he had reserved a table?

3. Ought he to tell them where to sit? If so . . .

However, things moved so quickly that he had little time to decide anything.

Julia disappeared through a door on the left. Brian was about to follow her through it when he realized that she had gone to a purely feminine institution. Lord William and Maurice then also disappeared through a door. This time he did follow, was stripped of his coat by a footman, given a ticket and pushed outside. Next, they were all walking together through many chairs, covered in rose-coloured silk. He had a momentary impression of bare shoulders, and rows of scarlet, insolent mouths, and then they were standing before a man with a dark smile who must be the head-waiter.

'Act! Act! you fool!' muttered Brian to himself. And so he said in a false and muffled voice:

'I believe you have a table for Lady Julia Cressey?'

But the man was not even looking at him. He was bowing low to Lady Julia. They seemed to know each other intimately. Then with many little beckonings and grimaces he led the way through more tables (on which Brian noticed an astounding and terrifying collection of exotic dishes) to a place in the corner. And they were all seated. How, God knows!

'I can't get over this young man.'

The voice came from Maurice, who was openly staring at him. It had the effect of making him sit up and take notice.

'He looks so distressingly healthy,' continued Maurice. He turned to Brian: 'How is it done?'

'I don't see what he means.' Brian glanced appealingly at Julia.

'I mean what do you use?'

Brian had memories of occasionally drinking fruit salts in hot weather, but surely Maurice could not want to be told that? He had also once used a patent shaving-cream which had brought his face out in spots.

'I don't use anything,' he said.

'Do you know, I believe he's telling the truth!'

Maurice eyed him enviously. He was so used to having things done to his own face that the sight of nature unadorned struck him as a personal affront. He invariably spent quite twenty minutes over shaving, had his face massaged twice a week, and, in lieu of sunburn, employed an ochreous powder which gave to his features a slightly less unhealthy appearance than they would normally have presented. It did not strike him as at all unusual to make use of these artifices. All his friends seemed to do the same. One simply had to, in London, or one would look like the wrath of God.

Brian, however, was becoming restive. He cast down his eyes, and then noticed something which made his heart leap with joy.

It was a menu, beautifully written out in a copperplate hand, conducting one gently from a cold *consommé* to a *sole marguerite*, from a sole to a quail, from a quail to something which sounded like a successful prima donna, and from the prima donna to coffee. Thank the Lord that was done! He looked up and saw that Julia was watching him. She turned to Lord William:

'You see, I told him what I liked.'

Lord William bowed. 'As long as he has not chosen prawns I shall be quite happy. I never take prawns. Prawns have far too much sex.'

'Nobody suggested them, darling. But . . .'

She broke off to bow to several people at the other end of the room.

'She does not really know so many people as that,' said Lord William, in a loud voice. 'She is merely dotting and carrying one. I do it myself sometimes, when I go to The Everyman, or theatres like that, where of course there is nobody whom one knows. I always choose a very old lady and bow to her frequently, with different expressions. It gives me a feeling of great brutality, which I adore.'

He paused. 'Julia, surely that is Anne over there?'

'Where?' She looked. 'Yes, it is.'

'Then I shall tell this young man a story which he may put in his paper. Do you see her – by the pillar?'

But at this point the waiter handed him the wine list. Frowning at the interruption, Lord William waved it in the direction of Brian, drumming meanwhile, with his fingers on the table. Brian took the list, full of trepidation.

Now, there are only two ways of looking at wine lists. That most commonly adopted by the English race is to study it with a flustered ignorance, as in the manner of schoolboys called upon to translate a portion of Æschylus, and then to ask the waiter if a certain wine is 'all right.' And after the waiter has firmly dragged the guest's finger to the bottom of the page, containing wines at double the price, to agree.

The other way is to give the list a haughty glance, indicating a prolonged connoisseurship, to close the book with a snap, and to say, 'A bottle of '57. A little iced. Only a *little* iced.'

Brian adopted a compromise. He could not look the wine list in the face as though he knew it, for, to him, there was no difference between Louis Roederer or Mumm or Pommery. (Nor, in all probability, is there much difference to most of us.) But he could at least avoid being intimidated by it. He would show the waiter that he was not going to be browbeaten. He would show . . .

But he had no opportunity to show anything at all. For Maurice solved the difficulty by saying, 'If anybody offers me anything but Ayala '15 I shall burst into tears.'

Brian looked at him gratefully. Then he glanced at Julia. She nodded. He felt like a ship that has glided into smooth waters after a storm.

Lord William could now continue his story undisturbed. 'Do you see that woman over there?' he repeated.

'The one with the odd face?'

'Odd is exactly the word. Look at her for a moment.'

Brian looked. And as he looked he felt a strange feeling of foreboding – one of those curious premonitions which occasionally come even to the most superstitious of mortals. It was to be a long time before he would realize the reason for this foreboding, or its justification, and as quickly as it had come it passed. However, he continued to look at her. She had a strange, tight look about the eyes, and a perpetual pout. Her face, indeed, was more like a mask than a human countenance.

'If he stares much longer she will suspect the worst,' said Julia.

'She is always hoping for the worst, and often getting it. Well,' he said, turning again to Brian, 'that is Lady Hardcastle. And she is one of the immortals.'

'Why?'

'Because I have decided to talk about her, and my scandals never die. They become part of the family history and are gravely repeated by nurses as examples of a great tradition. Shall I tell you my story of Anne?'

Maurice wriggled irritably. 'This is one of my stories,' he said.

'I admit that you gave birth to it. But when you sent it out into the world it was stunted and naked. I heard it crying in the wilderness and I adopted it. I clothed it with the richest adjectives of my own imagination, and fed it with my own wit. As a result, it has grown out of all knowledge. It is no longer your story. It is mine.'

Maurice pouted and consoled himself with an olive.

Lord William leant back and crooned: 'As the years passed by and Anne gazed into the mirror at the face which had launched a thousand ships – (she was once a great favourite with the Admiralty) – she wanted to know how she could possibly stop the wrinkles which time was writing on her brow. As a matter of fact, it was not so much her wrinkles which were worrying her as her mouth. She had a masseur who destroyed wrinkles as efficiently as a Scotch terrier destroys rats. But nobody could help her with her mouth. It seemed to grow larger and larger, and it had a most discouraging droop at the corners.

'It was in that distant era when facial surgery became so terribly fashionable. Every woman in London was rushing to be butchered, and Lady Hardcastle wanted to rush, too. But she was rather nervous about it. However, one day when the mirror had been particularly insulting, she decided to take her courage in both hands and have her face sewn up. As soon as the operation was over she departed, still bandaged, with her maid, to Florence, informing the world that she had suffered severe facial injuries in a motor smash. The unveiling of the face took place in a darkened room in one of the shabbier *palazzos* of Florence. A doctor, and a maid, were the only other persons present. As the last bandage was torn away she leant forward with a cry . . .'

'Go *on*,' cried Brian.

'She saw a woman with staring eyes, and a rose-bud mouth, and' – Lord William paused – 'what might best be described as a pout. The lips were pursed together . . . like this.' And he pouted absurdly.

Brian looked slightly disappointed. 'Is that all?' he said.

'Certainly not. The story now begins.'

He leant forward and fixed Brian with a glittering eye. 'Filled with gratitude at a blessing which was so evidently inspired from a divine source, Lady Hardcastle decided, on the same afternoon, that she would go to church and offer thanks. She set out alone, pouting with pious pride. She entered the church and knelt down, raising her face up to the fretted roof. She was alone with herself and her mouth.

'At least she thought she was. For hardly had she knelt down than a dark figure advanced out of the shadows. It was the verger. He touched her on the shoulder. She looked up at him, still pouting. Very gently he said to her, "*The signora is not permitted to whistle in the church.*"'

Lord William leant back, and beamed on the assembled company. After telling what he considered to be a good story he was always as amiable as a cat that has drunk a large saucer of cream. And if, instead of telling his own story he could tell somebody else's, and tell it better, he felt the same thrill as a certain amiable Persian of my acquaintance who leaves its own cream, makes a hazardous passage over a roof, across a wall, and down a tree, to gobble the plain milk of the infuriated cat next door.

Dinner was nearly over, and Brian was feeling almost happy.

He was already beginning to understand the technique of these people's conversation. The chief knack seemed to be in a stupendous exaggeration of everyday statements. If, for instance, the waiter forgot to give one a wooden 'spinner,' with which to take the fizz out of one's champagne, the right phrase was, 'this is *more* than I can bear,' or 'this is *agony*.' 'Divine,' 'amazing,' 'shattering,' 'monstrous,' were all employed for the most ordinary feelings and facts. He found himself wondering what language they would have to speak if anything really awful did happen. They would either have to relapse into Russian, or else express themselves in dumb-show.

However, he had managed to keep his end up in the conversation, wisely deciding that he would leave any intimate discussion on the habits of the aristocracy to the others, devoting himself to more plebeian affairs. He had told them the tale of Mrs. Pleat, and her Tuesday-morning complex, and it had been voted superb.

Most of all, Julia was invariably gracious. Oh! He could sing with joy.

'Don, darling. We must go.'

Lord William frowned. 'Why?'

'We shall miss the first act.'

'Does that matter? It's one of Evan's plays. And all his first acts are the same.'

'Darling, don't be too hideously tiresome.'

'It's entirely true. His plays are only produced because his uncle happens to be a duke. And he knows it! He was born with a silver spoon in his mouth, and he has been trying to swallow it ever since.'

'I can't help it. I'm going. Please, Don. We'll leave Mr. Elme to pay the bill.'

Oh, angel of tact! Brian had been able to carry off his task up till now, but the idea of paying for dinner with Julia's money, in front of Julia herself, and in front of Lord William and Maurice, who both knew that it was not he who was really paying, knowing also that *he* knew that they knew, would have been more than he could bear.

'We'll meet you outside.'

They rose to their feet. He was alone, with the waiter bending over him.

The bill came to nine pounds fifteen shillings. He felt inclined to laugh. Nine pounds fifteen shillings! Still, it seemed to be right. It must be right. He paid it. All that remained was to tip.

How much should he give? Memories of tuppences furtively pushed under plates in tea-shops. Memories of an occasional generous sixpence after a half-crown dinner. Would five shillings be enough? Or ten. It seemed fantastic. Then he remembered reading that the proper tip was ten per cent of the whole bill. He did a rapid sum in his head. Ten per cent of nine pounds fifteen shillings was nearly a pound. A whole pound. For a tip.

Madness. Complete madness. The whole world was mad. He placed a pound boldly on the plate and hurried outside.

CHAPTER FOUR

'I CANNOT think,' said Lord William, as they settled themselves into the box, some three minutes before the rise of the curtain on 'The Tragedy of Heloise and Abelard,' by Evan Spade, 'who it was who began the extraordinary legend that a first night was a brilliant affair. It always gives *me* the feeling that I am slumming.'

Brian looked at him in astonishment. He himself was at the acme of his mental, spiritual and social ambition. As soon as they had entered, he had been seized by that acute but pleasurable self-consciousness which assails most persons who sit in a box at a theatre for the first time. He was aware that a great many eyes in the stalls were directed at their party, and he was also aware that from this distance nobody could possibly detect any shortcomings in the set of his waistcoat. As a result he was holding his head very high and glancing almost haughtily at the inferior stalls. But Lord William's remark gave him to pause, especially as he followed it up by saying:

'The same flea-bitten crowd.'

Flea-bitten? Those gay, glittering creatures? Flea-bitten? Those stern men with horn-rimmed spectacles who were doubtless the critics? (Well, perhaps one.) But those brightly cloaked, laughing women?

He examined them more closely. Certainly, they were not quite the same as he had been given to understand by his perusal of novels. A great many of the women, with their cropped hair, their eyeglasses and their rough cloaks, appeared to desire to be mistaken for young men, whereas many of the young men had a positively maternal look on their smooth features. Several individuals impressed themselves upon his notice. There was a Scottish peer, carefully folding up his free programme in order to take it home in case his wife should desire to come to a later performance. There were quantities of young women in cloaks so spangled and glistening that one had a momentary impression of quantities of monstrous fishes. There was a bucolic-looking dramatic critic in a tweed coat, wrinkling his nose because the manager, who had a high sartorial standard, had placed him behind a pillar. There were heavily rouged leading-ladies, 'at liberty,' or, as Lord William expressed it, 'at large,' and thin and precious young men, holding their fingers in front of their faces, as though in prayer. The orchestra, with a charming disregard for Abelard and Heloise, was endeavouring to master the rhythm of a George Gershwin ragtime, with about as much ease as a British bulldog that had picked up a lump of chewing-gum in mistake for a bone. Everybody looked very tired and excited. But 'flea-bitten'? Surely not that?

He turned to Julia. 'They all look all right to me,' he said, a note of challenge in his voice.

'That's because you haven't got a liver.'

'No. It's because he reads female novelists. Every female novelist for the last forty years has been keeping up the illusion. They fill their stalls with duchesses who nudge each other at the entrance of Mr. Hannen Swaffer. They put a thinly disguised Bernard Shaw in one box, and a Prince Peculiar in another, and they scatter a lot of popular actresses about the house, who are always greeted by the gallery with uproarious applause. And yet, look what has just happened!'

'What?'

'Dear Sylvia has just come in. She is a very popular actress. And the only person who took any notice of her was a young man near the gangway, who mistook her for his mother, and is now burying his head in his programme.'

'I shall do the same,' said Julia. 'I see that the hero is a great friend of Maurice.'

'Darling – he *isn't!*'

'Oh yes, he is. You left Eton under the same cloud.'

Brian pricked up his ears. But Maurice stopped the conversation. 'I want to tell him all about the play,' he said quickly.

'Why – have you seen it?'

'No. But I know Evan. He's a terrible sentimentalist, and is so afraid of showing it that he makes all his characters positively inhuman. Mothers eat their young in all his families, and serpents are nourished in every bosom. As a result, Heloise and Abelard will not be allowed to kiss each other. They may have some form of sterilized connection, but otherwise they will say acid things about life, and drink a lot of twelfth-century cocktails. And Abelard will be given a sporting father, and Heloise a religious mother, and it will all be very nervy and brilliant and delicious. *You'll see.*'

The curtain went up. And in a few minutes Brian saw to his relief that Maurice was wrong.

The reader is now to be treated to a brief sentimental excursion, for a reason which will shortly become apparent.

The play, as we know, concerned Abelard and Heloise – those two lovers whose passion has been for seven hundred years the mirror in which successive generations have measured and reflected the colour of their own desires. It is also true, as Maurice had foreshadowed, that the drama was composed in a modern idiom. Yet the realities were there, the realities which had no relation to time or space, which spoke in the accounts of 1926 as truly as of 1192.

Heloise and Abelard! Brian and Julia! The coupling of the names is not my own. It is Brian's. In the present state of his mind it was inevitable that he should so join them. And when the curtain fell on the first act and the theatre was aglitter, and a babel of tongues was unloosed, none of the pleasantries of Lord William could break the spell in which he now found himself held.

And yet, Lord William was talking all the time, as though nothing wonderful were happening.

'Poor Bock,' he was saying, 'is still in the throes of his lighting apparatus. I hear he bought it in Germany, and certainly the sky in that act was terribly Prussian. There were things being done on the backcloth which looked exactly like the more rapid retreats from Mons in the *Daily Mail* war maps. How clever of him! We are all so anxious to see what shape the cloud is going to assume that we don't listen to anything that is being said on the stage. If only nature were as accommodating! If only one could arrange for thunderbolts just after one's best remarks, and a rainstorm when one was talking about Tchekov, or a Scotch mist whenever one condescended to remember the modern dramatists!'

Quickly over the interval and the second act, and the second interval as well. For in the third act, there came a moment which cut through Brian's life like a sword, killing his past with a single blow, propelling him into a strange and dangerous future.

The scene was laid in the study of Canon Fulbert in Paris. Darkness was spreading swiftly over the stage, and swiftly over the lives of the lovers, for it was at that blank hour before they were drawn apart, to be for ever alone. Tall windows gave on to the Seine, and outside one had the sense of a bitter, hostile sky.

Brian was lost – utterly lost. He *was* in Paris eight hundred years ago. He *knew* that just outside those windows there would soon flit the shadows of wolves from the neighbouring forests. He knew that in the new Cathedral of Notre Dame the incense was rising in a cold blue cloud, sweeter and more sharp from the icy air. He saw the men and women stumbling home over the rocky roads, and heard them whisper that there was snow in those sullen clouds, and that if the fall was heavy there would be more wolves from the east, and perhaps, for whole days, Paris might be cut off, as had been known some twenty years ago.

He moved, too, with the shivering students in the cloisters, hearing scraps of nominalism or the fierce phrases of some white-faced disciple of Roscelin, followed by the smooth and acid Latin of an orthodox priest. For no cold could daunt the controversialists. Paris was a city of theories. The very streets were thick with them. Theories were haunting men like ghosts, troubling the serene airs of morning, hanging like mists over the cheerless nights, following men to bed, stretching thin and tenuous fingers into their dreams.

And here was Abelard, the greatest theorist of them all, who had thrown aside these ghosts for the one reality in life, whose gay and brilliant brain had been clouded, who had willingly surrendered himself – he who had faced unscathed the intellectual arrows of the entire world – to a schoolgirl. No wonder that the faces in the cloisters were grey at the thought of this apostacy. No wonder that coarse and callous words hung on the dusk, seeming to linger like a damp and poisonous spell in the courts where he had held sway.

Yes – Brian was in Paris – he was in Paris now – he was Abelard and Julia was his Heloise. Through the streets he walked, gathering his coarse cloak firmly to him against the chill. Here he was at the door of the Canon's house, and here was the scared little maid who ushered him into the firelit hall. Memories – memories everywhere. How often from those book-shelves had he taken a Seneca or a Homer and how often, in that window-seat, had his head been close to hers while they studied, until, in the intoxication of sense, the words had seemed to swim before him, the book had been pushed aside, and all learning, all culture forgotten in the ecstasy of a kiss? There had been summer days when they had built their dream cities from Plato's mind, and when the clear light of Aristotle had shone more brightly in the golden, dusty beams which drifted through the windows. And days of spring when all was brilliant and alert, when the mind of Heloise was so keen for sudden, biting comment, or slow in plastic surrender that he had almost forgotten that she was a woman, and had argued with her as keenly as any man. But always learning had drifted to love. All the roads of controversy had led to that. All the sages and the prophets had pointed thither. All the seasons, the green and the golden, the leafy and the dark, had sped them along that enchanted way. It was as it had to be, ordained and irrevocable.

A sudden stir behind him, a flash of light, the silhouette of Lord William's figure (destined for the Bar), recalled him for an instant to the present. He was only one of the audience in the theatre. But the chilling shock of that realization was quickly clouded over. Once more he span through centuries. Once more he was in medieval Paris.

And now he was standing by the side of Heloise, looking out

with her over the steel-grey waters. How bare and forlorn were the trees on the distant river-bank! And the guttering lamps that ancient hands were placing in the windows were only brave signals against the onrushing dusk.

'Like those lamps,' he thought, 'are Abelard's own words. He speaks and a light is lit in her heart. They will help her through part of the night which she has to face. But long before dawn, the bright words will have flickered out, and she will be in darkness.'

Crescendo! Crescendo!

He leant forward. Abelard was kneeling at her feet. 'I know,' said Brian to himself, 'what you are feeling. I know it all. You ought not to be here before these staring crowds. It is wrong that we should be watching you, wrong that we should be sitting in judgment on your grief – wrong – all wrong.' So deeply was he moved that he lowered his eyes, gripping his hands together in pain.

And now, he saw an extraordinary thing. He saw a white hand – Julia's hand steal towards him. He saw, and felt, that hand settle on his own. He felt, too, the hand press his – not only press, but remain.

His heart was thumping so furiously that he was conscious of a sharp pain in his temples. He was also conscious – (it is my painful duty to record this unromantic sensation) – of feeling exceedingly sick. His mouth seemed to dry, his brain became thick and hot. Heloise and Abelard were blown away, two ghostly figures, far, far away, forgotten and unwanted.

Timidly he looked up. Julia had turned her head towards him. He thought he saw a reflected tenderness in her eyes. She was smiling, a little gravely, at *him*, at *him*. And still her hand was pressing his.

He then did an outrageous thing. In fact, to say that *he* did is almost a libel on so excellent a young man. Something outside him did it. Something outside him made him lift her hand with a swift gesture to his lips, and kiss it.

The hand was quickly drawn away. The smile faded from her face. In agony he could detect, on the profile that was now turned towards him, a frown.

CHAPTER FIVE

L ORD WILLIAM linked his arm in that of Maurice Cheyne and walked through the frost-bound square, up the sinister little sweep of Hay Hill, and so down the corridors, brightly lit and silver-floored, of Dover Street, into the queer and ragged thoroughfare of Bond Street. He was feeling well pleased with the world.

Firstly, he was about to eat oysters, and he had the curious faculty, common to most sensualists, of savouring in advance the flavour of any dish he had determined to consume. At the very moment ghostly oysters were, so to speak, rolling round his tongue, and the sparkle of untasted champagne began already to fill his veins with an imagined fire.

Secondly, he had Maurice by his side, so that he would be able to talk at his rather flashy best. That was the secret of his friendship with Maurice. He was a perfect audience. He could be snubbed, and insulted, and ignored, but he never, as long as one paid his bills, took offence.

Arrived at the Gaga Club, the two men made their way discreetly to the corner table which had been reserved for them, bowing simultaneously to various acquaintances who were scattered round the room. The Gaga Club was 'quite the most divine' of all London's night clubs. Its lights were the kindest, its bends the weirdest. And it had a terribly tactful head-waiter, who knew precisely the respective publicity values of dukes, divorcés, authors, and Mr. Michael Arlen. Yet, in spite of these delights, a slight frown suddenly obscured Lord William's countenance.

'Mrs. Grindhaven is here,' he said, 'and she will ask me to dance. She dances with one foot in Vienna and the other in New York, being unable to distinguish between a waltz and a jazz. Will you remember, Maurice, that I have a swollen ankle?'

'But she saw you walk in, Don.'

'Then you must have accidentally kicked me under the table. Here are our oysters.'

They ate their oysters. Lord William finished his first, and observed that Maurice had still two left. He stretched out a podgy hand and seized the largest.

'Don. You are incredible. I had been saving that one.'

But Lord William only smiled, his eyes glittering with the added pleasure of eating an extra oyster and annoying Maurice at the same time.

The champagne was excellent, and Lord William began to feel in the mood for delivering a diatribe against some of the recognized virtues of the British people. Unfortunately, as he was beginning to realize, there were so few virtues left to be recognized. Now that the works of Mr. Noel Coward were obtainable in cheap editions, now that even the universities were set swift on the road to decay, there was little about which one could justifiably complain. He put his thoughts into words.

'Over there,' he said, indicating the dramatist of the evening, 'is Evan. He informed me this morning that he is writing a play about a girl who is persecuted by narrow-minded, Puritan parents. I asked him where he discovered such people. And he confessed that they were only to be found in America.'

'He has evidently never met my father.'

'Your father is not a parent. He is a growth. I was about to say that I had a great affection for American Puritanism. Occasionally I send large and secret cheques to those numerous societies in the Middle West which aim at making bridge on Sundays a penal offence, and would permit the matrimonial act only to be accomplished on the first and third Thursdays in the month. I regard such societies as a terrific artistic blessing. No real genius, while he is working, has a sense of humour, and once one loses one's sense of humour such things as one finds quoted in Mr. H. L. Mencken's magazines are as red rags to a bull. If the artist is the bull, the larger and redder the rag the better. Unfortunately the modern artist is not a bull. He is a mild and amiable cow, who, if offered a red rag, would merely wipe his nose on it, or possibly caper round the field, purring like a kitten.'

'I believe,' said Maurice, 'that I am getting tight. And when I am tight, I am divine.'

'When you are tight you are merely expensive,' said Lord William, continuing in a slightly intoned voice. 'We have been rebelling so long against Victorianism that there is absolutely nothing left to rebel against. Consider our houses. If I were Prime Minister I should issue an order that everybody possessing Victorian drawing-rooms should be forced to preserve them intact, because of the inroads which good taste is making upon them. Nothing is so shattering as to live in an age of really good taste. It stultifies the soul.'

'There is always,' remarked Maurice dutifully, 'the Royal Academy.'

Lord William sipped some more champagne. 'I think you are mistaken. There is no real Royal Academy. Or rather, there are no real Royal Academicians. A few remain perhaps. Yes. I remember, on my last visit, recognizing the same six sheep which Mr. Joseph Farquharson has been painting for the last forty years, standing in the same snow. They had smiles on their faces and far too much Chinese White on their backs. They were perhaps a little woollier than when he first charmed us with them, but that only shows his close observance of Nature. The snow, however, had not melted, which shows his serene independence of it.'

'Don, you're insane. John Collier is still alive. Or ought I to say the Honourable John Collier? I think I ought. It makes him even more grotesque.'

'Yes. I had forgotten him too.' A look of painful regret came over Lord William's face. 'Those were great times, Maurice. Think of his problem pictures! Think of his men and women gazing at each other with expressions of such blatant stupidity that nobody could possibly tell which had done what! But, do you remember? they always *had* done something. That was the delicious part about it. 'She' really *had* dined at the Trocadero, or he really *had* cheated at whist, or loo, or whatever games they played in those days. But then – this marvellous designer of puzzles has practically ceased to function nowadays. And, anyway, what is one among so many? No. We live in a dreadful age, when everybody imagines themselves to be artistic and everybody is tolerant.'

'You're depressing me terribly,' said Maurice. 'I should feel hideously lonely if everybody agreed with me. But you're entirely wrong. Next season we will go to the opera together, and I will point out to you the exact moments when nobody but ourselves realize why Chaliapin is a great artist but would have been a greater politician.'

Lord William frowned. He did not like disagreement. He therefore ignored Maurice's remark about Chaliapin. 'Of course, the opera has always been more syndicate than singing,' he said, 'but until lately it was never more than a dress parade. As such it was quite amusing. But I am afraid that it is about to be taken seriously. We are breeding a public that is beginning to suspect that Wagner really did write music, and not merely an accompaniment to tiaras, and a painful silence descends on the house during the more obvious moments of *Boheme*. I never go to the opera now.'

'Well then – architecture. Look at Regent Street.'

'What hideous things you are suggesting. Still – it is possible to look at Regent Street, provided one is slightly drunk, and recover from doing so in a remarkably short space. And I glory in Regent Street. It is a perpetual provocation to anybody with the remotest sense of decency. By its revolting complexity and pomposity it is calculated to make an anarchist of everybody who walks down it. But we cannot all live in Regent Street.'

He paused and leant back, surveying the dancers with wearied eyes. The jazz band blared and screamed, the air was thick with smoke, the faces of the women were universally contorted. He had a feeling that he was witnessing a ridiculous parade of the wooden soldiers, in which the music had run to riot and the performers were all in thrall to the discipline of *ennui*. How unpleasant it all was! And yet one came here. One came because one didn't wish to think. Nobody could think in such a noise.

The band stopped.

'Of course, you are really a throwback to the nineties,' said Maurice. 'Your conversation to-night . . .'

'You are entirely wrong.' He raised himself on his elbow and lit a cigarette. 'If this were the nineties, I should be telling the whole restaurant that I had secret, scarlet sins, and that my sins were much more scarlet and much less secret than anybody's else's. Am I doing that?'

'No. But you will.'

'I shall not, because I find that there is something a little depressing about sinning *en masse*. It is like mixed bathing. Sin should be solitary, just as virtue should be companionable. There is the difference between worshipping a God and blaspheming one. The worshipper is at his best in a great crowd, lifting his voice in common praise. But the blasphemer is an egotist. He wants his little curses to himself. He has patented his own perversity. He must be silhouetted against a lonely sky, with a single fist clenched towards the sunset.'

'You would have fitted superbly with the nineties,' replied Maurice doggedly. Motley glanced at him. He *was* getting tight. How too tiresome.

'On the contrary, I should have been a gross misfit. I *was* a young man in the nineties, but I was not of them. I ignored them. If I had found green carnations growing in Hyde Park I should have suspected them to be lettuces. Besides, I have no use for an age in which one could gain a bad reputation merely by wearing a flower. A bad reputation was as abominably easy for people in those days as it is difficult to-day.'

'I don't agree.'

'Listen. When a girl in the nineties was bored, she could always electrify the family by announcing that she was going to be a New woman, or that she had read a novel by Mr. Grant Allen and had understood it, or that a pair of bicycling bloomers were concealed in her wardrobe. She could be sure that the confession would lead to violent opposition, and opposition was exactly what she wanted. It made her feel a martyr. It brought a sparkle to her unassisted cheeks.'

'But nowadays nobody ever opposes anything.'

'I have been endeavouring to point that out for the last quarter of an hour. As a result we are universally vicious, and therefore universally tiresome. To be forced to break all the ten commandments is much more wearing than to be forced to respect them. It is also infinitely less amusing.'

He sighed. 'That, to return to the subject of our agreeable young friend of this evening, is the fascination of Mr. Brian Elme.'

He is a good young man, and the breed is almost extinct. Because he is so palpably honest – (by the way, you *have* my gold matchbox, haven't you? Thank you so much) – because he is so palpably honest, one longs to see his first descent. Because he is so palpably virtuous, one longs for him to have affairs.'

'This is rather *vieux jeu*, isn't it?' said Maurice spitefully. 'To show the innocent young man the wickedness of London life?'

'Of course it is an old game. In other words, it has stood the test of time, as being eternally amusing. I intend to play it.'

He glanced slyly at Maurice, who, however, held his peace. 'What Master Elme wants,' he added, 'is a little course of a woman like Anne Hardcastle.'

'She would hardly corrupt him in a week.'

'Your ignorance of Anne's methods scarcely reflects credit on you, Maurice. Still, I believe she likes manly men, and nobody has ever accused you of *that*. Correct me if I am wrong.'

Maurice sulked.

'Anne can do wonders in less than a week. When the Italian cricket team stayed at Hardcastle, she made love to all of them, even the umpire. I wrote her a poem about it, called "The Decline and Fall of the Roman Umpire."'

'Yes. I remember,' said Maurice. 'It was a very bad poem.'

Lord William saw that he had succeeded in his task of upsetting Maurice and was therefore content to let the matter drop.

'I think we can safely leave his corruption to Julia,' he said. 'And here is Mrs. Grindhaven. My ankle is giving me great pain.'

'Don darling.' A woman with Chinese eyes and a flat figure leant over them.

'Laura. Come and sit down. What was that heavenly tango you were dancing just then?'

'It was a perfectly simple waltz,' she said hoarsely. 'And I have come to dance it with you.'

'But, my dearest Laura, I've hurt my ankle.'

'Don't lie. I saw you come in.'

'It has all happened since then. Maurice has kicked me under the table. I didn't utter a sound. I have been bearing it in silence like the Spartan boy and the fox. I always think,' he added, 'that boy should have been psycho-analysed. '

'Nothing but lies.'

'I will lend you Maurice,' said Lord William.

'He will kick me on the ankle, too,' she croaked.

'Not if you dance your tango, my precious. He would only be able to kick you on the elbow then.'

With a sigh Maurice rose to his feet. Mrs. Grindhaven grimly assumed charge of him. When they were safely at the other end of the room Lord William stretched out his hand for Maurice's glass of champagne, which was all that was left of the bottle. The last glass, he thought, was always the sweetest. And he knew that Maurice thought so too.

CHAPTER SIX

WHAT did Julia mean when she had pressed his hand in the box? That was, for Brian, the question on which his life depended.

Did people press hands without meaning it? Could there be some sort of involuntary action of the muscles which contracted the fingers, causing the same to squeeze any object with which they came in contact?

No. That was rot.

But – could people press a hand merely because it was there, and because they were labouring under the influence of some external emotion not connected with the person to whom the hand belonged?

He recalled the circumstances. The precise moment at which his hand had been pressed was when Heloise had been informing Abelard, in curiously blunt phraseology, that 'a little stranger' was expected. A striking announcement, no doubt, but hardly one to arouse in the audience any overwhelmingly sentimental feelings, considering the way in which it had been phrased.

A third alternative. Were exalted people like Julia – exalted in rank as well as beauty, virtue, wit, learning (and all the other qualities with which he was mentally endowing her) – were they in the habit of pressing hands as a sort of social custom? He meant, supposing an earl's daughter, and an ambassador, and a duchess, and a – well – a film star – supposing, that is to say, they all found themselves sitting together in a box in the dark, would they press each other's hands?

He pondered the question. He envisaged the ambassador and the duchess together – hand stealing towards hand. No. It didn't seem at all probable. However tightly he screwed up his eyes he couldn't make his ambassador place his hand on his duchess's knee. As soon as he tried to do so it became like something out of Alice in Wonderland. And the scene which had taken place at the Imperial Theatre the night before had been in no way legendary. It had been tremendously real. He could still feel the electric thrill in his fingers where she had touched them.

He held out his hand to the light. It seemed a very wonderful hand now. It belonged to her. So did his arms and his legs and his heart and his head.

'Catching flies?'

Brian turned round guiltily. 'Hallo, Walter!'

'What are you doing?'

'Nothing. Why?'

Walter looked at him and laughed. He knew better than to pursue the subject. Instead he said: 'It's jolly good of you to speak to me this morning at all.'

'Ass.'

'Still, you'd better give me a report. And you can begin with the soup.'

While Brian was explaining, Walter thought hard. He was worried and afraid. This woman – what did she want with his friend? He had never met Julia, but already, from Brian's halting references to her, he felt that he knew a great deal more about her than did Brian himself. Brian was such an infant where women were concerned. Still . . . if she made him happy. . . . But how could she? How could there be anything real, or . . . (he had to use the word) . . . 'decent' . . . with a woman like this?

Sooner or later, of course, one of them, or both of them, had to fall. That was inevitable. But how different was this from the romances which together they had imagined! He remembered a long summer evening on the Cotswold Hills when Brian had opened his heart on the subject of the girl he might one day love. It had been a curiously rambling confession, starred with moments of boyish passion which had surprised even Walter by its intensity. Lying back among a healthy crop of clover, he had painted his ideal upon the fading skies – an ideal such as only a boy could hold, of a virginity too rare for human flesh. Walter had never tried to destroy this ideal – that was one of the blows which Life must administer. But never had he dreamt that he would go so childishly astray as this.

Well – there was nothing to do. And so, when the recital of the dinner was finished, he said, 'Yes. But can't you tell me a bit more about Julia? What's she like? What tastes has she got?'

Brian flushed slightly.

'She said she liked men with fair hair.'

'Well – you score there, don't you?'

'Yes, thank God. I'd stand on my head all day in a bucket of peroxide if I thought it'd please her.'

'Anything else?'

'Well. She seemed to like birds.'

'What. To eat?'

'No. Flying about, you fool.'

'Well. I've got a parrot down at Portsmouth. That flies like hell. Only it's not very dainty in its habits.'

Brian looked at him in scorn. 'I wasn't talking about parrots. I was talking about thrushes and nightingales and larks and . . .' He paused ecstatically.

'And emus and wagtails and owls,' added Walter. 'You'd better take her to the Zoo.'

Brian ignored him. 'I think it's very wonderful to have tastes like that. I'm going to read all about birds. I'm going to learn when they mate and what their songs mean, and where they go to in the spring. . . .'

'And where the flies go in the winter.'

'You're damned funny, aren't you?'

He put his hands in his pockets and rattled a few coins together. 'I'd like to send her something,' he said casually. 'I'm passing Cartier's this morning.'

'Walter. That's not awfully kind.'

A shadow crossed Walter's face. 'Sorry, old thing.'

'If you knew how I longed to be rich,' said Brian, a little piteously. 'Because she loves green, I'd give her all the emeralds in the world. Because she loves the birds, I'd buy a place in the country, and there'd be nightingales in every tree, and a regular fusillade of larks to greet her when she got up in the morning. And because she likes fair hair, I'd have a bodyguard of blondes, even if they did make me jealous.'

'That's love all right.'

'Of course it's love. Of course it's love. Love!'

He threw up his arms and laughed. Life, which had seemed so meaningless, had become a tremendous palpitating adventure. So thrilled was he that, against his intention, he found himself confessing the episode of the hand, which he had meant to keep to himself.

'There's something else,' he said with a catch in his voice.

'Lord! You seem to have studied her closely.'

'No. It's something we did together.'

'Keep it clean, old man.'

He ignored the cheerful coarseness of Walter's remark. He was bubbling with a strange, halting pride.

'Well, we were sitting there in the box, watching the play, and – I don't know how it happened, but, you see, our hands . . .'

'Go on.'

'They sort of got mixed.'

'It's a way hands have.'

Brian looked at him suspiciously. 'And afterwards – she pressed mine – pretty hard – she did really.'

'Well, I never said she didn't.'

'D'you mean that's the only thing you can think of to say?'

'What d'you want me to say? I don't call that anything to boast about.'

Brian looked at him with bitter disappointment. 'Oh, I did think you'd understand.'

He walked to the fireplace, biting his lip with vexation. How could he explain to Walter all that he meant? How could he conjure up before him the crowded darkness of the theatre, the significant perfume of his worshipped one, the faint crescent of light on her shoulders, the sudden singing of his heart which that timid contact had impelled?

'B.'

'Oh. Get out.'

'Sorry.'

There was silence. He looked round. Walter was still there.

'B. I'm only chaffing because . . .'

'Why?'

'Oh – I don't know. P'raps because I don't want to take it too seriously.'

'But it *is* serious, I tell you.'

'Is it?' He put his hand on his shoulder and looked him straight in the face. There was a frightened expression in Brian's eyes, like a child standing lonely in the dark.

'I'm a selfish beast,' went on Walter. 'I want to go on living with you until the real thing comes. And then . . .'

'But, this is the real thing.'

'For you, perhaps.'

'Why do you say that?' There was agony in his tone. 'Why . . .' His voice trailed away into nothingness. For he had caught sight of himself in the glass. And he had noticed, not the eager face, not the sparkle of youth in his eyes, but a frayed collar and a rather worn tie. And beyond himself he had seen a shabby wall, with a few spotted prints hanging on it, a couple of faded curtains, a cracked window, and through the window a lowering sky.

'Walter, old thing.' He turned to him.

'Yes, B.'

'Am I making a fool of myself? Supposing it's absolutely hopeless? Supposing she was just laughing at me – pulling my leg? What then?'

'What then? I'll tell you what then.'

'Well?' he said breathlessly.

'I should go round to her, and I should put my hands on her

neck like this' – he suited the action to the word – 'and my knee on her tummy like this' – and here he gave Brian a dig in the stomach with his own knee – 'and I should throttle and throttle and throttle until she was lying at my feet. Then I'd remove my hat, give her a kick, and go off and have a bitter.'

'Ow! You brute. You're hurting.'

'Sorry, B.' He released him.

'And if you're ever disrespectful about Julia again, you're for it.'

He turned again to the window. The sky looked frozen and forlorn. The glass panes against his forehead felt like sheets of ice.

'Lord!' he said, 'it's cold. The whole world's cold.'

CHAPTER SEVEN

JULIA was now definitely decided that Brian should be her refuge against *ennui* during the next few months. She must have some such refuge, and really he was quite the newest and freshest thing which had been washed up on to the shore of Mayfair for a considerable period. One might play terribly amusing games with him.

It must be admitted that there were few cures for boredom which she had not sampled, either for her body or her soul. Last year, for instance, she had been principally intrigued by the latest mysteries of the medical profession, and had made, in company with her friends, pilgrimages to Harley Street which had often proved as entertaining as a first night. Standing before sleek and monocled physicians, she had been initiated into the devices of that strange instrument, Abram's box, which, as far as she could understand, claimed to diagnose, and cure, the most complicated ills of the human system by some electrical reaction from a spot of the patient's blood. A little farther up the street she had experimented in organotherapy, had sat in waiting-rooms surrounded by rich cretins and their despairing relatives, subsequently filling herself with the glands of goats (which, to tell the truth, toned up her system considerably). Still farther along she had indulged in a little mild psycho-analysis, but that told her little that she did not know already. As for osteopathy – 'the old maid's romance' – that struck her as rather too tame, and, after a single treatment, she gave it up. Another year, interior decoration had claimed her for its own. Plenty of her more prosperous acquaintances were always having their houses done up, so why should she not do it for them? And provided one possessed a temperament and a blank cheque one could obtain the most delicious results. So she had created bedrooms of the palest lemon-colour, with furniture of white leather and little green tables on which nothing more substantial than a lip-stick could ever rest. There had been dining-rooms hung with green brocatelle, and staircases with glass banisters, and corridors whose walls teemed with the bloated fantasies of Serck, and bathrooms of glistening silver (which caused agony to tired housemaids), and . . . But you know it for yourselves, do you not? It is a little obvious nowadays.

Then, of course, there was the great year when everybody was indulging in the strangest diets, in order to reduce. Julia had no need whatever to reduce, but she played the game because all the world was playing it. At one moment she nibbled lettuces, at another she chewed biscuits which seemed to be composed of a delicate mixture of sawdust and horse-flesh. Sometimes an eager friend would arrive hot-foot from the country, where he or she had been indulging in an orgy of milk and potatoes, and she would try their system for a while, until it was supplemented by the even more curious habit of a lemon-juice breakfast, followed by a lunch of raw vegetables and a dinner which it would be far too depressing to describe.

Ça passe. And unless somebody organized a trip to the moon there was nothing new in life. Hence the fascination of Brian. To meet anybody who really *was* thrilled by a first night, who opened his eyes wide at the sight of a woman smoking a cigar, who had never even crossed the Channel, who had never tasted Blini, who was frightened by one's butler, who swam in the Serpentine, who had read the works of Walter Scott, who thought Lord William brilliant, who stayed in London during August, and probably imagined that Marcel Proust was a form of infectious disease – all this was interesting in the extreme. Hence the following telephonic conversation, which must now be recorded.

'Is that you, Don?'

'Yes, Julia.'

'I want you to ask Brian Elme to lunch.'

'I have already done so.'

'Liar.'

'If you insist.'

'I shan't come. But I want you to ask him down to Hayseed, please.'

'Very well. You are going to have an affair?'

'Good-bye, Don. Good-bye.'

The above scandalous conversation floated a few days later over the wires that run unconcernedly across the noisy streets from Berkeley Square to Queen Anne's Gate. Had I the time in this narrative, I might indulge in some agreeable fantasies concerning the passage of words and passions and heart-throbs across those sober wires. Supposing, for example, that the wires were made sensitive, assuming the varying hues which were demanded by the conversations they were privileged to bear. Supposing that they glittered when the business men transacted their affairs in the city! What a golden mesh would hang over the black-coated throng that surges down Lombard Street, into the grey, mottled thoroughfares that circle the Bank of England. Supposing that they blushed a delicate pink as the ladies of Mayfair crooned their guilty secrets from scented rooms at dusk! What a pretty, fluttering array of ribbons would sparkle across the skies that vault the hallowed precincts of Berkeley Square and the Place that is called Carlos!

However, there being no time for those pleasant excursions of thought, one must make the telephone bell ring once more, this time in the office of *The Lady's Mail*.

Brian was writing a paragraph. You may think it an impertinence; but it was his humble way of paying tribute, even if, in substance, it was a lie. . . .

'I was in a little café the other day,' he wrote, *'and found myself behind Mr. Augustus John, who was dining with Sir William Orpen. They were discussing the perfect type of the female human face. Sir Wil-*

liam, in his quaint Irish brogue, was extolling the ancient Greek. John, of course, was inclined to revere the very modern. But both, curiously enough, agreed that both ancient and modern were perfectly combined in the features of Lady Julia Cres . . .'

It was at the close of this revelation that the telephone rang. Brian frowned. It was the office boy's job to answer the telephone, and the office boy's voice was in that slightly indecent stage which recalls a duet between Melba and Scotti, with a healthy crow acting as arbitrator. He waited until the duet should be over.

But the office boy, having put his ear to the receiver, started back in alarm. He glared at Brian.

'It's Lord William Motley,' he said, in a perfect mixture of soprano and bass. ''E wants you.'

Brian sprang to his feet. In awe the office boy regarded him. 'All right, this is private. You can go outside for a minute.'

'Yes, sir.' The crow this time was uppermost in the office boy's voice. He departed.

'Is that Brian?'

'Yes. Hallo!' (Damned silly remark, that.)

'Is it possible that you can lunch to-day?'

'I say, yes. I'd love to.'

'We'll lunch alone, I think. At the Gaga?'

'Just as you like.' (Lord, was that a brick?)

Brian learnt a great deal from that lunch, as indeed Lord William had intended. It began with his refusal of caviare. He would have loved caviare, but he observed from the menu that it cost seven shillings and sixpence a portion, and that seemed too fantastic a sum even to contemplate. Lord William saw through this subterfuge, and informed him that the habit of choosing cheap things on menus when somebody else was paying the bill was not only in exceedingly bad taste, but was a sure sign of an inferiority complex. Spurred on by this information, Brian proceeded to choose lobster cardinal, quail in aspic and foie-gras, a combination which Lord William heartily approved, although the sight of so healthy an appetite made him feel slightly faint.

'You should study Maurice,' he remarked. 'That sweet child has an eagle eye for expensive things, and he can tell a really prohibitive cigar merely by looking at it. People adore being imposed on by youth, if they can afford it. Don't you realize that? If you asked me at this moment to lend you five pounds I should be immensely happy. Aren't you going to?'

'I don't want it, thanks awfully.'

'Oh yes, you do. But that will come later, I expect. It is a pleasure still in store.'

This curious dialogue occurred as they were motoring back to Lord William's house in Queen Anne's Gate, of which the newspapers are always telling us so much.

They emerged from the car. 'Emerging' is indeed a gracious way of describing the scramble which descent from his lordship's car involved. He had designed the body of his car one day on a sheet of notepaper, when he had been slightly drunk, making it exceedingly narrow and drawing the roof with a single audacious curve. The sheet of notepaper had then been sent, by special messenger, to the coach-builders, who, having regarded it for some time with pained astonishment, had regretfully given it for execution to their workmen. The design had been faithfully carried out. As a result the car was undoubtedly a thing of beauty, but it could hardly be described as a joy for ever, or even as a joy for five minutes. The shortest journey in it (in spite of its immense chassis) involved curvature of the spine, sore knees, and a ruined temper. Still, Lord William stuck to his car. It was really so terribly *chic*.

The descent having been accomplished, they entered the house. A pale footman approached his lordship.

'The manicurist has been waiting since three o'clock, m'lord.'

'Send her away. I'm far too tired to be manicured to-day.'

'Yes, m'lord.'

'And bring some liqueurs.'

'Yes, m'lord.'

Brian leant his stick against a chair. In a Chinese stand were at least twenty varieties of sticks, topped with ivory, tortoise-shell, silver, gold, amber, polished bone.

'Slightly vulgar, aren't they? All presents, from people who think I go in for flagellation. Do take one.'

'Not really?'

'Of course.'

He stretched out a finger towards the silver one.

'That's the cheapest one,' said Lord William. 'Needless to say, it came from Maurice.' He looked at Brian curiously. 'If I'd asked anybody *else* to have a stick, they'd have grabbed a gold one.'

'I've been properly brought up,' said Brian.

'Yes. That's so clever of you.'

'I shall get over it.'

'Don't. Go on being more and *more* properly brought up. It always pays for a man. For a woman it's fatal. Anne Hardcastle is the only properly brought up woman I know, and as a result no bailiff will enter her house without a revolver or a dose of poison. Let's go upstairs.'

As they turned the corner of the staircase Brian suddenly stepped back in alarm. Through an open window immediately in front of them the head of a negro appeared. From the expression on his face he seemed to be in great distress. The head was followed by an immense body, clad in white. He scrambled through the window, bowed low, and then, with a frightened glance around him, he ran down the corridor.

'What on earth is that?'

'Only my servant.'

'But . . . coming through the window?'

'He comes through the window because he thinks the hall is full of devils.'

At any other moment Brian would have thought only of the superb newspaper story which this would make. 'Peer's strange attendant. Maddened negro who enters through the window.' As it was, he found himself wondering if Lord William were quite sane.

'But – do you let him?'

'Why not? I adore him. He adores me. But he's been taking drugs lately and they seem to have got on his nerves. He assures me that the hall is possessed by every sort of devil. I told him that must be because it is decorated by Fryers.'

'How does he get up, though?'

'I keep a ladder for him.' Lord William took him to the window and showed him a ladder stretching down into the courtyard. 'Really, Rastus would be thrilled to think of all the excitement he's caused. I must introduce you. He's the sweetest thing, and will try to poke hypodermic syringes into every part of you. What fun. But we'll leave him to himself just now.'

With a sigh of relief Brian followed Lord William up the stairs.

'Here we are. All the pretties.'

They stood in the doorway. A long room, with black painted walls and a silver ceiling, stretched before them. Round the walls, outlined with startling distinctness, were hung a series of masks, of every shape and colour. They stared into vacancy with sightless eyes, with fixed smiles and eternal frowns. A sudden wind blew in through the window and one of the masks fell to the floor. Brian shivered.

'Damn. Anne Hardcastle has crashed. Come and look at her.'

A little gingerly, as though the masks were about to speak, Brian advanced into the room. Lord William bent down to pick up the mask which had fallen.

'Doesn't she look horribly evil? It's a perfect likeness. The rather cow-like cheeks and that drooping mouth.'

'Is she really as awful as that?'

'She is. I'd love to introduce you to her. You'd be asked down to Hardcastle and given a liqueur which tastes of corpses.'

Brian went over to the wall. 'This is lovely, with the flower in her mouth.'

'Yes. It was a murderess I saw once at the Old Bailey. I feel that if I were clever I should give the flower some symbolical meaning. I suppose I shall have to call it life.'

He walked round the room pointing out mask after mask, some that were pale and perfect, some that were grotesquely contorted. There were masks that laughed with a painted frozen laughter, masks that were half turned aside, as though in fear of some mimic Medusa, masks with foolish pouts and semi-insane leers, masks so deformed that they were like the nightmares of a German caricaturist.

'They're my criticism of life,' he continued. 'That's how I see

my excellent friends. The masks in this room are all generaliza-
tions of types that are running about London to-day – types which
you will soon have the great pleasure of meeting. But – I sometimes do something more than generalization. . . .'

'What? Real people? Like Lady Hardcastle?'

'Exactly.'

'Oh, I say – do let me see.' Again Brian felt the journalistic value
of this remarkable revelation. '*Lord William Motley's strange hobby.*
Secret masks of the great and the notorious. Lady Oxford in green plaster
of Paris. Sir James Barrie in white soap-stone . . . *Anita Loos in pink*
papier mâché.' He sighed at the thought of so much copy wasted.

Lord William seemed to pause for a minute. 'Only two other
people have ever seen them. . . .'

Brian was touched for a moment with a medieval tremor. 'Perhaps you think I oughtn't to . . .' he said.

'I'm quite sure you oughtn't to. So you *shall.*' A rather feverish
smile spread over his immense cheeks. He drew a key from his
pocket, walked over to the wall, pulled back a piece of tapestry and
pushed open a door. He switched on a light which swung from the
ceiling of a tiny room. 'There!'

'Oh, God!' Brian stepped back. It was as though he had suddenly
intruded upon a party of all his new acquaintances and had found
them struck with some mortal plague. In the thin greenish light
he discerned the face of Lady Thane, wrinkled and decayed, and
by her side a coarse, brutal caricature of Lady Jane. A thin-lipped,
frowning Maurice stared at him from a bracket near the roof, and
a sallow, puffed-out Tanagra Guest (whom we shall meet later)
gazed white and blank from the only table. Other men and women
whose faces he had casually glanced at were here also, silent and
sightless, but strangely real. Most dreadful of all were those which
smiled.

'I've seen enough of those,' he said.

'How delicious and temperamental.' Motley took him by the
arm. 'Look! Look at Lady Thane.'

'I thought you liked her.'

'Look at her wrinkles and her double chins and her stupidity.
Look at her lovely daughter Jane. She only needs a waxed mous-

tache to make her perfect. Look at Tanagra – silly, bubbling, babbling Tanagra, thinking that she's going to escape from life because she can chatter anybody off the face of the earth. Look at him, and her, and this, and that. And look at Maurice.'

'I think you're rather beastly to Maurice,' said Brian quietly.

Motley clapped his hands with delight, though he was not regarding him. 'You're always true to type. Always the chivalrous schoolboy. One day I shall do a mask of you.'

'You'd better not.'

'It will be completely pink and innocent. And it will be winking. That's how I see you. So young and fresh, and with such an unbounded capacity for wrecking people's lives. But oh – aren't they lovely – aren't they lovely?'

He walked quickly backwards and forwards in the tiny room under the swinging light.

He leant forward and picked up a mask, fondling it, and sneering at it too. With a sort of drunken insolence he flicked a saddened face on the nose, stared suddenly into a pair of smooth eyes, fondled a grotesque, held to mockery a swollen cheek, snarled at a mouth with a hypocrite's twist.

Brian regarded him in amazement. He was as one possessed. His words, too, were hardly the words of a sane man. . . .

'It's true. It's all *true*. That's the terribly amusing part of it. This *is* Lady Thane. This *is* Maurice. This *is*——' and he named a dozen people, pointing a finger at them with trembling delight.

Brian shuddered. He could think of nothing to say.

'You'll see. *You'll* see. One day you'll find them out. You won't see their masks any more. You'll see their faces. Their beastly faces and their abominable souls. And then perhaps you'll think of this little room, and what I told you.'

He glared at Brian; and gradually the glare turned into a smile. The smile was the urbane, insincere smile of the old Lord William. When he spoke again his voice was smooth and calm.

'But, my young man, I forbid you to say anything about this in your horrible paper. Promise?'

'Oh rather. I promise.' He would have promised anything to get out of this room – this very sinister little chamber of horrors.

They went downstairs.

'By the way,' said Motley, as Brian was pulling on his gloves, 'couldn't you come down and spend the next week-end at Hayseed?'

Brian flushed slightly. A dinner and a lunch he had been able to manage, but a whole week-end, with fabulous tips and train journeys, and only two suits. . . .

'You're not engaged, are you?'

'No – no – not exactly.'

'Well, do come. They'll all be there. And, of course, Julia.'

At the mention of the last name he forgot all his fears.

'Thanks awfully. I'd love to. It'd be . . .' he hesitated, wondering if he could pronounce the adjective with conviction, and then, 'divine.'

'I should have much preferred you to say "ripping,"' said his lordship.

When the car had whirled his guest away, Lord William ascended slowly to his long black room. He felt suddenly bored and old. Brian had been so enthusiastic about everything, had eaten his lunch with such relish, and taken away his walking-stick with such pride . . . young fool. . . . Oh dear, why was one always so tired? He took up the rough basis of a mask and held it in his hands, staring at the opposite wall. There was the sound of a cart passing in the street outside, the purr of a motor-car, the lisp of footsteps. He had nothing to do till dinner-time. Five terrible hours of nothing. His fingers tightened round the mask. Then, very quickly, he got up and walked to his work-table, digging his fingers into a pile of moist pinkish clay. Flutter, flutter went the fingers. The room was silent except for the patting and smoothing of the mask. He was utterly absorbed in his work, and the daylight faded until the windows showed blue outside and the lights of the street-lamps shed pale beams on the polished floor. Gradually the mask assumed shape and life. And when, finally, he laid it down, a clay face was staring from the table, a face of extraordinary charm, but the face of a fool, with loose lips and half-closed eyes – a face curiously like that of the hero of our story.

CHAPTER EIGHT

B RIAN stood in the most sumptuous bathroom he had ever seen, trembling with agitation.

At every step, or fancied step, in the corridor outside he flushed, and took a quick step to the door. Then he drew back again, waiting till there was silence. Finally he sat down on the edge of the bath, wishing with all his heart that he had never come.

As he sat there, subconsciously he noted the glories of this bathroom. The walls were composed of tiny bricks of gold and blue and silver and black, giving one the effect of a large expanse of jewelled brawn. Along the side of the wall were a dozen bottles of Venetian glass, some very large, some very small, containing enough liquids, crystals and powders to make a healthy skunk pass unnoticed beneath the nose of Mr. Coty himself.

Upon the tessellated floor the figure of a highly-developed negress was worked in black mosaic, portrayed with such realism that Brian hesitated to step on her for fear that she would squeak.

The bath itself was sunk deep into the floor, and apparently quarried from a single block of marble. A fascinating bath. He would have liked to pour all the things from the bottles into it and steam in a soup of scent. Tentatively he put out his hand and turned one of the taps, ever so gently. A fierce snort and gurgle answered him, and a hiss of steam. Quickly he turned the tap back and wiped his forehead, which was sweating profusely.

What was all the agitation about? Well, it had happened like this. Arrived at Beaconsfield, he had jumped very quickly from his third-class carriage, concealed his ignominious green railway-ticket in his hand, and delivered his suit-case to a very smart and supercilious assistant chauffeur, who had said 'Is this all, sir?' as though he had expected a load of cabin-trunks in the guard's van.

That was bad enough. As he whirled through the country lanes, from which the miserly daylight was already fast fading, Brian drew the sable rug round his knees, pondering that sinister question: 'Is this all?' Well, he had his dinner-jacket, his tails, a Norfolk jacket and flannel trousers, pyjamas and a sponge bag, and the usual extras. What else could he want? Did they expect him to change his suit every minute? But that was not what really disturbed him. While they were driving up the broad sweep of the drive, he prepared a smile and a casual remark about the journey to deliver to his host and the rest of the party, whom he naturally imagined would be assembled to meet him. After all, one always *did* assemble to meet people who came to stay. He remembered how, in the dim days of his childhood, the whole household was dragged into the hall to greet an itinerant aunt. Brian himself was usually sent to the top of the drive to wave, the housemaid was couched expectantly behind the kitchen door, ready to leap at the visitor and transport her baggage to the 'spare' room, while his mother had always remained, for at least twenty minutes before the arrival of the cab, poised in the centre of the hall, with one hand outstretched and the other gripped tightly round the shilling which she invariably gave as a tip to the cabman.

He had expected something like this, though, of course, on a far grander scale. But nothing of the sort had happened. *Nothing.* He had emerged from the car and had been greeted by a butler in an empty hall. 'His lordship and the other ladies and gentlemen are out at the moment, sir.'

'Out?'

'Yes, sir. I'll show you your room.'

And that was all that had happened. It does not sound very terrifying, but to Brian it was terrifying in the extreme. Here he was in a strange house, surrounded by quantities of doubtless hostile servants, entirely alone. There seemed no reason why he should be there at all. They did not want him. He did not know any of their friends. He would only make himself ridiculous. He did not know the way about the house, and if he attempted to go downstairs, through all those corridors, he would probably wander into the servants' hall, and *then* what would he say? 'Good evening – I've come to stay?' Or – 'Oh – I thought this was the drawing-room?' Or – just 'Hallo!'? Life had never seemed more treacherous, more full of pitfalls.

And so he remained in his room. He had gone out once, only to come to a *cul de sac*, from which he rapidly retreated. He had occasionally peeped his head outside the door, but the last time he had done that a footman had been passing down the corridor, and he had hastily drawn in his head again. What would the footman think of him, popping his head in and out like a rabbit? What, indeed?

How long he stayed there he did not know. It was probably not more than twenty minutes, but it felt like an eternity. He would have liked a clean handkerchief, but to obtain it he would have to unpack his suit-case. And that, as he constantly had to remind himself, was the footman's job, and it would be too ghastly if the footman were to come in and find him unstrapping his case. He would be sure to think that he (Brian) had been intending to unpack his own things, and then what would they have said in the servants' hall?

However, his troubles were almost at an end, for there was the sound of voices in the hall, shrill, chattering, staccato, like a flock of noisy birds blown by the wind through the open doorway.

'Where is he?' He could distinguish Lord William's shout.

The chattering grew louder. Brian clicked his fingers nervously together. They mustn't find him standing here in the middle of the room, almost in the dark. What could he pretend to be doing? He rushed into the bathroom, turned on the light, and the tap at almost the same time, and began to wash his hands.

He was only just in time. For the door burst open and in frolicked Motley, followed by Lady Jane (Julia's sister), Maurice and Tanagra Guest. For the moment it suffices to say that Tanagra was tall and red-haired, and of American extraction, and that she was one of those parasites of modern London who make an excellent but precarious livelihood by flattering and entertaining their friends. As for Lady Jane, to say that she was unfeminine would hardly meet the case. She was about as feminine as General Pershing when young, to whom, indeed, she bore a certain resemblance. But Brian had no time to stare at this flat-chested, monocled creature, for Lord William said:

'Brian – will you ever forgive me – we've been buying up the village.'

'Rather. I've only just come. Hallo, Maurice.'

Thank God, Julia wasn't there.

'Have you had tea?'

He shook his head.

'They really are scandalous. Maurice, that butler must go. Brian's starving. Nobody meets him. Nobody gives him tea. Nobody does anything. He *must* go.'

'Give me a kiss, darling.' The voice was Tanagra's, very crooning and soft.

Brian looked at Lord William in agony. Was this part of the game, too?

Lord William puffed with delight. 'Go *on*. Tanagra offers you a kiss.'

Very well, if she wanted a kiss she should damned well have one. He reached up, put his arms round her, and kissed her on the lips, pressing her face to his until she gave a little high scream. She detached herself breathlessly.

'Really. These *boys*.'

'You asked for it, darling,' gurgled Maurice.

Brian felt giddy. They were mad. He was mad. Everybody was mad.

She raised her eyebrows. 'And I shall certainly ask again.' At which she airily took one of the bottles from a shelf and poured its contents into the bath, where it quickly ran away. 'Just to show you,' she added, with a glance at Lord William, 'that I feel at home.'

Brian had a fleeting thought that if *that* were all one had to do to show that one was at home, life would be very easy. He would go out and empty bottles of brandy in the garden, or throw a few boxes of cigars into the fire.

Tanagra strolled towards the door. 'He makes me feel so motherly,' she said.

'How very unnatural, dear,' gurgled Motley.

Jane's base voice broke in:

'Personally, I've never felt motherly. If I did I should go and see a doctor.'

Maurice piroutted up to him.

'Aren't they abominable? Let's go away and play by ourselves.'

But Lord William intervened:

'You can't take him off yet. He hasn't chosen his bath salts.'

More bath salts! A horrible doubt seized Brian. They surely weren't going to give him a bath now?

He blushed crimson. 'I really don't want any more.'

'But, *Angel*. . . .' Tanagra was standing in front of him. 'You *must*. These' – and she indicated the row of bottles – 'are just *ordinary* bath salts. You're going to be given a special sort.'

Brian became still more alarmed. What on earth were they going to give him? He felt certain that there must be something shady about them. Could they by any chance be drugged?

'You needn't use them if you don't want to,' whispered Maurice. 'But do pretend.'

Brian nodded gratefully. 'Of course,' he said, 'I'd love just to smell them. . . .'

Lord William beamed.

'This is quite my favourite game,' he crooned. 'Come on, everybody.'

Out of the room they went, and up another staircase, he leading the way, with Tanagra panting on his arm. Lady Jane, with a shrug of her shoulders, turned on her flat heels and disappeared.

At the end of a long corridor they halted in front of a cupboard. Lord William took a key from his pocket.

'I have to lock up all these things because of the servants,' he explained. 'I once had a housemaid who had such a passion for *Chypre* that we all swooned when she walked down the corridor.' He flung open the door.

'Ooh!'

Three noses, two male and one female, were stretched forward.

'Everything at once,' said Tanagra. 'I don't feel in the least motherly now.'

Lord William was taking down bottle after bottle.

'This is delicious,' he was saying. 'Tabac Blonde By Caron. Caron's scents are full of double meanings.

'What's this one that smells just like death?'

'Tanagra, you're too revolting.'

'I shall cover myself with it to-night.'

She seized the slim black bottle and held it to her breast.

'I think he ought to be fed on an exclusive diet of eau-de-Cologne,' said Maurice, who had been filling his pockets with Coty's 'Paris.'

Brian felt on firm ground here. He could remember having eau-de-Cologne dabbed on his forehead by cool hands when he was a small boy.

'I'd love some eau-de-Cologne,' he said.

Lord William snorted. 'I never heard such nonsense. If you want that you'll have to go to the village shop.' He suddenly jumped. 'Here's a perfect one. *Au fil de l'eau.*'

Tanagra was quivering all over.

'This one is *better* than death,' she said.

Brian looked at her. She had taken the stopper from her black bottle and, with eyes closed and parted lips, was inhaling the scent that drifted up, cloying and sweet. She seemed about to drift into a trance. The whole body was relaxed.

And then, a hand seized the bottle roughly from her. Her eyes opened suddenly.

'Now then, Tanagra' – Lord William's voice had a sudden harsh quality in it which amazed Brian. She flushed slightly and for an instant looked sulky. Then again she smiled.

'Well, and what shall we give him?'

He still looked at her, with something of a sneer. Then he too smiled. But the brief incident had registered itself permanently on Brian's memory. He was filled with a strange excitement.

'I think it should be *"Nuit de Noël,"* ' said Lord William. 'It's always used by the best Argentine co-respondents.' He rubbed some on Brian's hand. 'Isn't it divine?'

'Lovely,' said Brian. 'Like toffee.'

They all screamed shrilly. 'Perfect,' 'Delicious,' 'Isn't he *marvellous?*'

'Ooh!' Another bottle was taken down – a delicate thing of frosted yellow glass. 'This is *guaranteed* to make one forget everything that one's father taught one.'

'What is it?'

'It hasn't got a name. It was created for me on my twenty-first birthday.'

'Let me smell.'

Maurice took the bottle and undid the stopper. '*Pure* chloroform.'

'I've never heard anything so monstrous. *You* smell.'

The bottle was put under Brian's nose. The scent had a bitter tang in it that made him feel inclined to sneeze.

'It's rather strong,' he said.

'It's yours.'

'Thanks most awfully.' Gingerly he took the bottle. They were all looking at him to see what he would do. Having no ideas, he said:

'Can I have some bath salts to match?'

'I *knew* you had it in you,' cried Lord William.

Maurice sniffed with disdain.

'I still hold to the eau-de-Cologne theory.'

'Shut up.' Lord William was unscrewing an immense bottle of green bath salts. 'There's nothing that really goes with your scent, but this might do. Try it.'

Brian felt that if he smelt any more he would be quite sick, but he dutifully bent his head.

'Don't *snuffle* them so,' said Tanagra. 'Let me see.' She too sniffed. 'No. It's quite terribly obvious.'

Lord William, who was only too anxious to have an excuse for continuing these experiments, put the bottle back.

'I think,' said Tanagra, 'that it should be something sweet and subtle. Lilac, for example.'

Brian nodded eagerly. 'I adore lilac. It's my favourite flower.'

'I didn't know anybody but actresses had favourite flowers,' giggled Maurice.

'Well, I can't help that.' Brian's tone was a trifle curt.

Tears sprang into Maurice's eyes. 'I haven't *offended* you, have I?'

'No. Don't talk rot.'

Lord William was still rummaging in the cupboard. Slightly out of breath he dragged down a purple bottle.

'Here we are. *Le Temps des Lilas.*' He began to unscrew it. Tanagra leant against the wall. She sang:

'*Le Temps des lilas*
Et le temps des roses
Ne reviendra plus. . . .'

The voice was pure, strangely childish and sweet.

Brian looked at her in sudden admiration. 'I say, I didn't know you sang like that.'

She smiled at him. She seemed suddenly simple.

'There are lots of things you don't know.'

The bottle was again under his nose. But this time he drank in the scent eagerly – that most delicate and gracious essence that seems to hold in it the lights and shades of early spring. He remembered how he and Walter had once saved up to go to Cambridge for a week-end – how they had slept all night in a punt at Grantchester, under the purple sprays of an immense lilac that had hung the night with its lingering perfume.

'I love this,' he said quietly.

'Perfect. We'll put it aside and have it taken to your room. Don't forget this though.'

He held out the purple bottle, and closed the cupboard doors. By now the whole corridor reeked of warring odours.

'If only,' said Tanagra, 'somebody divine would call at this very moment. Somebody with thick boots and a heart in the right place.'

But the only person who came was the footman – to announce to his lordship that cocktails were served in the Venetian hall.

CHAPTER NINE

DINNER was over, and as far as Brian was concerned it was a great success. Nobody had put scent in the soup, for the moment the tide of cocktails seemed to have abated, and his shirt, of which he had entertained grave doubts, was doing its duty manfully.

We may, therefore, pass to the drawing-room, where the

ladies, to whom we must now add an æsthetic example named Gloria Woodroffe, from Chelsea, were discussing the best way of extracting money from men, with the minimum of pain and the maximum of profit.

'I have a marvellous way,' said Tanagra. 'I'm terribly nice to foreigners. I bring lots and lots of sunshine into their lives. And then they ask me to stay with them abroad.'

'But you never go.'

'Never. That's the whole point. I tell them that I can't get away from England for a few months, and they return home, leaving a cheque behind to pay for my travelling-expenses. Then I develop appendicitis.'

'But, my dear, that seems hardly worth while. The return fare to Paris, or even Rome . . .'

'Paris!' Tanagra wrinkled her nose contemptuously. 'I don't call *that* going abroad. *I* mean America, India – that sort of thing.'

'Oh, that's *marvellous.*'

'There was once a divine Indian whom I used to amuse enormously by imitating a cuckoo calling to its young. He said that he could not possibly live without me. The return fare to India, including a private suite, is quite a lot.'

'I wish I'd thought of that,' said Julia.

'You will, darling, next season,' droned Lady Jane.

'Then,' continued Tanagra, 'there have been quite a lot of Americans. They seem to need sunshine very badly. There was a dear old American millionaire who was studying English folk-lore. I read the lyrics of quantities of American plantation songs, translated them into English, and told them to him at the end of dinner. He said that I had a unique store of information, which was quite true. I've had appendicitis three times for him.'

'One ought to find you somebody in China,' said Julia.

'My ambition is an Australian. The return fare to Australia, if one does it really well, is nearly three hundred pounds. I once enraptured an Australian millionaire by playing Kangaroo games with his children. He loved to join in, too. However, it transpired that he was insane, and his keeper thought I should have a malign influence on him.'

'I should never be able to hold them in check,' said Gloria, who had discarded her stays and her scruples in the same evening.

Lady Jane stirred lazily. 'What makes you think that, dear?'

Gloria tossed her head, ignoring the question. 'That's why I'm so poor.'

'My dear, we all *know* your way, so why pretend?'

'My way? I don't do that sort of thing.'

'If forcing defenceless stockbrokers to hire the Æolian Hall while you draw caricatures to the accompaniment of six drums isn't "that sort of thing," I don't know what is.'

'You're incapable of understanding, Jane darling.'

'So are the stockbrokers. That's why it's so cruel.'

'Felix Waldo said . . .'

'Waldo! My God! You're not going to quote *that*?'

'Felix Waldo said that if it hadn't been for the strike he would have founded an institute for me.'

'Wouldn't that have been a little unbecoming?' asked Julia. 'To have an institute named after one seems to argue fifty years of public life.'

'What *is* public life?' said Tanagra.

'Everything that a man does before midnight,' replied Julia.

'Isn't that horribly like an epigram?'

Gloria was anxious not to drift out of the limelight. 'I shouldn't have cared. I shall have my institute one day.'

'Of course you will, darling. One can see it in your eyes.'

'Sooner than any of you expect, too.'

Tanagra leant back. She was wearing a spiritual expression. 'Gloria's given me an idea,' she said.

Lady Jane chuckled. 'It was an accident, I expect.'

'Religion!'

Gloria turned away with well-assumed disgust. The others leant forward.

'I am certain there is a tremendous amount of money in religion,' said Tanagra. 'Otherwise why should there be so many religious revivals in America? All organized religions are forms of insurance companies. An ordinary insurance company guards against being burnt on earth, a religion guards against being burnt in hell.'

But at this point the men entered the room, and the discussion faded away.

Now at last, Brian thought he would be able to talk to Julia. She seemed to have hidden all day, and apart from a few charming but evasive words at dinner she had said nothing to him all the evening.

But no. It was not to be. Julia pleaded the old-fashioned excuse of a headache and retired to bed. Brian, too, went early, for he was in no mood for the riotous charades which Lord William had suddenly decided to organize.

As he went to sleep, he swore that he would entrap her on the next day. But was there ever such a difficult house in which to entrap anybody? For when the next day dawned, things became more hectic than ever.

It began with breakfast. Breakfast had different interpretations for all the members of the party. For Julia it consisted in a little hot water and a couple of aspirins at eleven o'clock. For Lady Jane it meant porridge, and quantities of eggs and bacon in the dining-room at half-past eight, to the accompaniment of a frisking of dogs who mysteriously arrived from nowhere whenever she made an appearance. Gloria ate apples – (rather sour ones) sitting up in bed, clad in a bright orange dressing-gown. Tanagra drank quantities of very strong tea, under the impression that it was good for the nerves.

But to Lord William, breakfast was a ceremony of peculiar charm. It gave him, for instance, an opportunity of displaying some of his magnificent dressing-gowns, which hung by dozens in a cupboard specially set apart for them. He took, also, a malicious pleasure in observing the faces of those guests whom he could persuade to join him. Their pre-lunch complexions afforded such a strange contrast to their appearance the night before. And since nobody felt inclined to talk, he could croon along contentedly, making outrageous statements without fear of contradiction.

Therefore at ten o'clock, having arrayed himself in a bright green dressing-gown, with long golden tassels, he called for Rastus – (the negro servant whose acquaintance we have already made)

– and informed him that he desired the presence of Mr. Elme and Mr. Cheyne. His principal reason for having these two at the same time was to annoy Maurice, who found it very difficult to look less than thirty before midday.

Brian had slept till half-past nine. He had then woken, sprang out of bed, wondering if all the others would have had breakfast already. The complete silence of the house reassured him, so that he decided there was time for a cold bath. Just before he got into it he thought he might as well use some of his bath salts. Being ignorant of the true purposes of this luxury he poured a heap into one end, leapt into the bath, and sat down heavily. The accompanying shudder with which he scrambled from the water was not due only to the cold. He felt as though he had sat on some very sharp gravel, and as he peered in to see what it was, he realized that the bath salts had not melted, but were twinkling at him through the water. He therefore contented himself with a cold shower.

He had just finished drying himself when Rastus arrived with his message. Brian started. Would Julia be there? Perhaps. If so, what would she think of his mangy old dressing-gown? Oh, hell! It was in a depressed mood that he arrived in Lord William's little green 'rest-room,' and he was still more depressed when he saw nobody but Lord William and Maurice.

His lordship, however, was delighted, and pressed grape-fruit, and foie-gras, and chocolate, and fried sole upon him as though he were starving. For to Lord William, annoyance of Maurice was one of the chief of life's pleasures; and he delighted in observing his wounded vanity. Although this young man had shaved, anointed himself and brushed his hair, he looked pale and dissipated. Brian, unshaved and unanointed, had the appearance of radiant youth.

'How *does* he do it, do you think?' purred Lord William.

'Do what?'

'Look so amazingly fresh? You and I, for example, look like something that the cat has left on the lawn.' He sighed artificially. 'But I suppose it's only youth.'

At which Maurice spread more foie-gras on his toast, and wrinkled his nose with indignation.

But Brian took no pleasure in these compliments. He was thinking of Julia. And later in the day, when they did meet, it seemed impossible to talk to her alone, so utterly lacking in privacy was this strange house. For instance, somebody was always playing the piano. Maurice usually contented himself with the simple melodic progressions of Mr. Irving Berlin, which Lord William rightly described as 'so virginal and English,' while Gloria, at various times during the day, would walk hurriedly to the piano, and make sounds which she assured the rest of the company were Stravinsky.

Occasionally there would be some organized form of amusement. Lord William would propose a visit to the stables, and after a great deal of wrapping up, the party would assemble, clamber into cars, and whirl down the long drive towards a pleasant red-roofed group of buildings in the valley. But, much to Brian's regret, the stables were never reached, for half-way between them lay the hot-houses, and as soon as these were sighted, there would be fevered tappings at the window while the cars slowed down, and they all trooped over the short gravel paths to enter these more attractive institutions. And then they had to wander down long galleries of glass, chattering volubly, their breath steaming, their foreheads glistening, from heat to greater heat, fingering the damp speckled orchids, the murky man-eating plants with crimson veins, the hairy cactus and the evil-smelling lilies that protruded yellow lips above the surface of tepid pools. Each would come away with some souvenir, and when they eventually emerged, there was a fresh scampering to the cars, in which they were shiveringly transported back to blazing fires and frozen cocktails.

Cocktails, of course, were eternal. The chink of ice in a shaker began to echo in Brian's nerves in a maddening monotone. Whenever there was a pause in the fun, somebody proposed a cocktail, and they all flocked to the side-table in the hall. What effect it had on the others he did not know, but it seemed to be driving him crazy.

Brian began to wonder if all house-parties were like this. As a boy he had occasionally spent his holidays at the country home of a school-friend, but he could not recall anything in the least like 'Hayseed.' For one thing, people had always worn old clothes, whereas here the day was like a perpetual dress-parade. Tanagra had changed her frock three times since breakfast, and Lord William was always attired as though for Bond Street. He had timidly hoped that his host might propose a little shooting, but the hope was quickly extinguished. Everybody seemed determined to ignore the existence of nature, whether in the shape of the fields, the woods, the birds, or the air itself.

And still Julia evaded him.

All day he had been furtively glancing at her. He had tried to catch her eye, to read in it some open avowal or secret understanding. He had tried, too, to waylay her on the stairs, even taking up a position in the corridor outside her room, but the constant passage of footmen and housemaids, who seemed, at 'Hayseed,' to be swarming in every direction at every hour, had eventually dislodged him. She had been charming to him of course, laughing with him, even twisting his hair in full view of the assembled company, but otherwise there had been no personal contact. She seemed not to react at all.

As the day went on, he began to grow desperate. His mind was fevered with constant cocktails, visits to hothouses, and the tinkling of pianos. The adolescent passion which she had originally woken in him was deepening, it was becoming a fire which he could not control. He wanted to take her away, out of all this, out into the fresh air. He did not realize, at that time, how he hated the whole atmosphere of the place. He was still dazzled, doped by the eternal parade of luxury. Yet did he find himself dreaming of a courtship far different from any that could be imagined in such surroundings – a love, free and windswept, set against a background of such hills as only youth can climb, beneath a sky that only youth can paint so bright. Half-fascinated, half-afraid, wholly pathetic, he drifted with this strange crew who had sabotaged him, but always as one apart, as one who still believed that the drifting would end, that eventually the harbour would be reached.

> '*For a boy's will is the wind's will,*
> *And the thoughts of youth are long, long thoughts.*'

And then, after dinner that night, during a shrill game of amateur theatricals, she whispered to him: *'Come and talk to me to-night, won't you, when the others have gone to bed?'*

It was one o'clock. The menagerie of guests had retired to their separate cages. Brian stood at his door, listening. Had he not been stimulating his courage with several whiskies and sodas, he would not have dared to leave his room. And even now, he was afraid – sickeningly afraid – and he could not analyse his fear. She had told him to come. 'To talk!' *She* had told him. If she hadn't wanted him why ask? A sudden wave of courage surged through him. He walked down the long corridor and knocked, boldly at her door.

'Come in.'

She was standing near the window, waiting. How clear-cut, cameo-like she looked! In her red dress she seemed as a single scarlet line splashed against the curtain's gold.

His heart was beating so loudly that he feared she would hear it.

'You really did mean I could come and see you?'

'Of course, you silly boy. Come and sit down.'

He sat down at the end of the sofa.

'You're terribly young, aren't you?'

He looked at her silently. Then he shook his head. 'I feel very old to-night.'

'Really? Why?'

'Because I've met you.'

She laughed – the tired tinkle of a laugh that held for him so much magic. And then again her hand stole out to his, resting on it, pressing it.

'You did that once before,' he whispered.

'Did I?'

'Yes. At the theatre. I've been wondering ever since if it meant . . . anything.'

'What could it mean?'

'That's what I want to know.'

'Why do you want to know?'

'Because' – and he spoke very slowly, with a catch in his throat – 'because you're the most beautiful thing I've ever seen.'

She leant back her head. Why did these words always give her so much delight? Why, when she heard them, had she the sense of a curtain rising, with hushed music – a sense of being the heroine on that fairest of all stages, the stage of one's own mind, when the limelight is lit by one's own most secret vanity?

'Go on,' she said. And then, 'darling,' as an afterthought.

'Yes,' he said gravely, 'I must go on. I've got to go on. I've got to tell you. If I didn't tell you I should die.' There was no hint of mockery in his words.

He crossed his hands, as though in prayer.

'I've got to tell you something I've never told to any other woman in my life. Something I shall never tell any other woman again. The telling of it is rather hopeless. I know that. But I can't help it. I've got to tell you that I love you.'

Her hand, very slowly, came out to meet his. He took it. He was not looking at her. He was looking into the smouldering embers.

'You've come to mean life to me,' he went on. 'Just that. The curve of your neck – that's a sort of way to Paradise. The way you move your hands – they could lift me to heaven. Your smile . . .'

'Yes?'

He turned to her. His face suddenly seemed old, seared with pain. 'Isn't it all damnable?'

'Brian!'

'You see – to you it's such an old story.'

She closed her eyes. The child was becoming intelligent. This would never do. She achieved a very effective sigh, and turned her head.

'At least – I believe it is.' He paused. A burning coal fell with a foolish hiss on to the hearth. 'Isn't it?'

There was a faint shake of the head.

He tightened his grip on her hand. Oh – that hand – that arm – that body. . . . 'You have heard it all before – haven't you?' He leant towards her. 'All this is old to you. Old.'

She frowned. Her fingers closed mechanically upon the old brocade cushion by her side. Old! Why had he said that word? Oh – she was a fool to bother with him. Impatiently she drew herself up, and looked into the flagging, languid fire.

'You're terribly complimentary.'

'Darling. For God's sake don't be angry.'

'Angry?' She laughed. 'Am I being angry?'

It was exquisite to see the pain which this sudden change of tone caused him.

'I'm such a fool. It's because I feel so – so fearfully about it all.'

'Really?'

Oh! the chill in her voice. He turned away, and studied the carpet. There were lots of silken shapes on the carpet. Roses and formal flowers and crimson circles. Crimson circles and formal flowers and roses. Damned funny. Oh – so funny! His forehead lifted itself, and something outside him seemed to twist his mouth into a smile – then, he realized that he was being theatrical and absurd. He got up and walked to the window.

'Sorry. I'm an idiot.'

'Brian. Come back.'

There was a note of real entreaty in her voice.

He came back and sat by her again.

She put her hand on his, and looked in his face. He could not read her expression.

'I wish I knew. I wish I could feel sure.' She paused. 'I wish I could feel *anything*. But I can't. Or if I can, I don't know. But go on loving me, please. Please don't stop that.'

He kissed her hand, and the knuckles glistened as he raised his head.

CHAPTER TEN

As the weeks shivered themselves away, and the fogs of December melted into the fogs of January, Walter began to grow more and more anxious about his friend. He was changing more rapidly than he could have believed possible.

It was a pale Brian now who greeted him every morning – a Brian with dark rings under his eyes and a bored listless voice. It was a Brian who seemed totally uninterested in his old life, who did not care for the peculiarities of Mrs. Pleat, who was no longer amused by family jokes. Only in the evenings, when he rushed home to dress for dinner after calling at the house of one of his new friends for a cocktail, did a flush come back to his cheeks – a hectic flush which had more of fever than of health.

He seemed utterly to have lost his head. The telephone was ringing all day long. He never came in before the small hours. And every penny of his tiny capital had been invested in new clothes, while he had ordered more for which he would never be able to pay. Walter himself would not have been in the least worried by such a predicament, because as long as he had half a crown in his pocket he was perfectly content. But it was quite unlike Brian, who had always prided himself on never owing a penny, and had never cared what sort of clothes he wore provided that they were a fair fit.

However, one frosty night towards the end of January, when he had at last pinned Brian down to a date for dinner – (Brian, who used to dine with him night after night!) – he determined to put these gloomy thoughts away from him, and behave as though nothing had happened.

They dined, as usual, at a small restaurant in Soho, at which the *chef* had a genius for making plaice taste like sole, and rabbit like chicken. Violently futuristic designs adorned the ill-lit walls, contrasting strangely with the meek and battered foreigners – mostly Spaniards – who huddled beneath them.

As soon as they had sat down, Brian called the waiter – an old friend of his. 'This cloth is filthy,' he said. 'Get another one, please.'

The waiter looked at him rather in the manner of a dog that had been unjustly kicked. But he removed the cloth.

Walter studied Brian from under lowered lids. He looked tired and sulky. This episode of the cloth was typical of his new attitude. He had never complained of the place before. He sighed. He was puzzled and worried, not for himself, but for B. He hated to see him unhappy. However . . .

'A bottle of the usual?' he said.

Now this remark was usually followed by a nod from Brian, the production of half a crown, which was joined to Walter's own half a crown, and pressed into the hand of a beaming waitress, who would dart into the street to return with a bottle of good, coarse Spanish wine. But the thought of such wine to-night revolted Brian. So he frowned and said:

'I'll have a brandy.'

Walter did not comment on this revolutionary statement. He merely ordered half a bottle of the usual and a brandy.

The waiter then approached. The two friends knew all about this waiter. They knew that he was saving up to go back to Spain, and that in ten years' time, if all went well, he would have enough to do so. They knew him as a consummate liar and a staunch friend, who would allow them to owe the price of many dinners, without security, confident that eventually they would pay him.

But to-night, Brian dismissed him briefly, for he seemed shabby and shameful. He resented Walter's cheerful ragging of him. He little knew the effort it cost Walter, nor guessed that it was all done for his benefit, in the hope that sooner or later he would freeze out of his isolation, and become the old 'B' again. He was thinking of Walter not at all, whereas Walter was thinking very acutely of him. He took out his handkerchief. A faint smell of sandal-wood – an echo of 'Hayseed' – floated over the table.

'Somebody seems to have stepped in something,' said Walter cheerfully, helping himself to some sweet corn, and looking fixedly at an innocent woman sitting opposite.

Brian blushed guiltily, and stuffed his handkerchief back again. 'What do you mean?' he said.

'Only that foul stink. But it's gone again now.'

'I didn't notice anything,' remarked Brian, and began to pick at his 'steak Barcelona.'

'I expect the steak's jolly good at "Hayseed," isn't it?' said Walter without the flicker of an eyelid.

'I expect it is,' replied Brian, without the flicker of an eyelid. 'I didn't ask the butler.'

'Oh – good for *you*.' Walter's eyes sparkled. 'But,' he added, 'I expect the butler lives on ortolans and caviare. In fact, I believe I read it somewhere in the paper.'

Brian munched on solemnly. He was in that ghastly mood

where one wants to laugh, but has, in a moment of pique, jumped on to a pedestal of dignity from which descent is impossible.

'What sort of bitter does his lordship drink?' asked Walter, who felt like continuing in this strain indefinitely.

'Oh, all of them. Mixed up.'

'I thought so. That's where he gets his complexion.'

'You can't talk about complexion. You've got a face like a beet-root.' (An unkind way of describing Walter's healthy flush.)

'Thank God! That means more credit.' He looked at Brian with excessive gravity. 'I expect his lordship can get any amount of credit, can't he?'

'How should I know?'

'I mean' – and here Walter gulped down another glass of red wine – 'he could probably go down to the village pub and order a whole case of Guinness on tick?'

'You're not in the least funny.'

Walter ignored him. 'My word, that's a man!' he went on. 'That's a friend. I don't wonder you like him so much.'

'Oh – for God's sake shut up!'

And there was a tone of harsh irritation in Brian's voice which plunged the rest of the meal in silence.

The dinner, this terrible, silent dinner came to an end. Brian felt ashamed, Walter miserable. The streets of Piccadilly – those dark, rumbling thoroughfares of adventure – seemed void of promise, even of interest. Of old, the two friends had found those streets a sort of poor man's theatre. Together they would set out, warmed with wine, when the lamp-posts were flickering like foot-lights along an endless stage, knowing that they could choose their scene as they willed, that the curtain could be raised or lowered at their disposition, and that the cast which they could call to play for their delight was numberless. The sound of a barrel-organ down a wind-swept street was as thrilling as any orchestra, the garish lights against the warehouse would glitter with a subtler beauty than the shimmer and sparkle of the most luxuriant beauty-chorus. And the occasional human contacts, when they drifted, unprepared but welcoming, into the lives of strange men and stranger women

– these were laden with a drama more moving than any in a dramatist's brain.

But to-night – no. The curtain would not go up. The drama would not begin. The streets were only streets. Life was not a stage, nor were the men and women in it players. Life was life, and men were men, and as soon as one comes to that horrible and unreal conclusion, something is very wrong indeed.

There was only one thing to do, thought Walter, in order to drag Brian out of the depression in which he found himself, and that was to take him forcibly into a public-house and make him drink. It sounds a dangerous remedy, but there are worse ones.

They were just passing a little bar that stands at the corner of Bryanston Street and New Quebec Street. A cheerful glow came from the inside, and the place was crowded with soldiers in scarlet coats, taxi-men with blue noses, Hogarthian women, an occasional thin prostitute with patched stockings, and various loungers.

'Come on, B. We'll go and have one in here.'

Brian took Walter's hand from his arm. 'That filthy place,' he said bitterly. 'Have you come to that?'

And as soon as he had said it he could have bitten off his tongue. For apart from the essential priggishness of his question, its true vulgarity, he knew that he was hitting at something which Walter held sacred. A dirty public-house may seem a curious thing to hold sacred, and in America, where such places are called 'saloons,' and where beer is parodied under the name of 'liquor,' such a veneration would be merely regarded as part of the essential madness and perversity of the conventional Englishman. But to Walter a public-house meant England. It meant the England of Chaucer and Johnson and Dickens. He knew the whole lore and custom of these places, their rich humanity, their little tragedies, the riotous humour of their patrons. He knew where the beer was good and where it was bad, and the temperamental peculiarities of barmaids held no mysteries for him. He knew, too, of many strange and furtive bars in the by-ways, where one could drink long after closing hours, and speak with strange companions till the early hours of morning. In dealing with a 'drunk' he was superb. But he was very seldom drunk himself.

It had been a long time before he had been able to persuade Brian to come into a bar with him, for to Brian, in the first days of their friendship, a bar had been merely a rather dirty place, its counter wet and dripping with stale drinks, a sawdusted floor, and highly unsavoury people. He felt ill at ease in these surroundings.

But gradually he had allowed himself to be persuaded, learning little by little to appreciate, from an outside point of view, the qualities which appealed to Walter. Even the smell of them, as warm and racy as the smell of a stable and the colour of them – the scarlet coats of the guardsmen, the blonde hair of the barmaids, the rich browns of the woods, the variegated labels on the bottles – even to these things he eventually responded.

But he had never admitted this capitulation to Walter. He still pretended to enter a 'pub' with reluctance, still feigned an ignorance of its customs and traditions. And this pretence was indeed one of the charms of friendship. It was part of that 'technique of opposites' which is the true basis of companionship.

Thus, if Walter said, 'Shall we go and have one?' – Brian would reply, 'Have what?' At which, one of them kicked the other – it did not matter which. Or if Walter said, 'When do they open?' Brian answered, 'They? What do you mean by they?' In reality he was charmed by these expressions, which are the international language of the drinking fraternity.

And there were many country inns where together they had passed glorious hours. Never would he forget an evening on the South Coast late in May, when they were tramping down a lonely road towards the sea. There was a savour of salt in the air, mingling with the creamy scent of blackthorn, and a mist hung over the meadows in which a few cows were crunching the lush grass. Suddenly, round a bend in the road, they came upon a little white inn, with an open door, and a lamp spilling golden shadows on to the gravel road. And there had been long, long drinks at that inn, cool and translucent and dark, first in the low-ceilinged bar, with its solemn rows of pewter, and then in the garden, where lavender stood stiff and prim against the broken walls. Through the still air, stabbing it with sweetness, had drifted the song of nightingales,

rapturous and unending. No, my friends, they were not drunk.
One does not get drunk in such surroundings.

But to-night – everything seemed changed. He did not want to
drink beer. He wanted champagne. He did not want to stand in an
atmosphere of coarse tobacco. Poverty, which had before seemed
so natural and so lovable, appeared suddenly hateful and strange.

'Come on,' said Walter. 'They'll be closing in another quarter
of an hour.'

Brian stood on the pavement, undetermined. From inside came
the clink of glasses and the shouting of a song:

> 'The Lord Mayor of London,
> The Lord Mayor of London.'

Roughly Brian shook his arm free from Walter. 'You'd better go
in by yourself,' he said. And he was off down the street like one
pursued.

He could have cried aloud at his own beastliness. He could have
gone down on his knees and apologized. He longed to go back and
say, 'I'm sorry – I've been a brute – an utter brute.' But he could
not. His feet would not turn. They carried him, almost against
his will, down the deserted street, up the silent staircase, into his
flat, and across to his desk where there lay the little photograph of
Julia, which he had cut out of a paper. And something apart from
himself seemed to force his fingers to lift the picture to his lips, and
kiss it hungrily, with the loneliness that only those can know who
have betrayed a friend for a lover.

CHAPTER ELEVEN

No 'gossip' writer should ever meet his victims in the flesh.
Brian was beginning to find life more and more complicated as he was introduced into a widening circle of the
aristocracy. When, for example, he met Lady Monk, whom he
had so often characterized as 'vivacious' in The Lady's Mail, it was

acutely embarrassing to discover that, in reality, she was crippled with rheumatoid arthritis, and of so jaundiced a mentality that her favourite topic of conversation was the imminent downfall of the British Empire – a subject upon which for hours at a time she would intone with lugubrious relish.

Even more embarrassing was it to meet Lady Monk's son, about whose prowess at baseball in the University of Yale he had not failed to keep his readers well informed. For Patrick Monk proved to be so shortsighted that his large and clumsy feet were constantly tripping over the edges of the pavements. Indeed, Brian very quickly decided that as soon as this young man had returned to his University, *The Lady's Mail* would be forced to chronicle his desertion from baseball to Science.

As for the Dowager Lady Macrael, whom he had credited with the enterprise of turning old Scottish tunes into modern jazz – that was a brick, if you like. For this tiresome woman proved not only to be almost deaf, but to possess so violent a distaste for modern fashions, that life at Macrael Castle was carried on in almost medieval state. Even when she dined alone, the bagpipes must parade her in to dinner. Even on the bitterest of winter mornings, family prayers must be celebrated in the ice-bound chapel. And if the humblest and obscurest kitchen-maid were to vary the monotony of existence by shingling her hair, out of Macrael Castle she would go, by the first ferry-boat that crossed the forbidding lake. Brian thanked the Lord that this alarming woman would have considered it beneath her dignity to subscribe to a Press-cutting agency.

One would have thought that the more people he knew, the easier would be his task. The very reverse proved to be the case. For as soon as he met anybody he had to cease writing about them, unless he wished to be detected. When, for instance, he was the sole witness of the complete intoxication of old Lady Gaveston at one of Lord William's parties, he could not even refer to her ladyship's connoisseurship in the matter of wines without grave risk. The accounts of Lord William's activities had long ago ceased, and as for Lady Julia – no money would have persuaded him to write a word about her, unless it were in the form of a sonnet to an anonymous goddess.

He was, therefore, forced to carry his investigations much farther afield, until the gossip columns of *The Lady's Mail* eventually
presented the appearance of a page from the *Wide World Magazine*. For some weeks he contented himself with chronicling the
peculiarities of Colonial Governors' wives, attributing to them
favourite flowers, noting how they longed for the sight of English
roses, telling of parties which they had never given and excursions
which they had never made. If, for instance, he said that the wife
of the Governor of Australia had shot a kangaroo, he was perfectly
safe for, at any rate, three months, even if the wife of the Governor
of Australia should desire to deny so singular an honour.

Having exhausted the Colonies, he turned to the big-game
expeditions. Some members of the aristocracy were always obligingly departing to the wilds in order to shoot harmless animals,
and as soon as they had left London, Brian would get to work
describing their voyage. He discovered the shop where Lady Stillhaven had purchased her outfit, and wrote quite a pretty little
paragraph about her, headed 'Crêpe de Chine to catch Caribou.'
He also imagined that so delicately complexioned a lady would
not altogether dispense with the articles of the toilet, and spent an
enjoyable morning on a leader entitled 'Powder and Peril.' It began
in this manner:

*'All British women will be interested to learn that Lady Stillhaven
(whose expedition to Central Africa is so intriguing Society) has not omitted to include in her travelling-kit a selection of Coty's perfumes, with
powders to match. The stern male may scoff at such an item in so grimly
practical an undertaking, but to many women Lady Stillhaven's action
will appeal as a gesture at once fine and significant. For a woman, even if
she is to face danger, sees no reason why she should not face it looking her
best.*

*'Is not that as it should be? Is there not in it something calculated to
arouse a thrill in the breast of every woman (worthy of the name) – this
prospect of a gallant little lady powdering her nose in the presence of
panthers?' etc., etc.*

Meanwhile, Mrs. Gossett was beginning to give more and more

trouble. Her eagle eye had not failed to detect the change in him, his faintly dissipated air in the early morning, his new clothes, his casual references to the distinguished people he had encountered. And Mrs. Gossett was quite determined not to be left out of the fun.

She was actuated by several motives. Firstly, she was more deeply than ever attracted by his appearance. She would make excuses for coming into his room, and would dart furtive glances at him as he worked, marvelling at the fresh gold of his hair, drawing unholy deductions from the boyish pallor of his cheeks. Secondly, he was her only male acquaintance who, somehow or other, provided her with a constant stream of remarks by which she could be shocked. To be shocked was Mrs. Gossett's constant ambition, and Brian, by his turn of phrase, or the rather tired droop of his eyelids, somehow or other gave her that sensation. At the back of her mind she was perfectly aware that his remarks were entirely innocent, but she refused to admit so depressing a conclusion to herself.

And thirdly, Mrs. Gossett was a snob. It was hardly possible that she could be anything else. When one spends one's entire life poring over photographs of peeresses, writing genteel captions beneath the stolid faces of the British aristocracy, weaving romance into their lives, flattering them, fawning upon them, giving them honour where precious little honour was due – how could one avoid being tainted with this most comical complaint? She *was* a snob, and she admitted it, if not to others, at least to herself.

In Brian, therefore, she saw a splendid stepping-stone to higher things. And when she obtained, by certain ingenious manipulations known only to herself, two invitations to a very exalted dance at the house of a certain 'exclusive' duchess, she was determined that Brian should be her partner.

'I suppose I *must* go,' she said to him, with assumed diffidence one afternoon. 'It's a bore, but one has to do these things, hasn't one?'

Brian agreed that one had to do them.

Then, quickly, with amazing ingenuity, she cornered him. How,

to this day, he could not tell you. But there was no escape. He had
to take her to the dance. And since the anticipation of it weighed
heavily upon him, and would make depressing reading, we may
pass quickly to a certain second-rate 'smart' restaurant, where the
two may be observed dining before the entertainment, he in his
new dress-suit, she in a confection of salmon-pink, trimmed with
lace arranged in an archaic design, her head crowned with a coiffure that nobody could overlook.

'Will you have a cocktail?'

Mrs. Gossett bit her lip, paused, and glanced at the tablecloth.
Then, with a sudden, girlish twist of the shoulders . . . 'You won't
think me *dreadful?*'

'Of course not.'

'I'd adore one. Don't let's bother about *anything* to-night.' Her
eyes rolled round rapidly in two complete circles, and at the same
time she began to drum on the table with her long thin fingers,
while a tremulous hum escaped from her lips, which bore a faint
resemblance to '*Annie Laurie.*'

Brian called the waiter. 'What sort would you like?' he said.

'Something beautifully strong.' The beginning of a giggle was
heard in Mrs. Gossett's throat, and then, realizing the presence of
the waiter, she again became the duchess. 'I weally don't know.'
She glanced disdainfully over her shoulder at a bank clerk who
was swallowing a steak with more appetite than grace. The sight
of this person caused her to add in a frosty voice: 'Stwange people
one sees everywhere, nowadays, doesn't one?' At which she negli-
gently drew her rabbit-skin cloak over her left shoulder.

Brian felt that any very powerful stimulant would, in the circumstances, be more than Mrs. Gossett could stand, and so he
ordered two dry Martinis.

'How divine,' said Mrs. Gossett. She suddenly melted, and
observed the existence of the waiter. 'And mine with a cherry,
please.'

'Certainly, madame.'

'I think the chewy's the nicest part,' she confided to Brian, when
the cocktails were brought. 'Is that naughty of me?' Her head was
much on one side when she asked this question.

'I think it's very like a woman,' replied Brian, to order.

Mrs. Gossett's eyes narrowed to two slits, and she held her head very high. A faint smile which she conceived to be cynical played about her thin lips.

'What do you know about women?' she said. And, overcome with the daring of her question, she lowered her eyes and began to drink her soup very quickly, crumbling a roll at the same time with such excessive delicacy that most of it fell on to the floor.

While Brian was thinking of an answer, he could not help observing that Mrs. Gossett was making a great display of her fingers. At one moment she would place an elbow on the table, and spread out her fingers fan-wise under her chin, at another she would pat her hair with many spiral gestures. He suddenly realized the cause of these manœuvres.

Mrs. Gossett had been manicured! And manicured with a vengeance. Her hands were covered with liquid powder, which ceased, somewhat irregularly, in the neighbourhood of her finger-nails. The latter were fiercely pointed, in the shape of talons, and were coloured a deep sparkling ruby red, which gave the impression that Mrs. Gossett had been careless with the red-ink pot.

She must have observed his scrutiny, for while the soup was being removed, she leant forward and said:

'Do you believe in palmistry? Do you? *I* do.'

She leant back again, both her hands stretched before her on the tablecloth, like blood-stained symbols. Brian made a movement as though to examine one of them.

Mrs. Gossett snatched her hands in mock terror from the table, and held them behind her back. 'I *won't* let you see,' she said. '*I won't.*' She looked at him with a gay challenge. As, however, the challenge did not seem to be very provoking, she timidly relented. 'Well – p'r'aps . . .' The hands were once more produced, with many quivering little withdrawals, and were lain out for his inspection.

Brian studied a little hopelessly the moist palms before him. 'But really,' he said, 'I don't know anything at all about it.'

The head was again put on one side and a great deal of white of eye appeared. 'You're teasing.'

'Honestly I'm not.'

'Of course you are. I can see it in your eyes.' Mrs. Gossett suddenly bit her lip violently. 'I haven't said anything *dweadful,* have I?'

'Of course not.'

'Oh, I *have.* I know I have.'

'Really you haven't.'

'I never know when I say things. It's too embawassing. But then – we said we wouldn't mind to-night, didn't we?' With a daring gesture she tossed back her head. A loose lock of mouse-coloured hair fell gently over her left ear.

Her palms were still outstretched.

'Don't you think we'd better finish the sole?' said Brian.

Mrs. Gossett shook her head.

He began to feel exasperated.

'But I tell you I don't understand these things.'

Again she narrowed her eyes. 'You're cheating yourself, you know,' she remarked, with great solemnity. 'I *know.*' She continued to stare at him. Then the eyes again rolled and her mouth broadened into a timid smile. 'Still – we'll talk about that some other time, shall we?'

And she began to 'pick' at her sole. Mrs. Gossett seemed to consider it indelicate to eat any dish in its entirety. She would take her 'portion' of whatever it might consist, and slide it from side to side of her plate, playing with it as a cat plays with a mouse, occasionally dabbing it with a fork, and still more occasionally transferring a small piece of it to her mouth, where it was chewed absent-mindedly, with prim lips, until it apparently melted away. The same procedure was adopted in respect of the bread. The cherry-tipped fingers would delve into the centre of the crisp roll, extract a portion of white bread, and knead it into a rather disgusting pulp on the tablecloth. Then a minute portion of crust would be taken between scarlet thumb and scarlet forefinger, and placed, with a certain rumination, between her irregular teeth.

'You've eaten nothing,' said Brian, towards the end of the meal.

'I've *adored* it.'

'It's not a bad place, is it?'

'Heavenly. So much nicer than the Savoy or the Berkeley or

the –' her memory failing her for a moment, 'or any of those old places.'

'Yes, isn't it?'

'One gets so *bored* with them, doesn't one?' She was once more the duchess, in spite of a suspicious flush on her cheek-bones which owed more to Beaune than to nature.

'Dreadfully bored.'

'The same old people. The same old ways. Whereas *this* . . .'

She made a sweeping gesture with her arm, wiping as she did so the remainder of the bread on to the floor. The gesture included the bank clerk, whose steak was now thoroughly absorbed, the guzzling provincials, the tired waiters and the dreary aspidistras.

Mrs. Gossett now began to fumble under the table. Brian watched her with considerable curiosity. After a moment she produced a large crocodile bag, which she laid on the table. She gave the impression of a female professor about to demonstrate a problem in physics. The analogy might indeed stand, for she was about to make up.

She made up with carefully calculated devilment. A lip-stick as large as a small carrot was firstly applied with grim precision to her mouth. A large puff, similar to a housemaid's mop, was then flicked round her nose, where it left patches like snow on a somewhat trampled Eden. A brand-new pot of rouge was finally produced, and dabbed in all the wrong places.

Brian stared with something akin to horror at the metamorphosis which was taking place before him. Mrs. Gossett at the end of this proceeding was looking positively clownish. Had she been about to appear in a circus as a comic turn she could not have prepared herself with greater effect. Something had to be done. And so he leant forward and said, with as much affection as he could put into his voice:

'I like you better as you were before.'

Mrs. Gossett lowered her eyes.

'You see,' he added, 'you don't *need* all that.'

She put her head on one side.

'I suppose,' he concluded desperately, 'it's because I'm old-fashioned.'

Her eyes fluttered up again. A smile which she imagined to be radiant spread over the large and glistening lips. She suddenly rose to her feet, swept her cloak round her, and disappeared.

In a minute she had returned again and Brian sighed with relief to observe that her face had returned to the normal. 'How wonderful of you,' he said. 'Shall we go on?'

They were whirled in through the great doors, she one way, he another. He received a ticket in exchange for his hat, and stood waiting for her at the bottom of the staircase.

And as soon as she appeared, his heart sank. She was all wrong. In the midst of these exquisite, glittering creatures, she stood out as a conspicuous frump. Among the crowd of sleek, shingled heads, her tousled mop appeared barbaric. Against the simple delicious confections around her, the pink, bunchy dress had all the disadvantages of extreme rusticity, without any rustic charm. By the side of the pale, ivory complexions of her companions her skin had an appearance of health for which the word 'rude' was an inadequate description.

He forced a smile, and gave her his arm. For the moment she was being the 'Duchess,' which was at least something to be thankful for, since it would tend to moderate her behaviour. She waved her bedraggled fan at a mass of superb orchids which were heaped in white and purple profusion near the top of the stairs.

'Quite pwetty, aren't they?' she observed casually, as though she had just caught sight of a few geraniums.

'Marvellous,' said Brian.

'Oh,' he said to himself, 'I want orchids. I want orchids. I don't want this thing on my arm. I want Julia – Julia – Julia – Julia. . . .'

An awful thought seized him. Supposing Julia were here to-night? What on earth would she say about Mrs. Gossett? The idea made him sweat with sudden fear. Fool that he was! Why had he not thought of it before? They might all be here. Julia and Lord William and Maurice, and Tanagra and Lady Thane. They might see him dancing with this . . . with *this*!

Pale, and almost tearful, he glanced again at Mrs. Gossett. In the light of this fresh alarm she seemed positively obscene. He knew he ought not to feel that way about her. He knew that he was being snobbish, and contemptible. But he couldn't help it.

He saw, or thought he saw, mocking eyes directed at him and his companion. He heard, or thought he heard, whispered comments upon the pink dress and the tattered fan. He knew, or thought he knew, that they were both creating a sensation, the unenviable sensation that always comes to those who are out of the picture. He would have liked to sink through the floor. He would have liked to carry Mrs. Gossett up to the roof, and keep her there in the darkness, under the stars, until all the rest had gone away.

But no such plan of campaign was possible. For they were already in the entrance to the ballroom, and Mrs. Gossett heard the band as a war-horse hears the trumpet. She forgot her 'Duchess' manners. She became instantly a shy young debutante. She let her fan dangle ponderously from her wrist. Then she placed a napthaleened glove on Brian's shoulder, and looked up in his eyes.

Suppressing a groan, he began to dance.

'Isn't this heavenly?'

'Superb.'

It was worse than he thought. For she danced with an allure that could only be matched by those ladies who, in the side-shows of the Folies Bergères, nightly exhibit to American business men the remarkable elasticity of the female abdomen. She curved here, and willowed there. She bent, and swayed and sidled, until it was with the greatest difficulty that Brian could steer her at all. And from time to time she would throw back her head, very suddenly, and give him a 'look,' lowering her eyes immediately afterwards in much confusion.

When the first dance was over, Brian began to make for the door.

'But, oh – we *can't* miss one!'

He faltered weakly. 'No. Of course we can't.'

She clapped her hands in loud isolation, then kittenishly put them behind her back, alarmed at the attention she was calling to herself.

Swaying on one foot, she said, 'Did'm's think I was tired?'

'Are you sure you're not?' he said eagerly.

She shook her head rapidly from side to side. 'Not the very least. Not the *vewy* . . .'

And then the band began again, and once more they were making the circuit of the room.

Brian was almost desperate. Something must be done. He felt instinctively that Julia was in the room. She must not on any conceivable account see him with Mrs. Gossett.

But how could he conceal his identity? Should he pull extraordinary faces, so that nobody could possibly recognize him? Should he try to appear patronizing, as though he were the owner of the house and were doing his duty by dancing with the cook? Should he even try, by a series of apt manoeuvres, to trundle Mrs. Gossett round the sides of the room, keeping his face grimly set to the wall, and only turning round very quickly, when necessity demanded?

All of these manoeuvres, in varying degree, he essayed, but he had to give them up as hopeless.

'*Too* lovely,' she murmured after each dance, grimly remaining in the centre of the floor.

That was the most hideous part of the whole business. Mrs. Gossett was obviously becoming violently infected by the gaiety around her. Her cheeks were flushed, her chatter became high and shrill, and a lock of hair detached itself from the main structure of her coiffure, drifting inconsequently into her eye. She would then remove it with a whimsical gesture, or toss it aside with a girlish, muttered imprecation. Once, she even said 'damn,' very softly, and then, overcome by the abandon of her behaviour, hid a scarlet and coquettish face in the lapels of Brian's coat.

There was only one thing to do in these circumstances, and that was to hide. After about the third dance, Brian said:

'Suppose we go and have a drink?'

She turned huge dolls' eyes upon him.

'Alweady?'

'Oh – I mean any sort of drink.'

She pursed her lips, and then simpered. What on earth she was supposed to convey by that Brian could not guess. Nor did he care. It was enough that he was in mortal fear of detection. He therefore took her by the arm, and steered her feverishly through the crowd, up the staircase, and into a gallery where, on a long table, a series of typical dishes and drinks were arranged indicating the spirit of charity more than that of taste.

'I always think that sitting out's the nicest part of a dance,' he said, as soon as he had securely hidden her behind a bust of Disraeli.

'Well – of course' – and here her eyelids were working at top speed – 'that *depends*, doesn't it?'

'Depends on what?' asked Brian.

'Really, Mr. Elme.' With mock nervousness she toyed with her gloves.

Brian forced a grin. He had no idea that smiling could be so fatiguing. Smiling at Mrs. Gossett was as arduous as lifting heavy weights. He could feel permanent creases coming round his eyes and mouth.

'I don't think it depends on anything,' he said fatuously.

For answer she shook her head, and lifted to her lips the glass of lemonade which he had obtained for her.

There was silence for a moment. Brian surreptitiously glanced at his watch. It was only just after eleven. He could not possibly suggest leaving before one. Two hours more of this! It was enough to make one weep. If it had been merely a question of looking after Mrs. Gossett, he would not have minded. But this horrible business of hide and seek – this concealment . . . he shuddered.

'Cold?' a sweet voice crooned.

He looked at her.

'Yes – rather.'

'I'm *deliciously* warm,' she sighed, with head well back.

She certainly was, thought Brian. She was purple in the face.

Suddenly, Mrs. Gossett, with the impetuousness not merely of a girl but of a positive babe in arms, leant forward, thrusting a diminutive handkerchief under his nose.

'Smell,' she said. 'That would make *anybody* feel warm.'

A sickly aroma of stale carnations made itself evident.

'Yes,' he gulped, 'it would.'

'What do you *mean*?' she cried.

'I only agreed with you,' he said in desperation.

'But I didn't say anything like *that*.'

'Like what?'

'Well – like, like, ll-l-like –' (God! thought Brian, she's going to stutter. That's the worst sign of all.)

'Like what?' he repeated.

'It was the *way* you said it,' she murmured, oh, so virginally!

'I didn't think I said it any particular way.'

She turned her head, arching her neck like an acrobatic swan.

'You're such a tease.'

'Honestly, I'm not, Mrs. Gossett.'

'Never mind.' Her mood changed as suddenly as it had begun. 'I forgive you.' She sprang to her feet almost knocking over the wicker chair in which she had been sitting. 'And to show you I forgive you, we'll have another dance.'

And gaily, with hand on hip, and fan fluttering by her side, she was already walking away down the long corridor, in the direction of the ballroom.

Brian followed miserably. There was no escape.

On all sides of him were delectable maidens, slim and chic – maidens with whom he might have been happy, maidens with whom he might have danced deliriously. And somewhere, perhaps, was the one particular maiden of his desire. . . .

Mrs. Gossett suddenly drew up short. 'My *dear*!'

'Yes?'

She raised her arm to point, and then remembering her gentility, quickly let it fall again.

'Surely that's your friend?'

Brian's heart leapt. 'Who?'

A sly smile spread over her face, and she coyly glanced at her somewhat tarnished slipper. But as Brian looked in the direction where she had pointed, he saw at the other end of the corridor, Julia.

He stared at her, his lips parted, a quick flush dyeing his cheeks and fading away again. She was in white, with diamond shoes that glittered, even though she was standing still. By her side was a young man of no particular interest or attraction.

She had seen him. Here was the man walking quickly towards them while she waited. Brian was rooted to the floor. He wanted to fly, he wanted to stay, he wanted . . . oh, Lord!

'Lady Julia wondered if it was you.'

'Oh yes – of course.'

'Will you come over?'

Brian glanced plaintively at Mrs. Gossett who had assumed a pose of powerful nonchalance a few yards away.

'I'm awfully sorry, but . . .'

The man grinned. 'Well, I'll deal with that for a bit.'

'I say . . .' Thank God. . . . He could have hugged this chap. 'What's your name?'

'Molyneux.'

Together they went to Mrs. Gossett.

'May I introduce a great friend of mine? Mr. Molyneux. He's longing to meet you.'

Mrs. Gossett was almost inarticulate. The air was so full of romance. At one moment she felt she should be haughty at Brian's desertion. At another she felt that it was a sublime opportunity for saying things which could be 'misunderstood.' And again, she had to rally all her battery of woman's wiles for the subjugation of Mr. Molyneux. Fortunately, the latter motive was uppermost. So she bit her lips, fluttered her fan, and gave to this new conquest a look of undiluted enticement.

Languidly she lifted her blood-red fingers on to his arm, and darting a glance at Brian, uttered the one word 'Later?' Then she dragged Mr. Molyneux away.

Why can one never plunge straight into Romance? Why are there always so many antechambers in which one must kick one's heels, growing tired and cold and dull? Why, in fact, could he not lift Julia in his arms, and carry her out into the night, sealing her lips with kisses until she should say the one thing he longed to hear her say?

Instead, there was a most prosaic beginning.

'Darling – who *is* your girl friend?'

Unaccountably, Brian suddenly felt inclined to defend Mrs. Gossett.

'She's the Duchess of Pentecost,' he said. 'In other words, Mrs. Gossett.'

'Why didn't you introduce me?'

'Listen, Julia. I know she looks peculiar. But she's my editress. It's agony, but it can't be helped.'

'How terribly chivalrous you are.'

Brian swallowed a lump in his throat, but did not reply.

Julia watched him. She was more happy than she dared to confess, even to herself, that she had found him here. But she would not show it – yet.

'I'm being horrible,' she said quickly. 'We'll go and sit down somewhere.'

It was nearly ten minutes before they found a place – a shadowed corner near the ballroom, where the sound of the bands came only fitfully, as though blown on the wind. Nor could they yet talk as they desired, for no sooner had they sat down than the screen trembled, and a head appeared from behind. It was Molyneux.

'Sorry to interrupt,' he said. 'But I've called for my halo.'

Brian's face fell. 'You haven't brought her back *yet*?'

'No. Guess who she's dancing with now.'

'Who?'

'Maurice!'

He could have shouted with joy. Julia peered beyond the screen.

'It's true,' she said. 'Look!'

He looked. From where they were sitting they could see the open doorway of the ballroom. And at that very moment, the linked figures of Maurice and Mrs. Gossett slid into view. The dance was a tango, and Mrs. Gossett was extracting from it every possible curve, pirouette and posture. She clung to Maurice like an excited leech. As for Maurice himself, it was only too evident that he was exceedingly alarmed. He held his head as far from hers as decency admitted, and glanced wildly round the room with staring, horror-struck eyes. She was a far greater problem in life than any he had hitherto encountered.

Brian felt at peace with all the world.

'She's good for another hour with him,' he said.

'Angel,' whispered Julia to Molyneux. 'You can take your halo.'

And they were again alone.

Julia sank on to the sofa, over which a tangled spray of yellow orchids had fallen.

'Do you like all this sort of thing?'

'Now you're here.'

'Yes – but forget me. Do you like being fearfully smart and gilt-edged and – you know?'

'It's rather new for me.'

'Would you like to do it always?'

He looked at her boldly. 'Is that an offer?'

She was silent for a moment. Then: 'How you've changed.'

'Why?'

'You wouldn't have known what a remark like that even meant a few months ago.' She leant forward. 'Don't change, darling.'

He studied his finger-nails. 'I've got to grow up some time.'

'Physically, yes. But not in other ways.'

'You mean you still want me to go on dropping bricks, and being awkward, and not knowing whether you eat caviare with a spoon or a fork?'

'You eat it with a knife, my dear, but that's beside the point.' She was amazed at herself to find how difficult it was for her to keep this conversation flippant.

'Simplicity's a rather futile rôle,' he said. There was the suspicion of a sulk in his voice.

'No, it isn't. It's a wonderful rôle. You used to play it perfectly.'

'Did I?' he asked eagerly. How wonderful it is to be analysed by somebody one loves!

She nodded. 'When you first called on me – what ages ago it seems – you were an absolute child. I felt it was almost wrong of you to be allowed to smoke cigarettes. And as for a cocktail . . .'

He laughed happily. 'You gave me the first I ever had.'

'I know. I was a brute.'

'Julia – really – that's overdoing it a bit.'

She pursed her lips. 'Perhaps. But even if a thing's got to be destroyed one doesn't take any particular pleasure in being the one to destroy it.'

He was too puzzled to reply. And she, too, was puzzled by herself. She had imagined that the maternal feeling, the desire to shelter, which sooner or later is bound to make its appearance in the romances of any popular novelist, was reserved for the pages of fiction alone. It was more than tiresome to feel like this, but she could not help it. And having said so much, one could hardly draw back. She went on:

'Somehow, I hate to see you here at all. I hate to know that you're learning to talk in the same silly way as all the rest. Sometimes I hear you say a thing's "divine," or "too adorable," and each time you do that a cold shudder goes down my back. It isn't *you*. You've learnt it from Don or Maurice or somebody and it means nothing.'

'But they're your friends.'

'Yes. And look at them.' She laughed quickly to cover the bitterness in her voice. 'You used to say things were "jolly," and I even believe I heard you use the word "topping" once. Why don't you do that any more?'

'Because I've stopped being a sweet little schoolboy, I suppose.'

'That's the trouble.'

He looked at her moodily. 'I believe you're making fun of me.'

She half closed her eyes. 'That's the last thing – the very last thing.'

'I'll put on my old dress-suit again, if you like. With the patched trousers.'

'No. For God's sake don't go as far as that!' She laughed in spite of herself.

'Thank you for laughing at last.'

There was a mist across her eyes. 'Oh, my dear, you are a kid.'

'I'm not.' He squared his shoulders heroically. 'I'm a terribly smart young man-about-town. I breakfast on dry martinis and sweet corn. I'm going to write a brilliant novel and make thousands and thousands of pounds and give you bracelets which are so utterly modern that they'll be dated before you have time to wear them twice.'

'Are you?'

'Yes. And I'm going to dance with you now. Like a good old lounge-lizard. For hours and hours and hours. Oh, Julia, isn't this priceless?'

She gave him her arm. 'You've said it at last.'

CHAPTER TWELVE

B RIAN's education proceeded apace. A fortnight later he went to a party given by the famous Tanagra Guest. People still talk of that party.

Tanagra was as much a product of the war as Monsieur Poincaré, and some people were inclined to think she was equally regrettable. Her profession was, ostensibly, that of a miniature-painter. She had painted miniatures of almost everybody in London, and she had the reputation of being able to compress the largest possible woman into the smallest possible space, rather in the manner of an animal-tamer persuading elephants to squeeze through paper hoops.

Her appearance – six feet tall, thin, with a red Eton crop and large horn-rimmed glasses, was mysterious enough. But not so mysterious as her past. Speculation as to her origin was rife. Some said that she had begun as an attendant in a Ladies' Cloak-room in Boston, others that she had been employed in a chewing-gum factory. As a matter of fact, she had been a mistress of drawing in a small school in New Jersey, from which she departed owing to a slight disagreement on the subject of the nude. What happened to her during the war, nobody knows.

She had a mother somewhere, but she had not seen her for many years. But that did not matter much, because mothers were not among her friends' more popular hobbies. All they cared about was 'parties' and they looked upon Tanagra to provide them.

Provide them she did. Of party-giving she made a trade. Who paid for her parties one never quite knew. Somebody paid, of course, because one could not fill that huge studio in Chelsea with Easter lilies, and provide cases of champagne and buckets of caviare out of the mere practice of miniature-painting.

Still, what did it matter? Tanagra's parties were always such fun. Everybody did their stunts so much better than in other people's houses. Evan Spade, for instance, swore that the only place where he could imitate Beatrice Lillie was on Tanagra's sofa, and that, surely, was enough to make any party a success nowadays? And nobody minded, at Tanagra's, if Mrs. Grindhaven danced a polka to a palpable valse, or if couples disappeared, a little oddly, into the backyard, or if Lady Jane put her cigar ash down one's back. For Tanagra had the only two essential qualities of the successful party-maker. She knew the meaning of shaded lights. And she did *not* know the meaning of the word 'hock-cup.'

The present party was a new idea, and Brian, in his new capacity, as a bright young person, had been invited. Everybody was to be dressed as a child. And not only to be dressed, but to act as a child as well. The idea of Lord William, garbed in crawlers, lisping childish words, seemed too good to miss. Besides, Julia was going. She had said, 'You must go. You'll look so adorable in shorts.' At which he had held his head very high.

His invitation was written on children's note-paper with pink woolly lambs at the top, and said:

'Dear Brian, will you please come to my party on the fourteenth? Yours affectionately, Tanagra.' And in the bottom right-hand corner was written, 'Please tell your nurse to call for you at 4 a.m.'

Had Society always done this sort of thing? He asked himself this question, as he stood, clad in shorts, socks, a tight-fitting jersey and sailor hat, prior to setting out. Did Mr. Gladstone and the Earl of Beaconsfield and the late Duchess of Argyll so attire themselves, and make merry in such scanty garments? Or had he got into rather a peculiar set of people? The question answered itself as soon as it fluttered through his mind. Shame on him to doubt these new friends! Julia, Lord William, Maurice? How could they possibly be 'peculiar'? Shame indeed!

He was to call for Maurice, who had insisted that they should go to the party together. He was a little nervous about this arrangement because it was becoming only too evident that Maurice was beginning to dislike him. However, he had to go to the party with somebody.

When he arrived at the studio at a quarter to eleven, fifteen minutes before his time, a weary-looking housekeeper informed him that Mr. Cheyne had been forced to go out for a few minutes but would be back at eleven. Brian was rather glad, because he had never been in the studio before, and he thought it might tell him something about its owner. It did, but in a way which he had hardly expected.

The first revelation came at once. He wanted to have a cigarette. On a painted table near the fireplace lay a small papier-mâché box. He opened it, then started back in astonishment.

Inside the box was a slip of paper, laid across the cigarettes – and written in large block capitals was the word

THIEF!

This was very odd. It made him feel quite uncomfortable. He found himself blushing as though the accusation were intended to apply to him alone. There was no doubt that Maurice had written it. The 'THIEF!' was in his handwriting. He closed the box guiltily and went away to sit on the extreme edge of the sofa.

Then he thought – 'this is ridiculous. It must be some absurd joke.' A little self-consciously he got up from the sofa, whistling, his hands in his pockets. He approached the box again, and stretched a tentative finger towards it. THIEF! No. Better leave it alone. Perhaps these were very special cigarettes. Perhaps they were filled with some exotic drug. Anyway, there must be *some* reason.

He decided he would have a drink. He spied a tantalus and a soda-water bottle on a sideboard near the door. Maurice surely wouldn't mind. He approached the sideboard, and lifted up the decanter.

Another slip of paper fluttered on to the floor. He put down the decanter as though it had bitten him, then stooped down, wondering what he would find this time. There was another message.

'YOU THINK I DON'T KNOW, DO YOU?'

Brian stared at the paper with wide-eyed amazement. Who thought that who did not know? And what was it that they didn't know? Did it mean that Maurice had a sixth sense that enabled him to discover automatically who had been at his whisky? Did it mean . . . He began to feel slightly indignant. If wherever he turned he were to be silently accused of incipient kleptomania, he would prefer to go outside.

Then curiosity seized him. There might be more slips of paper. It really would be rather fun just to see. Would the sponge in the bathroom squeak out the word 'robber' if one squeezed it? Would the bath-mat be inscribed with the legend, 'Thou God seeth me'? He tiptoed across to the door of the bedroom, opened it, and peeped in.

A truly remarkable sight met his eyes. For, all round the walls were pinned sheets of note-paper, large and small, bearing a series of singular messages. Forgetting the fact that he might be regarded as guilty of indecent curiosity, he stepped inside.

On the first piece of paper he read:

'WHAT IS TEN SHILLINGS?'

He felt slightly dizzy. If Maurice did not know what ten shillings was, nobody did. Underneath this question was drawn the face of a man, contorted into a sneer, pulling a long nose at ten silver disks.

More and more singular. For the next slip of paper bore the single word:

'YET!'

By the side of this word Maurice had drawn an emaciated woman, lifting a long green-tipped finger to her lips.

He turned to the adjoining slip.

'TEN SHILLINGS *EVERY* WEEK FOR A YEAR EQUALS . . .'

What did it equal? The next slip told him.

'TWENTY-SIX POUNDS.'

Underneath the 'twenty-six pounds' were depicted several touching scenes illustrating the powers of this sum for the purchase of happiness. The first represented a pink youth with large hips lying on the sands of the Lido. The second showed three cases of champagne. The third showed two suits, one blue and one black. The fourth was a somewhat attenuated drawing of the Eiffel Tower, standing stark against a roseate sky.

Brian began to see light. These legends represented Maurice's method of curbing his expenditure. It had never been exactly reckless, and in the circumstances he did not feel inclined to wonder at it. To wake up every morning, in the shadow of this artistic deification of parsimony, would be enough to put anybody off buying anything. There were many other legends, at which he took a cursory glance:

'BISMARCK USED TO WORK TILL DAWN.'
'WHY NOT A BUS?'
'GIVE YOUR STOMACH A REST. WE ALL EAT TOO MUCH.'
'DO YOU *NEED* IT?'

Had he been able to assimilate all these injunctions his mind would have been in a state of hopeless confusion. However, he was saved from that by the sound of steps on the stairs outside. He had just time to tiptoe out of the room, close the door, and sit down on the sofa when Maurice entered, dressed in a very tight sailor suit and carrying a bucket and spade in his hand.

'I'm terribly sorry to be late. I had to wake up all the children I know to borrow these. Shall we go on?'

And so quickly did he whirl Brian out of the room that we shall have no time to investigate the meaning of these strange wall-messages – not, at least, till nearer the end of this book.

CHAPTER THIRTEEN

THE party was at its height, and as a typical social phenomenon of the post-war period it is worthy of study.

The large studio was packed with men and women of all shapes and ages, dressed as children. Through the smoke-laden atmosphere one could distinguish the forms of immense women wearing 'crawlers,' old men with paddling-drawers and shrimping nets, sophisticated, pale-faced girls in pinafores, an occasional young man in long clothes. For the rest, there were quantities of sailor suits, flimsy white skirts and jerseys.

This amazing crowd fox-trotted and fox-trotted round the room to the sound of a negro jazz band, members of which were uniformly garbed in shorts, blue shirts and white straw hats. Everybody in the room was acting up to his or her part (Tanagra, moving hither and thither like an anxious spectre, was seeing to that), so that the general effect was of a children's party conceived by Aubrey Beardsley, executed by Benda, and held in one of the more obscure cafés of the Rue de Lappe. If you know the Rue de Lappe, you have nothing to learn. If you do not, you would be wiser to avoid it.

One heard, for instance, this sort of thing.

1st woman (aged 53). 'How old is 'oo?'

2nd woman (aged 48). 'I'm seben.'

Tired young man. '*I'm* eight.'

At this point, a grey-haired, cat-like man advances and says, '*I'm* nine.' And they all scream, and gulp more champagne, are dug in the back by hot elbows, and dance away together through the swaying crowd.

Or this would happen.

1st woman (aged, perhaps, 61). 'My daddy's very *rich*.'

2nd woman (a slim slip of 20). 'My daddy's *richer*.'

Old man. 'But my daddy's *dead*. He! he! Ho! ho!'

And again they scream, and light cigarettes with fingers itching with impatience, inhaling the welcome smoke as though it were a draught of fresh air to those who are suffocating – as indeed it was, to them.

Now, too, the band has become infected with the universal 'infantility' – if there is such a word. Black, vibrant voices cut through the din. The song is a jazz rendering of Little Jack Horner. Fighting against the saxophone and the drum one hears:

> 'Little Jack Hor-Hor-Horner
> Sat in a cor-cor-corner
> Eating plum pudding and pi-eeee.
> He put in his th-th-thumb
> And pulled out a pl-pl-plum
> Saying, oh what a good boy am I-ee.'

From the general to the particular. Brian was sitting in a corner with Julia. Champagne had driven away his self-consciousness. He really did *feel* like a child, and with his flushed face and his tousled hair he looked only like an overgrown boy. He said to her:

'Would you like to be a baby with me?'

'I am.'

'Would you play with me then?'

'Yes.'

'Would you play postman's knock?'

'What game is that?'

'Shall I show you?' (Incredible daring!)

'Ssh. Not here!' Her hand fluttered to her mouth. A pretty gesture, even if it was second-hand. To him it was like the memory of a white flower glimpsed in the age of innocence.

'We'd build a house in a wood,' he said.

'What sort of house?'

'A lovely house; with a green door that you had to bend your head to get through, and peaches growing out of season round the windows.'

She nodded.

'And,' he went on eagerly, 'an enormous ditch to keep out the bears.'

She pursed her lips. 'Not the Teddy bears too?'

'No; they'd have a smaller bridge which they could walk across.'

'But supposing the other bears used it too?'

'They wouldn't. I'd put up a notice saying that it was only for the Teddies.'

'But supposing they couldn't read?'

'All bears can read. And even if they couldn't, they'd pretend to. So it comes to the same thing.'

'How deep would the ditch be?'

'Oh, awfully deep.'

'As deep as this room?'

'Deeper.'

'As deep as the Grand Cañon?'

'Well' – he paused gravely. . . . 'Perhaps it wouldn't be quite as deep as that. We don't want to be vulgar, you see.'

'No. I see. Would it keep out the alligators?'

'Yes. And the boa constrictors too.'

A childish frown obscured her forehead. 'Which sort of boa constrictors?'

'The ones with the big blue tails.'

'Ooh! Could you keep *them* out?'

'I would. For *you*.'

They laughed happily. The dance went on, and now the melody was muted – an innocuous tune that moved one's feet in the manner of a nurse playing with a baby's toes.

'And I'd build you a boat,' he whispered.

'What sort of boat?'

'A big boat with a jade-green sail. And we'd sail away on the lake.'

She gripped his arm more tightly. 'Where should we sail to?'

'To an island with a yellow beach, and sands made of powdered diamonds. And we should find pearls in blue pools.'

'Big pearls?'

'Big and little. And medium too.'

'How big would the medium ones be?'

He took her little finger and kissed the tip of it. 'As big as that.'

'Would you give me the pearls?'

'Yes. All of them. I'd string them round your neck. And then I'd sit you down and look at you. I'd look at you all the morning, and all the afternoon, and all the evening, and all the night. By twilight and by sunlight and by moonlight. Sometimes your pearls would look white, and sometimes they would be red with the sun's blood, and sometimes green, because there would be a mist over the moon.'

'Why would there be a mist over the moon?'

He whispered very softly, 'So that I could kiss you without the boa constrictors seeing.'

'They'd be asleep.'

'No. They only sleep on Tuesdays.'

'How do you know?'

'Everybody knows *that*!'

'But suppose the alligators saw?'

'They never look at things like that.'

'Why not?'

'Because they're alligators, all cold and gooy. Alligators never kiss each other.'

'Don't they?'

'No. They try sometimes, but their leather faces rub together, and that sets their teeth on edge.'

'Darling! Thank God you're not an alligator.'

He pressed her hand so tightly that she bit her lip. 'Don't drive me mad,' he said.

The music stopped abruptly, with that queer, strangled cough that is so characteristic both of modern tunes and of modern life. Julia was claimed by somebody else. She whispered to him that she would be dancing with him again in a few minutes. Reluctantly he let her go, and stood in his corner, watching.

And then, as he was standing there, he saw a woman looking at him so intently that, had he not drunk more than enough champagne, he would have felt strangely embarrassed. Even as it was, he shivered slightly, as though a cold draught had blown across the room. He had a sudden and disquieting sense of something beautiful ending and something ugly beginning. A foolish sense, he told himself, for the picture he saw was merely grotesque. The woman was standing on the other side of the room, dressed in a short frock of broad blue check, with ribbons in her hair. The face seemed vaguely familiar – and as he turned away to avoid her gaze, he tried to remember who she was. The difficulty was solved for him by Lord William, who suddenly appeared by his side, with the cryptic remark:

'Never sell your virtue for a cigarette case.'

'I don't know what you mean.'

'Yes, you do. She's still looking at you.'

'What – the blue thing with a head like an Easter egg?'

'Yes. Anne Hardcastle.'

'Lord! So *that's* Lady Hardcastle!'

He looked at her again. A feeling of foolish shyness came over him. To the initiated all nymphomaniacs are a little alarming. And Lady Hardcastle, by reputation, by theory and by practice, was a perfect type of nymphomaniac. Even the seven surgeons who, at various times, had sliced the wrinkles from her face, tightening her cheeks and carving her neck until she gave the appearance of an animated intaglio, had been unable to take away the hunting look which she perpetually wore. Brian returned her stare openly. And, to his horror, she came over, greeted Lord William, and said, 'I want to play with *this* little boy.'

'Darling, we're all wondering why you haven't done already. It was so obviously indicated.'

She pushed him aside. 'Don't want 'oo,' she said.

Looking faintly sick at this perpetual baby-talk, Lord William briefly introduced the two and took his departure.

'Good evening. How is 'oo?'

Brian started. Then he remembered the game. 'I've got a pain,' he said gravely.

'Where is 'oo's pain?'

'Tummy.'

''Oo's been eating cocktails. *Naughty.*' And she dabbed him with one of her tiny talons.

Brian wanted to giggle. The woman before him looked so very queer. Her face, as we have already learnt, had the uncanny smoothness of all women who have had their features 'lifted.' But she had purposely puckered it to give the effect of a perverse child. As a result, the wrinkles were in all the wrong places. The skin about her eyes was quite smooth, but a curious network of lines had appeared round her pouting lips. Her chin was as clear cut as if it had been carved (which, indeed, was literally the case), but the base of the neck seemed to have 'come unstuck.'

'Does 'oo think I'm pwetty?'

'I think 'oo's beautiful.'

'As pwetty as any other little gel in the woom?'

This was too much. Brian said, 'I'm awfully sorry, but I can't keep it up.'

She allowed her face to relax, and smiled. She again looked young and pretty.

'Shall we dance, little boy? The great thing about life is never to stop still for more than a minute at a time.'

'I'd love to.'

Marvellous record for Anne! She had talked to him for two whole minutes before enunciating one of her 'greatest things about life.' Later on, as Life itself was to bring them closer together, he would have more than his fill of those definitions. They were her philosophical stock-in-trade, the ribbons with which she bedecked her emptiest thoughts.

However, Brian did not know that. And so he merely said, yes, he would like to dance.

They danced. And somehow the news that they were dancing together seemed to spread round the room before they had been together for more than a minute. Everybody knew Anne and her amours. In fact, one could play quite a good parlour game on wet days in writing down on a sheet of notepaper as many of her lovers as could be remembered in a quarter of an hour. It used up a lot of notepaper, but it seldom failed to amuse.

And now Brian was the latest recruit of all. 'I do think it's a shame,' said Mrs. Grindhaven, who was dancing *round* Lord William rather than with him. 'That nice boy. Why did you let her speak to him?'

'I cannot interrupt the forces of nature,' he said, his eyes almost closed and his shoulders aching from her swinging motion.

'There's nothing *natural* about that connection?'

He opened his eyes wide. 'Connection? Tell me more.'

In another part of the room Lady Jane was booming about it to Tanagra. 'She ought to have been a man,' she said.

'But that wouldn't have been quite nice, would it?' replied Tanagra, smiling at six new arrivals, yet giving all her attention to Jane.

'It would have saved a lot of trouble.'

'Yes. But I'm terribly glad she chose my party to meet him. Anne's enthusiasm is so infectious. They'll all be following her example soon.'

And certainly, whether 'they' were following Anne's example or not, they showed themselves hectically amused by her and her new companion. There was, indeed, a pathetic cause for amusement. Brian had obviously drank too much; he was miserable at being away from Julia, but he saw no escape. Julia had disappeared and Anne refused to let him go. She held on to his arm like a leech, gazing into his eyes, prattling ridiculous baby nonsense. He felt acutely self-conscious. What did the woman want? And if she did want it, what would she do when she found she wouldn't get it?

Then he felt a hand on his shoulder, and he saw Julia standing by his side. She had taken in the whole situation, and she was looking at Anne with a smile of contemptuous amusement. Brian sighed with relief and withdrew his arm from Anne's.

'I'm so sorry, Lady Hardcastle, but I'm engaged for this one.'

She still held on to his hand. 'Oo's not going away? I want to play with 'oo. 'Oo's my new toy.'

Brian looked at Julia hopelessly. She stepped forward, ignoring her.

'But *I* want to play with him,' cried Anne plaintively. Her resemblance to a spoilt child was unmistakable now.

Julia whispered to Brian, 'She's impossible.' Then aloud, 'Brian dear, give this golliwog to the little girl to keep her quiet.'

Keep her quiet! If only that were possible. For the little scene had drawn an audience. Over his shoulder he could see Maurice and Tanagra, watching with ill-concealed delight.

With a tremendous effort, he tried to cover it up with one of her favourite, fantastic children's gestures.

He held out the golliwog, and in a strained voice he said, 'This is for 'oo.' And then he put his arm round Julia's waist, waiting for a clear space through which to steer her. A shrill cry came to them before they had started: 'She's got my toy! She's got my toy!'

Brian, suddenly sobered by the queer harshness of her voice, stopped still, the ridiculous golliwog held aloft in his hand. And in that frozen moment the face of Anne Hardcastle and of those around her remained permanently stamped on his memory. They were like an obscene parody of Reynold's Heavenly Choir. Anne's features were twisted into a grotesque that was all the more horrible because it still retained, like a coat of surface paint, the assumed vacuity of childhood. Maurice, powdered and pouting, stared with eyes which were wide open with the mimic innocence of youth, yet were tired and darkling with the shadows of an age greater than his own. And Tanagra! She, too, had masked herself in a smile of childhood. Her scarlet lips hung foolishly apart. Monotonously, insanely, she clicked her tongue.

He realized with a shiver of disgust what was happening. *They really were becoming children.* The game had turned to reality. A warped, misshapen reality, of course. But the fact was evident that they had forgotten their adult restraint and that old passions were creeping out under a mask of innocence. He shivered, and Julia shivered too. There was a sudden blare of sound from the jazz band, the room started once again to whirling life, and they danced away. They danced slowly, with set faces.

Nor did they say a word until, on the stairs, they whispered 'good night.'

CHAPTER FOURTEEN

THE dark tale of this night must continue. Looking back on it, long afterwards, it seemed to Brian that of all the nights in his life it was the most ominous.

Shivering with the cold airs of early morning, he let himself into his house in Seymour Street. As he closed the door, he leant his face against the wall, cooling his hot forehead, closing his eyes, aching with fatigue.

The bleak silence of the little hall contrasted with the clanging uproar of his brain. In his head the party rioted still. The tunes still echoed strident and clear, faces drifted like leaves on a swirling, ceaseless stream, lights shone, blinding and pitiless. If only some one would turn out those lights and give him peace! His fingers clutched tremulously at the wall in search of a switch. They found nothing. He opened his eyes, saw only the darkness, and mocked himself for a crazy fool.

With an effort he roused himself. He was sober now, and he walked slowly upstairs. On the topmost step he halted. There was a light from under the sitting-room door. Walter must be still up.

Thank the Lord for that! If ever there was a time when he wanted Walter it was now. Nobody else. No languid lovers, no screaming wits, no twisting pantaloons, nobody but his friend. He wanted to slip his hand through Walter's arm, and lie back on the shabby sofa and say nothing. And then to sleep.

But could he do that? He had hardly spoken to Walter for a fortnight, and even then it had ended in some futile arguments. What was wrong with him? Were they never to be as they had been? Couldn't he make it up now?

He opened the door. Walter was standing by the fireplace filling his pipe. His back was turned towards Brian.

'Hallo, Walter!'

'Hallo!'

He did not turn round to greet him. Brian frowned. He slipped off his overcoat, revealing his crumpled costume, and went to the fireplace, warming his bare legs. Silence.

'What's the time?'

Walter glanced at his wrist watch. 'Only about four. Early for you.' He turned and noticed Brian's clothes. 'What the hell . . .'

'I've been to a party.'

'Pretty queer party, I should think.'

'Everybody was dressed like this.'

'Must have looked sweet.'

Brian clenched his fists tightly. Why were they speaking to each other like this, flinging icy sentences from two remote peaks of pride? Why couldn't they get together? Why couldn't he say, 'I know they were a lot of freaks, but it was fun, and anyway, what's it got to do with you, you old devil?' But he couldn't say it. Instead he said:

'What have you been doing yourself?'

'Getting drunk.'

'Alone?'

'No. Some chaps.'

'Exciting for you.'

'Awfully. Had a fight with a policeman.'

'That was elegant.'

'Fearfully.' He went to the sideboard and poured out a whisky. He swallowed it neat.

'Do you ever stop drinking?'

'Not when I can help it. Cheers my lonely hours.'

'Is that a veiled hit at me?'

Walter knocked out his pipe on the mantelpiece.

'Not particularly veiled. We don't see such a terrific lot of each other now, do we?'

'Is that my fault?'

'Frankly, yes.' He looked at Brian as though he were looking at a stranger. 'You keep rather late hours for me nowadays.'

'Well, I can't help that.'

'Can't you?'

Brian turned to him angrily. 'If you're going to preach . . .'

He laughed. 'Preach! That's funny. To you of all people.'

'Well then, don't do it.'

Walter looked at him from the corner of his eye. 'You must have brought quite a lot of brightness into people's lives in those trousers to-night.'

Brian did not answer.

'I expect they wanted to adopt you, didn't they?'

'Oh, shut up!'

'I'm only trying to learn about this wonderful party.'

Brian sat down and began to take off his shoes. 'Wouldn't interest you.'

'Is that exactly matey?'

He threw the shoes irritably into a corner of the room. 'Well, it wouldn't.'

'Anything that was ruining your health and your temper ought to be interesting. Otherwise it seems hardly worth while.'

'What?'

'You heard me.'

'If I understood, then, you're mad.'

'Oh no, I'm not. You *are* ruining your health and your temper. You've suddenly been taken up by a lot of – well, I won't characterize them. You've become a social success – a sort of social success.'

'Go on.'

There was a dangerous calm in both their voices.

'I say "sort of" social success because it's obvious that, with seven pounds a week, no other friends, and precious few clothes, your success will be – shall we say? – of a certain kind.'

Brian stared at him coldly. 'I don't know what you mean,' he said, 'but you sound damned insulting.'

'It isn't insulting to tell you that you're successful, merely because you're something *chic*, for the moment, and because most of these women would like to have an affair with you.'

'You're damned clever, aren't you?'

'I'm six years older than you. I've seen this happen before. As a matter of fact, it rather amused me, till it happened to you. I've seen other fellows taken up like this, just because they were good-looking and amusing – taken up out of the gutter . . .'

'Are you suggesting that I was taken up out of the gutter?'

'No, but you're damned well putting yourself on a level with people who were. I could show you pageboys out of second-rate hotels dancing with your friends at the Embassy. I'd probably do the same if I were a page-boy, but still . . . I could show you poisonous swine out of dancing academies who've now got their flats in Half Moon Street. How? How? You know how.'

'Do I?'

'Yes.'

Brian walked up to him.

'Do you mean to say . . .'

Walter held out his arms. He wanted to put his hands on Brian's shoulders, but Brian shook him angrily off. He said:

'Brian, old thing, I know you. I'm not suggesting anything. It's only what other people are suggesting.'

'Have *your* friends been talking?' There was a sneer in Brian's voice that he instantly regretted.

Walter lowered his eyes. 'My friends aren't much. I know that, thank you. But they're better than yours.'

'You think so?'

'Think!' He blazed up again. 'Think? Your friends may be brilliant and æsthetic and God knows what, but they're no damned use to *you*. If you weren't a childish ass you'd see that. You'd see that you'd got into the rottenest set in London with about as much rapidity as a little lost boy in an American society film. Tanagra Guest! How does *she* get her money? You can't give her sort of parties on the proceeds of miniature paintings. She lives merely by arranging nice little dinners for people and then going out of the house. That's all.'

'You're foul. You're absolutely foul.'

Walter's hand was on his wrist, holding it in a vice.

'As for Lord William, your other great friend, he's so filled up with vice that he can't see out of his eyes. He's so desiccated himself that he wants you merely because you're young and vital and healthy. Soon you won't be any use to him. And you'll be dropped *flat*.'

'For God's sake leave go of my wrist.'

He held it tighter. 'Now we're on this we'll have it out. Look at Maurice Cheyne. Charming manners. Perfect clothes. Dances like a well-trained snake. Doped all day and all night. Would do you down for sixpence and make a good story out of it.'

Brian was struggling violently. 'You'll be sorry for this.'

'I couldn't be sorrier than I am now. Look at that freak Jane, the sister of *your* lovely lady. Do you call her a normal woman? In a civilized society she'd be put into corduroy trousers and locked up. Look at the life they lead. It isn't life – it's a revolting parody. They're none of them ever in a state of anything but intoxication of some sort or other. They're a mass of nerves. You're a mass of nerves, too. You're pale and jumpy and impossible. . . .'

'My life's my own. *Will you let go?*'

'Just one more thing. Julia. Yes, this'll hurt. I don't care. If ever there was anybody less worth wasting twopennyworth of affection on, it's her.'

With a breathless effort Brian freed himself.

'You'll go too far.'

Walter came close to him. 'She cares about as much for you as for a new bottle of scent. Because she's beautiful, she thinks it's her right to have affairs with anybody she damn well pleases. She's as foul as the rest of them; fouler, because she's making you foul too. . . .'

With a sob of anger, Brian hit him across the face.

Walter staggered back. Instinctively he prepared to hit back. Then he checked himself. A look of utter misery came over his face. He turned towards the door, and went out without a word.

It is, of course, all wrong that a young man should weep. Weeping, according to the psychological chart which mankind has mapped out for our guidance, should be the strict monopoly of women and children.

Yet, there are occasions when young men do weep – when the stream of tears which they thought had dried up in childhood proves, after all, to have been running underground, all the time, and with an agonizing travail forces its way to the surface. To-night was such an occasion. For a whole hour Brian had been weeping. From head to foot he had been racked with sobs. Almost he had seemed to drown with sorrow. It was not only that his face was wet and glistening with tears; his whole body ached with the violent physical contortions which it entailed. For a few moments he would have calm, and then again the agony would seize him, and he would bite his lips, while his breath came in shuddering and spasmodically, and his face twisted itself into a mask of pain.

'This is all wrong, all wrong,' he told himself. 'Mustn't give way like this. All wrong.'

Gradually the storm spent itself. He felt as though he had been whipped until he could not stand. He lay on his back on the bed, too tired to move, too exhausted even to raise his hand to wipe away the tears that still trickled, salt and warm, on to his lips. Still, at least now, he could breathe without that fearful shuddering effort. He heaved a deep sigh and shut his eyes.

He did not remember falling asleep. But he must have done so, for when he woke it was already dawn, and he could hear Mrs. Pleat moving about in the little kitchen outside.

He felt stiff and weary and forlorn. Why? Suddenly he remembered. He looked down at his still clothed limbs. Then, with a start, he rose to his feet and began to undress. Mrs. Pleat mustn't find him like this.

He had only just got into his pyjamas and sprung, shivering, into bed, when Mrs. Pleat entered.

She surveyed Brian with a watery eye.

'Not slept well?' she said.

Brian pretended to be sleepy. 'Oh – not so badly.'

''E 'asn't come in at all.'

'Who?'

'Mr. Walter.'

'Not come in?'

'No. That is to siy, not unless 'e's come in and gone out again, and made 'is own bed, which isn't exactly like Mr. Walter.'

She was studying him intently. Brian thought furiously. She must not guess that anything had happened.

After a pause he said, 'Now I come to think of it, I believe he said he was going to stay with friends.'

'Hoh!'

She shut her mouth grimly. *She* didn't believe that. *She* knew there was something in the air. Still, it was none of her business. She bustled to the window and shut it, her face wrapped in profound gloom. Then she turned and blinked.

'It's Toosday,' she said.

It's Toosday! Somehow that seemed the bitterest thing of all. For Brian knew now that Walter had gone for ever. It had been inevitable. After what had happened last night, even the stanchest friendship must break. Mercifully, for the moment he did not realize all that the breaking of such a friendship implied. He did not realize that the room below was empty, that never again, perhaps, would he have his morning 'rags,' never again find a face to welcome him home. Like all men who come to the parting of the ways, the first steps on the new road seem very much like those that have gone before. It is only when the road winds away into the distance that one begins to understand what it has all meant.

But the little phrase, 'It's Toosday,' hurt – hurt as though she had bruised his heart. It was one of the most precious jokes he had ever shared with Walter. He would share it no more. Walter had flown into his life like a bird. Like a bird he had flown away.

He turned his face to the wall.

'Yes,' he said, 'it's Tuesday.'

CHAPTER FIFTEEN

'TOOSDAY' went by, and Wednesday, Thursday, Friday and Saturday, and still Brian stayed in bed. For two days he lay in a high fever, which peopled the room with hectic shapes and painted crimson shadows on the ceiling. He had no company save a thin, rusty old doctor, who uttered platitudes about burning the candle at both ends and prescribed the obvious medicines, which Mrs. Pleat dispensed with grimy fingers, standing over him with that morbid interest in every phase of his condition which is one of the greatest delights of the very poor.

Then on the Friday visitors were allowed. First there was Mrs. Gossett, who was so thrilled at the idea of being in a man's bedroom that her eyes almost popped out of her head, her speech became tremolo and inarticulate, while she sat on the other side of the room, keeping her gaze primly fixed on the centre of the opposite wall in order that she might not see anything *too* . . .

'Oh – won't you stay and chaperwon me?' she had cried to Mrs. Pleat, as that lady had announced her intention of departing.

Mrs. Pleat regarded her for a moment with dark suspicion. 'I ain't a trained nurse,' was her sole reply. So that Mrs. Gossett for twenty delirious minutes was left with Brian alone, and if any woman could have been compromised by looking it, Mrs. Gossett was that woman.

Then the rest of them had come sweeping into the flat, filling it with scent and chatter, until he longed to be really ill again that he might get rid of them. Lord William brought masses of roses, which he thrust into the arms of the astounded Mrs. Pleat, and a strange machine which was supposed to give oxygen to the air, but only succeeded in fusing the lights and slightly electrifying Maurice, to his lordship's great delight. Tanagra came too, with a scent by Lentheric, and Mrs. Grindhaven, with the works of Mr. Michael Arlen (in each of which she fondly imagined herself to be the heroine), and Lady Jane, with a pair of green pyjamas. And they all went away saying how 'delicious' he looked, lying there in his little room. They also made other comments concerning the room itself, but those were not so kind.

Finally, Julia.

She had emerged from her car on the evening of Saturday just as Mrs. Pleat was coming out of the front door to go home. So appalled had Mrs. Pleat been by the vision of loveliness before her that she merely muttered something about 'the secon' floor up,' and fled. Julia had therefore tiptoed upstairs, found Brian's card on the door, and walked softly in, alone.

So this was Brian's room. She took it all in with one glance – the worn carpet, the cheap chairs with their lumpy corduroy cushions – and again the strange motherly protective feeling – one of the few feelings in which life is true to fiction – swept over her. She stepped across to the mantelpiece, and then she saw a thing which changed the motherly feeling into something else – her own photograph, cut out from a page in *The Sketch*, set in a frame which, she realized, must have cost him half his week's salary.

'Who's there?' A tired voice from the next room.

'Guess.'

'Julia!'

There was the sound of somebody rising up in bed. She walked quickly to the half-open door and stood in it.

'Ssh!' she whispered. 'You're not to get up.'

'I'm all right. Honestly. Oh – my dear.'

Her fingers were on his forehead. She stood over him, looking into his uplifted eyes, which were wide and bright after a day of sleep. She bent down and with her face touched his fair, tousled hair, rubbing her cheek softly against it. In such a way, during her flashing childhood, had she rubbed her cheek against the silken mop of a worshipped golliwog.

'Hot hands,' she whispered.

The hands clutched hers tightly.

'Just lie back!' She patted the pillow for him.

He did as he was told. 'I'm in heaven.'

She kissed him lightly, brushing her lips with his, and his bare arm came round her neck, drawing her face to his, keeping it there, while he closed his eyes.

'Shall we stay like this for ever?' His voice was only a drowsy murmur.

'If you like.'

'I should have grown a huge beard, though.'

'And my hair would be falling down my back.'

'And we should have nails like eagles.'

'And all our family jokes would be exhausted.'

'I wouldn't mind. I'd go on holding you like this.'

'We'd have to have some food now and then.'

'We could have it in tubes, very quickly.'

'And somebody would have to rub your back with methylated spirits.'

'You could do that. And when we died, in about sixty years from now, we'd do it together. You would wake up one morning and say, "I rather think I shall die to-day." And I'd say, "Very well, if you insist." And when the actual moment came I should give you a terrific kiss through my beard. Then I should say, "On the word one, take a deep breath. On the word two, let the breath out. On the word three, make a huge rattley noise in your throat and die."'

'Ooh. You're frightening me.'

'There's no need, because we should shoot up to heaven.'

'What's heaven like?'

'Just an empty room. And you.'

'Oh, darling. *Something* else.'

'You don't love me if you want anything else.'

'Only sometimes.'

'Well – I think it's horrible of you. Still, we might arrange it. . . .'

But no. There are limits. Nobody can be expected to read somebody else's idea of heaven. It is about as dreary as Tchekov on a wet Wednesday afternoon. The clock must be set on six hours, to one o'clock in the morning, the scene changed (with that agreeable ease which is one of the chief compensations of the novelist) to Julia's bedroom in Berkeley Square, which is panelled in faded yellow brocade, with white leather furniture, lit by the cool silver flame of naked candles. And there the amazing secret is revealed that Julia, for the first time in her life, is really in love.

It is not as dull as it sounds, if you take the trouble to read on. For common or garden love was the very last emotion of which Julia, or anybody else, conceived herself capable. Passions with a new twist, certainly, sentimental states, mental processes of a sweetly sexual nature, which lent themselves to analysis – all these caricatures, variations and attitudes of love which today we welcome as the real article – all these things she had known, had practised, and had adored. But love – the sort of love which has no complexes, which is so simple that it passeth understanding, that was a new and quite singular emotion. No wonder, therefore, that she stood at her door, undecided, radiant, as though she heard melodies which, for the rest of the world, were muted.

She walked across the room slowly and sat down at her ridiculous desk, with its notepaper that matched the coffee-coloured carpet, its precious Venetian inkpot, its spray of yellow orchids that leant tired and bloated fingers over the lacquered edge. The light from a faded parchment shade shone on to a pile of white paper that she had laid there before she had dressed for dinner. She began to write.

The first words tell her secret:

'Brian, I love you. For a whole hour, I believe, I shall love you. And then the other "I" will wake again, and I shall look at what I have written, and laugh.

'*This is not a letter to you, darling. It is a letter to myself. It is a letter that is written by this curious real-unreal "me," that sometimes comes out from its shell, to the other "me" that you know, and I know, and the rest of the world knows. Oh – it's too involved. And I don't want to analyse myself. I want just to drown in my own feelings – my real feelings for a minute.*

'*I love you. Isn't it dreadful that one can write those words so easily, so glibly? Love ought to be a word that could only be carved with a sword, or painted with one's own blood. It should be something difficult, that called for strong sacrifice from the singer, that could only be pleaded in pain – it should not be so easy. I love you. I write it again and again, because it does my heart good, dearest, to write to you.*

'*Remember, only a little bit of me. Only this aspect of me that comes out, like a ghost, in the small hours. I am loving you now because I have stepped out of myself. Julia is lying in wait for me somewhere. She's lying in the shadows, laughing at me, sneering at me, telling me I am a fool. That is why I am writing so quickly, beloved, because at any moment she may come and stay my hand.*'

There was a sound outside the door – a whisper and a scuffle, and at the same time the heavy curtain, caught in a draught, billowed slowly and massively forward, paused, and sank back again with a hiss. She caught in its movement the tarnished glitter of a mandarin's robe, the embroidered smile of a Chinese grandee. Then all was still again.

Guiltily she had laid down her pen. Guiltily? Julia was writing a love-letter. She was writing from her heart. It was, perhaps, the only thing which she had ever done from her heart, and for this precise reason she was ashamed of it. And thus she put her feelings into words:

'*I am ashamed, and yet proud, of every word I write. I am ashamed because it is so ridiculously "ordinary," and I hate to believe that I'm an "ordinary" creature. I hate (or rather, the traditional part of me hates) to believe that I can fall in love in the same way that people love in penny novelettes and popular songs. I had theories of love – cheap, pseudo-intellectual, if you like, perhaps even a sort of bastard Anatole France – but still, they were, in form if not in quality, a little higher than my present feeling. My present feeling is purely vulgar. It's in harmony with all the cheap ballads, all the silly little stories in magazines that one glances at and puts under the seat when one is travelling in a train. It makes me want to walk with you in the moonlight, and kiss you, and give you roses, and read notes from you – oh, how second-rate it all is.*

'And yet, I'm proud of it all. Or rather, this little part of me that emerges towards the dawn is proud. Because I feel – (don't think that even for a moment I'm forgetting that I am being ridiculous) – because I feel that in loving you like this, this purely primitive, selfless, absurd way, I am in some vague way putting myself in harmony with the rest of Nature. A tiresome thing to do, one might say, but in these small hours, when I am feeling like this, it is only wonderful and fine.

'Even now I feel the other Julia stepping towards me, bringing me back, cooling my adjectives, checking my pen. Oh, darling, if only I could wait! If only life would slow down – even for a moment. If only we could stop dancing and drinking and being amusing, and let ourselves be plain and bored and real. You would say, if you could read this, that I am merely expressing the obvious emotions of a rather spoilt girl who has been burning the candles at both ends and needs only to go and vegetate in Scotland for a month or so.

'But it means more than that. This life we're all leading – (and you, poor darling, are dancing into it so gaily too) – this life is killing us. I'm not weak or stupid. I'm not merely a bored fool who goes on and on because there is nothing else to do. I merely know that one has to go on, that we are all caught in a trap, that we must dance till we drop, and that there is no alternative. You will never know, dearest, that I have written this letter to you. You'll never realize. I shan't let you. When the morning comes, I may read it again, and laugh, and think myself a silly fool, think that this fine prose is merely the aftermath of a few cocktails. But I shan't tear it up. Something will prevent me doing that. Something that may be overlaid and stifled, snubbed and ignored, but something that is yet stronger than myself . . .'

Suddenly she stopped writing. Behind the heavy curtains there was a tinge of grey which told her that dawn was already here. She got up, went to the fire, and fitfully kicked a log with her green slipper. A shower of sparks fled up the chimney.

She had been writing? Oh yes. A sentimental mood. How amusingly temperamental one was! Should one tear it up? She walked to the desk again and saw a pile of paper, covered with a quick, scrawling hand. Had *she* written that? She? That was terribly funny. One's moods! Where mightn't they lead one next? With cold fingers she stretched out for the manuscript. Better to throw it in the fire. The paper crumpled beneath her hand.

And then she stopped. She stayed very still. Slowly her eyelids drooped, and for a moment she stood there with eyes closed tight. In the grey and cruel light her face looked haggard and old. With eyes still shut, she folded the manuscript and laid it on the table. Then she went to the window and looked out into the beginning of another day.

CHAPTER SIXTEEN

LORD WILLIAM MOTLEY was exceedingly interested in disease. In his Louis XIII library in Queen Anne Street were long shelves of books dealing with the more picturesque maladies of the body. His taste in such matters was catholic. He took as much pleasure in the latest theory of influenza as in the prettiest example of elephantiasis, and would trace the pranks of a recalcitrant pituitary gland with as arduous an interest as he studied the works of Mr. Havelock Ellis (which, one understands, are to be found in the desks of every right-thinking schoolboy).

The convalescence of Brian Elme was therefore a matter which he took as a personal responsibility. Brian was an ideal convalescent, because he was sure to be grateful for anything that one could do for him and would probably submit to the most exciting treatments. Most of one's friends, Lord William had discovered, were otherwise inclined. They refused to be benefited. He had never recovered from the disappointing reception which they had given to his young Russian osteopath, whose habit it was to sing strange and fiery Russian folk-songs while he continued to crack one's bones. They had all been frightened of him ever since he dislocated Mrs. Grindhaven's back. But then, that woman never possessed any ear for music.

Nor had they shown any true interest in the little gymnasium which he had caused to be erected on the top floor of his house, where every form of exercise could be obtained merely by sitting still. There were chairs which bumped one up and down, and sofas with electric rollers for massaging the back, and rapidly-working pistons, padded at the end, which percussed the stomach. These devices seemed to fill his friends with alarm. But that was possibly due to the unfortunate circumstance that one night, after dinner, somebody who had drunk too much champagne had strapped Lady Hardcastle on to the artificial camel, and had left her to rock furiously backwards and forwards in the dark until she had been rescued in a state of exhaustion by an astonished butler, who had imagined that a cat-burglar was having fits in the attic.

He decided to begin Brian's convalescence with a little artificial sunlight. As he imagined, Brian proved eminently tractable. A party was therefore arranged, consisting of Brian, Lord William and Maurice, at which they lunched at Claridge's, and afterwards departed to their destination in a taxi, for reasons which will immediately become apparent.

Maurice was a champion 'Fumbler.' Whenever he rode in a taxi in company with others, his conversation took on a fierce vivacity towards the end of the drive and, on arrival at the destination, developed into a breathless succession of anecdotes. This habit gave him many excuses for gesticulating on the pavement while his friends were feeling in their pockets, allowing him even to look slightly pained that they should concern themselves with such mundane things as fares while he was telling them stories.

On this occasion he was quite determined that Lord William should pay for his bath-ticket, while Lord William was equally determined that he should pay for it himself. A grim smile illumined his lordship's face as they drew up at the door of the hotel where the sunlight baths were situated. Maurice, by ingenious physical contortions, had managed to be the last out of the car, and, as usual, had dropped his handkerchief on the seat, so that he had to return for it while the others were crossing the pavement.

This was a subterfuge that Lord William knew of old. He determined to go one better.

'We won't wait for Maurice,' he said. 'Let's get into the lift.'

Two footmen were waiting for them at the top.

'Violet rays, sir?'

'Please. Two tickets.'

Brian could not understand what the hurry was about. Lord William had almost leapt from the lift, he had his money ready in his hand, and he kept on glancing back over his shoulder as though pursued by fiends.

'Come on. Take off your shoes.'

His elaborate suède shoes were already scattered on the floor. He stood tapping a large cobweb-socked foot. The lift bell rang impatiently from downstairs.

'That's Maurice. We'll go straight to the changing room.'

He grabbed Brian by the arm, precipitated him down a corridor, into a long white room containing six beds.

This haven reached, Lord William sank into a chair.

'Why this tearing hurry?'

He kicked his heels in the air.

'Maurice will have to pay for his ticket. I've *never* been so thrilled.'

Brian stared in polite astonishment.

'Of course, he's my greatest friend. But he is so terribly mean. If he dared, he'd take the pennies out of a blind beggar's cap, but he's such a cynic that he wouldn't even believe the beggar *was* blind.'

'But he's got pots of money, hasn't he?'

'Not pots.' Lord William shook his head. 'But three thousand a year. And he's never paid for anything – ever. That's why he has such odd friends. There's a terrible wine merchant with only one eye who's always at the studio, simply because Maurice gets free champagne out of him. He tells him that he's going to get it drunk by the King, or something equally weird. Then there's that dreadful Miss Garside who writes all about actresses' clothes. He almost *smothers* her with affection, and she gives him seats for first nights. Ssh! Here he is.'

To Maurice: 'Where *have* you been?'

Maurice looked pale but determined. 'I'm terribly sorry,' he said, 'but I entirely forgot to bring any money.'

Lord William paused in the act of taking off his trousers. 'Well?'

Maurice sighed. 'I asked them to put it down to you.'

Lord William turned an outraged face to Brian. 'You see. . . .'

'Oh really. What difference *does* it make? I'll send you a cheque to-night.'

Lord William was not looking at him. 'One day,' he said, 'I shall write a ballad to those words and send it to Maurice. "I'll send you a cheque to-night." He'll be able to make it sound so improper.'

The arrival of the attendant interrupted this passage of arms. He was a fat man, of a worm-like body, with large kind eyes. He commented on the rain and said that his garden was not doing at all well. Lord William and Maurice appeared to be bored with him, but Brian would have liked to carry the conversation farther. However, he concentrated on the problem of undressing.

Up till now he had always considered his underclothes adequate, if unpretentious. His shirt was of plain blue cotton, his vest was of the sort known as 'cellular,' and he wore no pants. But as he observed the elaborate disrobing of Lord William and Maurice he began to have his doubts. Both had shirts of the purest silk, with open-work monograms embroidered on the sleeve. Instead of putting these garments over their heads, with a consequent ruffling of the coiffure, they undid them, in the manner of jackets, and gracefully slipped them from their shoulders.

Beneath each shirt was revealed a vest, again of silk, again heavily monogrammed. Brian could not help thinking that if either of them were to fall into the Thames identification would be a matter of a few moments only. Even the pants were monogrammed.

At length they were ready, draped in towels. Lord William and Maurice both shivered with joy as the attendant opened a door, through which one could see the lights and shadows cast by three great arc lamps.

'Marvellous. Sunshine. Let's *leap* into it.'

The attendant put out an officious arm. 'You just put on your glasses first, sir. There's a danger of conjunctivitis.'

'I *knew*.' Lord William's voice was hoarse with excitement. 'I knew we were all going to risk our lives.'

> '*Oh to be in England*
> *Now that April's here* . . .'

Ridiculously, inconsequently, the lines flitted through Brian's head. Analyses of mental states are often tiresome, but Brian's was so unusual that it is worthy of note. Here he was, a healthy young Englishman, standing clad in a bath towel before one of the latest triumphs of civilization. His companions seemed, apart from a forced hilarity, to take it all for granted. They cared not that outside the building the rain was slashing down in torrents. They cared not that they, human animals, were about to precipitate themselves before two glass bulbs, thereby transforming themselves, in essence, if not in fact, to the Sahara desert. They were merely enjoying a 'stunt.' To him it was more than a 'stunt'; it was a marvel. The fact that he was here at all was sufficiently extraordinary. But the fact that he was about to bask in a man-made sun was more extraordinary still. He felt as though he were participating in some savage rite. To be perfect, there should be the sound of tom-toms in the air, and a whirling sweating chorus of those who had scarred themselves in the service of this unnatural god.

However, he quelled those feelings. One must be *blasé*. One must not be amused. He controlled his features. He even tried to yawn.

Maurice was putting on the thick, fur-rimmed glasses. He glared in front of him.

'I feel like an American in hell,' he said.

Lord William put on the glasses also. 'This is more than delicious. I'd adore to have a bathroom done in this shade. Doesn't Brian look marvellous? Like a war-memorial. Do put on your glasses.'

Brian did so. He felt in some queer way that the action was symbolical, as though at this moment he were definitely renouncing the real for the sake of the false. It is true that the English climate affords every excuse for such renunciations.

As soon as his glasses were fixed, the attendant moved the disc from the face of the lamp and the room was flooded with mimic sunlight. The faces of his companions appeared suddenly chilled and sinister. He forgot what they were saying, reflecting that in some such light must dwell the people of the moon, moving with greenish limbs in a world of monstrous shadows.

'Now, gentlemen. Lie down on your faces, if you please.'

They disposed themselves on the beds. A faint sickly scent of ozone assailed the nostrils.

Brian felt he must at all costs play the part of the hardened roué.

'I feel like something that has been washed up on Brighton beach,' he said. 'But,' he added, 'I think something *is* biting my back.'

Maurice pouted. 'You always get all the sensations. Nothing's biting *me*.'

The attendant put his hand on his forehead. 'You'll feel it soon, sir. You must wait till your lymphatics are stimulated.'

'I don't believe he's got any lymphatics,' crooned Lord William.

The attendant assured his lordship that all men have lymphatics.

Maurice became petulant. 'I'm sure I've got dozens,' he said. 'What I want to know is, when shall I be sunburnt?'

'Not till after the sixth or seventh treatment, sir.'

Maurice raised himself indignantly on his elbow. Six more treatments meant another three guineas, and since Lord William was so disgustingly mean . . . 'Can't I be sunburnt *now*?' he asked plaintively.

'No, sir. We can't over-stimulate the lymphatics.'

'Damn my lymphatics. I really think it's absurd. *Why* can't I be sunburnt *now*?'

Lord William was delighting in this conversation. 'My dear, you'd go mad,' he assured him. 'You'd rush out of the room quite naked, one mass of lymphatics, and you'd dart away to call on Anne Hardcastle. And that would be dreadful, because it's exactly what she's been wanting you to do for years.'

Brian felt a slight burning on the back of his neck. 'I think I'm getting sunstroke,' he said.

The attendant slightly moved the lamp. 'Will all you gentlemen please turn over on your backs?'

With groans they did so. Maurice peered across the room. 'You look exactly like an earlier work by *Picasso*,' he screamed to Brian. 'All mottled and speckly.'

'Well, what do you expect me to look like? Venus?'

Maurice screamed again. 'Oh, my dear! My knee's turning pink. I swear it.'

'Probably dirt,' muttered Brian.

'Your conversation has a schoolboy freshness which suggests years of practice,' sighed Lord William, who had overheard this remark. 'How you manage to keep it up in this atmosphere, I can't imagine.'

'It *is* rather hellish, isn't it?' Brian could no longer pretend that this situation was anything but singular. 'Like something out of Poe. I feel this must be exactly the same as a premature burial. To wake up with a droning noise in one's ears, to see this greenish light, which seems as if it were creeping down through wet earth, and to find one's body almost phosphorescent. . . .'

'You're hideously morbid for a schoolboy.' Maurice was becoming more and more jealous of Brian's 'schoolboy' reputation. He had so long enjoyed a similar reputation himself that he bitterly resented anybody poaching on his preserves.

Lord William, still malicious, realized the significance of Maurice's remark, and quickly added:

'Yes – isn't he? Exactly like a schoolboy. All schoolboys are morbid in England. They believe in nothing. That is why they grow up into strong silent Empire builders. In Germany they believe fiercely in heaven. And so they all commit suicide.'

'I think his lordship is feeling the heat.' Maurice's tone was exceedingly acid.

'Only one more minute, sir,' said the attendant.

'But really. *Nothing's* happened yet.' Maurice felt that he had not nearly got his half-guinea's worth.

'Nothing that you can feel, perhaps, sir,' said the attendant, with the omniscient air of all semi-educated persons who possess a little specialized knowledge.

Silence for another minute. Then the lights were switched off and they emerged into the drab daylight to dress.

'I think,' said Lord William, 'that was the most marvellous thing I have ever done. I feel like a sun-god; my lymphatics are singing inside me like young cherubim. They seem to be lifting me up to the skies. There is nothing of which I am not capable. I am . . .'

Maurice interrupted him. There was a harsh impatience in his voice. 'One would think you'd had something more than mere sunlight,' he said. 'What's that?' And his fingers stretched out quickly, trying to seize a tiny gold box which Lord William was slipping into his waistcoat pocket.

There was a sudden silence. The two men's fingers grappled, interlaced. Maurice retreated with a cry of pain.

'Now you *shall* pay for your ticket, my young friend,' muttered Lord William.

Brian took no notice. These chaps were so very odd.

The sunlight treatments may, or may not, have done Brian good. It is difficult to say, because he immediately plunged back, with a sort of desperate futility, into the mode of life which had been responsible for his condition. Had Julia been with him always, things might have been different. As it was, now that Walter had gone he felt alone, utterly alone among a crowd of chattering friends.

And bored! Only those who have lived at top speed, cramming every minute with some engagement, can realize the æons of boredom which a single unoccupied evening can contain. There were nights when he was left alone, and would wander down the roaring streets to dine in Soho. The evening paper would be propped up in front of him, and after he had read it he would sit down and stare gloomily at the opposite wall. What was there to do after dinner? Visit the pubs? That would be deathly without Walter. A theatre? He had seen them all. A cinema? He would go mad, sitting by himself in the dark with loving couples all around him. Walk the streets? There was not much fun in being accosted when one happened to be in love.

And so, on the top of a bus, through the chill slanting rains, he would return home again. Up the stairs. A peep into the room that had been Walter's. Whistle a bit of tune to stop one growing morbid. Up again to his room. Strike a match. Pop goes the gas-fire. Draw the curtains. Only ten o'clock. Read a book. And the lines swim before one's eyes, the characters flag and fall, the vision is blurred. And there is nothing but the gas-fire, and the distant roar of buses, and the gas-fire – and – God! – the utter futility of it all!

CHAPTER SEVENTEEN

A GENERATION which knows a great deal about love is usually a generation which produces few great lovers. And to-day we know everything about love. We put Cupid under the microscope. With delicately adjusted instruments we gauge the heat of the divine fire. We have searchlights which lay bare the secrets of the mind, penetrating far into the dim and delicate desires of child-hood. In fact, there is nothing about love which we do not know, except how to love.

Julia was a typical product of her generation. She knew every-thing about love, and when one knows everything about any particular thing, the thing becomes, *ipso facto*, slightly ridiculous.

Yet, here it was, producing a surprise with regard to Brian. Her feeling for him fitted into no recognized niche. Had they been continuous feelings – had she, that is to say, entertained the same feelings during the morning and the afternoon as stirred her in the small hours of the morning the situation would not have been so difficult. But her feelings were not continuous.

In fact, as she stood in her room on a bright spring morning, reading again the effusions which she had written with such genu-ine ardour the night before, she felt it difficult to believe that she could possibly have written them at all. Had she discovered letters of this type written by anybody else, she would have presumed that they were the outpourings of an hysterical nursery-governess.

She was genuinely fond of him, of course – as genuinely fond as she could ever be fond of anybody. She adored the perfect cast of his features, his colouring, his eagerness to please, his rather old-fashioned politeness, his happy smile, and the air he gave, whenever she smiled back at him, of longing to turn somersaults

out of sheer exhilaration. But these letters! They were crazy. They
had no rhyme or reason – or rather, they had a great deal too much
rhyme and far too little reason. If anybody should discover them
. . . Quickly, as though she were being watched, she shut them
away in a drawer.

She sat down and looked out on to Berkeley Square. It was
a glorious day – one of those days in which the English climate
apologizes so winningly for its past misbehaviour that it is readily
forgiven. The baby leaves on the trees were already a vivid green.
A lorry clattered by in the street below, full of daffodils growing
and blowing. Next there was a hansom cab, with its horse stepping high and brave, as though it refused to be regarded as a relic.
On the other side of the square there was a furniture van, which
meant that Max Beitheimer had been forced to sell another set
of his Chippendale chairs. Coming round the corner was Mrs.
Grindhaven, with her new German dog, which made everybody
remember the war so painfully.

To-day she began to feel almost amused by life. Was it part of
Brian's infectious example? She remembered that when they had
last gone out together she had noticed dozens of things to which
she had hitherto been blind. They had undertaken a tremendous
walk after a very bad lunch which he had given her in Soho. Anything more calculated to send one into acute hysteria than a bad
lunch and a long walk she could not previously have imagined, but
she had actually adored it.

He had shown her a new London. They had wandered up
Farringdon Street and treasure-hunted among the stalls of fruit,
flowers, old books and cheap jewellery. They had bought peaches
at twopence apiece, and eaten them there and then, so that the
juice dripped on to the pavement, and long sticks of pink London
'rock,' in which the word London appeared in the centre however
many times one bit it through. They had purchased spectacles for
sixpence, which broke as soon as they attempted to put them on,
and old prints of the Haymarket aflutter with crinolines, and an
isolated volume of Boswell's *Life of Johnson*, which was discovered
to contain only the index, so that they had to go back and indignantly demand the return of their shilling.

And the purchase of Boswell had suggested to Brian that he should take her to see Johnson's house, so that they continued through narrow streets, up dirty alleys where boys were playing hopscotch, past the blackened offices of obscure papers, into a little cobbled haven where a mellow Georgian house was basking in the sun. Through a swinging gate they had walked, and up the broad uneven stairs. It cost but sixpence to enter the house, and one would have thought that it would have been full of chattering tourists. But no. It was empty. With true British carelessness, old books lay on the shelves in untutored profusion, so that anyone who cared might take them away. But they paid no heed to the books, nor to the old prints, nor the chairs which Johnson had used, nor to the windows from which so many times Boswell must have sat gazing on to the darkening street, while waiting for the Doctor to end one of those silences which must have been so far more terrifying than his keenest thrust of words. They had cared not for these things, for they had been far too interested in themselves.

Yet, had they? That Brian had been utterly absorbed by her she knew well. But had she been utterly absorbed by him? She knew equally well that she had not. It had been herself that had really absorbed her. She was interested in studying herself in this new position. She was interested in studying the motives which made her behave like – like a housemaid. It was only on those rare occasions, late at night, when she wrote those secret letters – it was only then that she completely forgot herself – only then that she really loved.

She moved impatiently in her window seat and turned away from the bright picture which the square presented. Mrs. Grindhaven and the German dog had vanished, and a woman strangely like the Countess of Oxford and Asquith was clattering by in heavy boots. But they interested her not at all.

She thought: 'Oh! If I could only get away from this ghastly self-consciousness! If I could only say, "This is a moment in itself. This is a day to be lived for itself, without questioning, without thinking of to-morrow, without caring whether the day will come again, without caring whether I am growing older, or whether I look my best, without caring about the transience of things. . . ."'

She was becoming morbid. She would go and have a cocktail with Don. And after that she would buy a new hat. She took up the receiver. Yes. His lordship was in.

He was standing there, in the long black room, where the spring sunlight seemed to touch the masks to an unwonted life. In his hand was a new mask to which he was putting the finishing touches. It was a white, sullen face of a girl with twisted eyebrows. He held it out in front of him, not looking at Julia.

'My ideal woman.'

'Put it down.'

'One day, Julia darling, you will realize that there are degrees of rudeness.'

She made no reply.

'I am going to design a set of masks for the Cabinet,' he continued. 'The Prime Minister will have a face which looks both ways at once. The Lord Chancellor will be given a green wig. The Home Secretary will have a little house on top of his head. And the Chancellor of the Exchequer will be given a permanent and highly irritating smile.'

She threw her cigarette into the fireplace and lay back, looking at the ceiling.

'You know why I've come to see you.'

'Brian?'

'Yes.'

'You're terribly *éprise*, of course.'

'He's so different from all these wrecks.'

He laughed. 'I thought the-tired-lady-of-quality-and-the-lusty-boy combination was a little overdone. Look at Anne Hardcastle.'

'The last thing I want to do.'

'Of course, she's not particularly a lady of quality, and I always think her boys look quite washed out after their first week-end at Hardcastle. Still, it's the same thing.'

'Can't you be serious?'

With a sigh he laid down his mask. 'I see. We are to have one of those boring discussions about love. You will say to me that your affection for Brian is quite different, and that you want to keep it fresh and fragrant. You will expect me to sympathize and buy you a cottage in the country. I shall do nothing of the sort.'

'It's curious how I suddenly hate talking to you about him.' She spoke more to herself than to him. 'Quite curious. I suppose it's because he seems almost sacred.'

Lord William heaved a sigh of relief. 'Excellent. All sacred topics are barred in this house. Now . . .'

'Do let me go on.'

'Oh, Julia. You're impossible.'

'We're all impossible. I'm sick of this damned London. I want to take him away from it all.'

He sat down.

'You have obviously been reading the articles of Mr. –,[1] who has been selling his virtue at the rate of eight guineas a column for the last twenty years. He discovered, after the war, that London was an immoral city. He was publicly pained. I made the same discovery. I was privately pleased. I should have hated to have to live in New York.'

She gave a vicious tug to her hat. 'I don't know why I talk to you.'

'You talk to me because I am sane. Now let us consider the position. Take Brian first. As we are being so charmingly frank, we may admit that your love for him is entirely physical.'

She stirred wearily. 'That's a lie.'

'Nobody's blaming you. Audrey Forster almost had a seizure when she met him at Tanagra's last party. He's an exceedingly attractive young man. And infinitely more so now that he knows it.'

She forced a smile. 'We'll consider this discussion closed.'

'No.' He held out a glittering finger. 'There are several things yet. You say that Brian is spoiled. I fail to see why.'

'Anybody who got to know our friends with the rapidity with which he has got to know them . . .'

'Really.' He moved impatiently. 'Brian's merely had a social success. You seem to regard it as a tragedy.'

---

[1] *Author's note.* The name of this famous journalist, on second thoughts, had better be omitted.

'It is a tragedy.'

'I've no patience with you. Listen. The subject under discussion is London. Nobody pretends that it's a particularly edifying subject.'

Her lips tightened. 'You appear to have been reading – yourself.'

'I certainly have. I read him because he makes me feel that my friends are, in some way or other, an adventure. He makes me feel, by the naïve way in which he is shocked, that I am living in a really exciting age. He titillates my vices. He makes me imagine that I am almost original in doing . . .' he paused . . . 'whatever I do.'

Her face was shadowed in melancholy. She seemed hardly to be listening to what he was saying.

'The fact remains that it is all very amusing.'

'Amusing!'

'Terribly so. Nothing gives me greater pleasure than to see one of those lovely large American women weaving a new-world halo round the head of an English peeress whose jewels are paid for by a Jewish Company promoter and who spends her week-ends learning about the sorrows of the male chorus at the Gaiety.'

Julia turned her head. 'You're pathetically obscene.'

'I am equally thrilled,' continued Lord William, 'by the sight of a number of English gentlemen accepting the hospitality of a very dirty Argentine, whom they would hesitate to employ as an under-gardener, simply because he pays their tailor's bills with such delicate discretion. That is really amusing to me. Nothing is so interesting as decay. I am watching the final and utter decay of a large section of the British aristocracy. Soon the only respectable people left will be impoverished Scottish families, who live surrounded by dogs in Inverness and eventually become almost indistinguishable from their pets. And even they will be forced to capitulate before long. The whole spectacle gives me great satisfaction, especially as I believe I may claim to be regarded as one of the plague-spots myself.'

He took up the mask of a girl and carelessly painted a large moustache across the lips.

'There,' he said blandly, 'that was a sensation I've been longing to have for days. And now I've had it. It was quite divine. Whenever I'm bored in future I shall go to the Underground railway and paint moustaches on the faces of all the pretty ladies on the posters. What fun it will be, Julia. Will you join me? If we were found out, we could always say that we were working for a wholesale firm of depilatory merchants who had bought up all the spaces on the walls.'

She beat an angry tattoo on the floor with her feet.

He looked at her anxiously. 'In fact,' he continued, 'I think we ought almost to go at once. You are obviously in need of a very strong sensation.'

She sprang to her feet. 'Yes, Don, I am. But who am *I*? Where am *I*? I've got a brain and a body and a will, but I can't feel anything. I can't. I can't. I don't believe you can, either. We aren't either of us *here*. We're never here. We're over the border somewhere. We can't catch ourselves. We . . .'

She stopped suddenly, breathlessly. The black face of Rastus was peering through the door.

'Cocktails, Rastus,' said his lordship with a yawn.

Julia turned her back.

CHAPTER EIGHTEEN

T HE evening of the same day.

Brian was rushing round his flat in a state approaching panic. For Julia had just rung him up to say that she was coming to pay him a visit – 'after dinner, for a cigarette' – and it was already nearly ten.

What ought to be done first? The lights, obviously. Julia could never bear to sit under these glaring globes with their china shades. But how could he improve them? He had an inspiration, and hurried to a drawer in his bedroom, from which he produced two handkerchiefs, one red and one blue. Then, standing on a chair, he fastened these round the offending bulbs.

The effect was singular. Half of the room was bathed in a lurid blood-colour, the other half plunged in a depressing shadow. Moreover, bright chinks of white light escaped and mercilessly illuminated the cracked ceiling. Besides, even if the radiance had been uniform, the things themselves looked so odd. Like trippers on the beach with handkerchiefs tied round their heads to keep off the sun. No. It wouldn't do.

With fingers that trembled he removed the handkerchiefs, and the room was once more flooded with brilliant rays. What the devil could be done? He had once, as an experiment, painted a bulb with crimson lake, but it had only filled the room with a foul smell of burnt feathers and then exploded, deluging him with red-hot glass and fusing the lights. That would be a pretty way to welcome his lover, wouldn't it?

Candles! What a fool he had been not to think of them before. He knew that there were some candles somewhere, and some shades too. A few minutes routing in a cupboard produced them. The candles were suspiciously nibbled in parts, but they were unmistakably candles. The shades were not so good. They were all smeared with black patches where they had been allowed to burn. Still, the patches were so numerous that they might almost be said to constitute a design. Well, that was the only way to look at it.

Now for the candlesticks. He paused, and bit his lip. For he remembered a pair, fashioned from old brass, which Walter had given him on his last birthday. After Walter had gone he had put them away, swearing never to take them out again. However, it was a question of necessity. He went to the cupboard, and from the lowest shelf he produced them, tarnished and covered with dust.

Poor candlesticks! Walter had possessed them for years. They had been in many pawnshops, had held the light to many sordid rooms. Finally they had been given to Brian, and the threat of the pawnshop removed from them, a threat which should never have been levelled, for, as Walter had said, those candlesticks were 'gentlemen.' And indeed they were gentlemen, with their sober, Georgian frames and their solid workmanship. He decided that he would never put them out of sight again, however painful might be the memories which they suggested.

However, he must get busy. There were only two candlesticks, and he needed four. A distracted search revealed nothing that could, even with the best will in the world, be said to resemble a candlestick. Wait a minute though. There were four blue coffee cups. They would do. And indeed, when the candles were in them, with their shades duly placed, and the handles of the cups deftly concealed behind photograph frames, they did not look so bad.

He postponed the lighting of the candles and confined his attention to the carpet. If he put a newspaper down carelessly, as though it had dropped, it would cover the hole in the corner. But there was also the hole by the door and the hole near the fireplace. And one could not scatter newspapers all over the room, or it would look as if the ceiling were leaking. He therefore took the mat from his bedroom and put it over the hole near the door. As for the fireplace hole, it would have to remain. If it became too offensive he would sit on it.

Thank the Lord, he possessed some flowers. It had been a blessed influence which prompted him that very afternoon to purchase six yellow roses. Very gracious and fragrant they were, too, and now that he placed them against the mirror on the mantelpiece they were no longer six, but twelve. Twelve yellow roses! There was nothing to be ashamed of there.

Concerning the fire, there was nothing to be done. It was the same old fire, and that was an end of the matter. If allowed to burn too fiercely it emitted a curious odour, so that he turned it very low, and propitiated it by placing a small bowl of water in front – a hint he had learned from Mrs. Pleat, who assured him that a bowl of water 'took away the fooms.' He wished he had done something about the beastly fire before, because, after the manner of its kind, one of the white clay things had fallen out, so that one received the impression of a row of grinning, irregular teeth. Still, it was too late to alter.

Everything seemed to be done now. He went into the bedroom to see if that was presentable. A pair of dumb-bells caught his eye. He seized those and secreted them under the bed. It would be ghastly if Julia perceived this secret sign of 'heartiness.' He also took his pyjamas, which were very plain and unpretentious, and stuffed them under the pillow. He then sponged his face, combed his hair, took out a clean handkerchief, lit the candles, and waited.

'*She is coming, my own, my sweet,*
Were it ever so airy a tread,
My heart would hear her and beat,
Were it earth in an earthy bed. . . .'

Shamelessly he spoke the words aloud. Shamelessly, for were Maurice or Lord William aware of his affection for Tennyson they would be provided with enough epigrams to last them for an entire season. Had not Lord William composed, for the benefit of an American motor merchant, an acid parody of this very poem, which began:

'*Come into the garden, Ford,*
For the great Rolls-Royce has flown'?

But Lord William knew nothing of the affairs of the heart. Nothing. He did not know anything about passion. Well, did Brian himself?

He caught sight of himself in the glass. His eyes were unnaturally bright; his face had a flush which was more than the flush of youth; his lips were parted.

Did he not?

Certain things must be left to the imagination of the reader. When two hearts are beating high, it seems almost cruel to linger over the sound of a car drawing up to a door, to chronicle the shedding of a satin cloak, to trace that long relentless crescendo by which the words of a lover's pleading begin to glow more and more brightly, until they seemed to be ringed with fire. One must hurry, plunging straight into the dialogue which echoed in that room an hour later.

'Why don't you *say* you love me?' he pleaded.
'I've never said it to anybody.'
'Can't you say it now?'
'I can't.'
'Please, please. Can't you?'

'I don't know.'

'Say it. Say it. Even if it doesn't mean for ever, even if it's only just for a minute or a second. Can't you?'

She drew him very close to her. Something seemed to be battering at a thick wall in her brain. She did not know whether to fight or surrender.

'Darling,' he repeated, 'can't you say it? Only once? If you said it, I'd feel I hadn't come into this damnable world for nothing. I'd feel that I'd been made complete. I might be broken up again, smashed to pieces; I might be destroyed utterly – anything might happen – the end of the world even – but if I'd heard you just once whispering that to me, I'd feel that nothing else would matter afterwards. You'd have given me something that you could never take away again. I'd have that till I died. . . .'

Oh, that hard wall of her brain! Batter, batter, batter! Each of his words was like a blow against the barrier that for so long had stood unassailed between her heart and her head. Not once had the words 'I love you' echoed across that barrier. Something had always stopped her from making the ultimate declaration. Perhaps a sense of the ridiculous, or a too keen knowledge of the mechanics of desire, or an inability to escape from the perpetual domination of self. She had never climbed over that wall into the limbo of folly, where self and sense are forgotten, where all the past and all the future are swept into a breathless present.

And then something seemed to snap. She said, 'I love you.' And as she said it, for the first time she escaped from her fortress of self, jumping over the wall. Lying there with half-closed eyes, she seemed to hear a burst of music, to dip her hands in a riot of flowers. She was young, young, young. The air was rapturous with bird song. She wanted to dance. She drew Brian to her, laughing and crying.

Nothing in the world now but love.

It is an hour after midnight and Julia is back in her own room. She lies on her own bed, very still, looking at the ceiling. Her face is contorted into an expression which, had one seen her by chance, one might think almost ridiculous. Yet, in reality, the expression is a little terrifying. The eyes are half-closed, as though they no longer wished to see the world; the face is very pale; her upper lip is curved over her teeth, as are sometimes the lips of the dead. The result is a hideous parody of a smile – a still, sneering smile.

And, indeed, she was smiling. She was smiling at the lunacy of which she had shown herself capable. She had known her hour of love – (oh yes, it *had* been love) – and it had gone. It had left her in no way changed. She was precisely the same. She had clambered back over her wall, waving good-bye to the aforesaid limbo of folly, and here she was again, as she had always been, as she knew she would always be.

The only change which had taken place was in her attitude to Brian. For a moment after she had left him she had felt nothing but an acute disgust – not for any conventional reason, either moral or physical, but because, for him, she had descended from the pinnacle which she had always occupied in the past. For a moment she had ceased to dominate. She had surrendered. And with Julia there was no question of the 'sweet surrender' beloved by lyric poets. It was a bitter surrender, in spite of herself, in spite of her inherited traditions and the acquired code of life which had guided her ever since she had seen the world as it was.

Well, her disgust had been short-lived. Now it had turned to indifference. He had ceased to have any interest for her. In two brief hours he had become just – 'an affair.' He was a dear child, of course, but after this he would be a bore. Oh, such a bore. A crashing bore. Still, she would let him down lightly. Delicately, so that there would not be any disagreeable fuss.

She sighed, and slowly rose to her feet. Well, that had been an experience. Decidedly an experience. She would never forget it – no, never. And for that reason she would still be quite charming to the young man who had provided her with it. But there must be no more scenes such as had occurred to-night. To-morrow she would go to Paris for a few weeks.

Meanwhile, she went over to the telephone.

'Is Miss Guest in?' A pause. She tapped her fingers impatiently on the receiver.

'Tanagra. Yes, it's Julia. I'm so bored. What? It isn't, it's only half-past one. The Ambassadors goes on till three. Do be an angel. Will you? Oh, my dear! How marvellously sweet of you. And will you be terribly amusing? I've been so – so . . .' She did not finish the sentence, but jerked the receiver down.

Then she went to her dressing-table and slashed her lip-stick savagely across her mouth. Her underlip was trembling in the strangest way, and it was some time before she managed to make it look presentable.

CHAPTER NINETEEN

HAD not Brian been walking on air, in an unreal opalescent city where the men and women moved like ghosts, and had not Julia departed so suddenly to Paris, it is improbable that he would ever have accepted an invitation to lunch with the *très connue* Lady Hardcastle. As it was, when her phantom voice glided over the telephone a few days later, he murmured that he would be delighted. He did not visualize her as the grotesque figure who had caused him so proper a horror at Tanagra's party. She, like all other humans, had become an abstraction.

But if, after the supreme experience with Julia, his fellow-creatures faded into a grey obscurity, he himself became far more vivid and significant than ever before. With a single breath, the mists of adolescence (which still cling to some men, though they know it not, long into the twenties) had been scattered. He was a MAN. In his own eyes, at least, his figure was taller, his voice deeper, his bearing more authoritative.

And, like an ancient picture which has been cleaned by patient hands, the world itself, as distinct from the people in it, became brighter and more clamorous. A sharper green painted the leaves of the plane tree outside his window. Higher and more shrill sang the sparrows that spluttered in its branches. The uniform greys of London split and dissolved into multitudinous tints – from the silver pavements of St. James' Street to the faded cedar hues of Bloomsbury, and the rusty blacks of the city. He had a sense of inanimate things reviving. Nelson from his column almost waved

his hat as he sped through Trafalgar Square, and even Mr. Land-
seer's painful lions were endowed with a dormant life, as though
they might begin, if not to yawn and stretch, at least to emit a
subterranean purr.

But his lunch with Anne – as one really must call Lady Hardcastle – was poignantly to remind him that there were other people in
the world besides Julia, people with whom one must reckon, and,
if necessary, fight. Let us skim through the lunch, with its fat *hors
d'œuvres*, its sleek sole, its immoral *mousse* of chicken, and faintly
rude angels-on-horseback, until the time when:

'The great thing in life,' said Anne Hardcastle, powdering her
nose in that generous post-prandial fashion to which we have lat-
terly become accustomed, 'is never to miss an experience.'

Brian, as he surveyed her face, with its hunting eyes, its loose
mouth, and its cheeks drawn tight by the manipulations of many
surgeons, thought the number of 'experiences' which she must
have missed could be counted on the fingers of one hand. However, he agreed with her.

'That's why I asked you to lunch,' continued Anne. 'I saw that
we might be friends. And I think that's the greatest thing of all in
life – making friends, don't you?'

She had enunciated so many 'Greatest Things About Life'
during their sumptuous meal that he was losing his sense of pro-
portion. He felt that he had already sufficient material to compose
an Anne Hardcastle Calendar with one 'Greatest Thing About
Life' for every day of the year. Yet, again he agreed.

He was wondering how he could decently escape. Luncheon
had been like a dance of the seven veils, in which, with each
course, his hostess had thrown aside one of the normal conventions – I had almost said decencies – which exist between men and
women. She had begun by asking if he had ever been in love, gone
rapidly through courtship, passion and divorce, and had ended up
by asking, in a loud whisper, if he did not think the head-waiter
had delicious eyes – a matter upon which he had not felt qualified
to express an opinion.

In fact, it will already be evident that no medical examination
was necessary to convince even the most casual observer that

Anne Hardcastle was one hundred per cent WOMAN. And as far as the domain of the Spirit was concerned, her mind was situated somewhere between Elinor Glyn and the Marble Arch.

Perhaps her friends, after the modern habit, were a little prone to exaggerate the amatory qualities of her disposition, but she certainly afforded them ample excuse for doing so. She liked lying on sofas, waving handkerchiefs that were saturated with 'Fleurs du Harem' (at 500 francs the litre). She kept in her bedroom a row of little handbooks in French and American on the enticement of men, rather in the manner of a keen fisherman who cherishes a well-thumbed collection of essays on flies and baits and tackle. And in every room of her many houses there were cupids. Cupids were painted on the ceiling. Cupids were inextricably woven into the carpets. Cupids pranced on the staircases. Even her bells, in Grosvenor Street, were formed from two cupids who kissed each other when one desired to summon the footman for a cocktail.

There is a legend, that a young engaged couple who had been asked down to Hardcastle for a week-end, found themselves after dinner alone in a room that was full of cupids. They decided that they would pass the time by counting the cupids. And after they had counted sixty-nine they grew tired, and did something which they regretted for the rest of their lives. But why do people say such nasty things?

The point of importance in this narrative, however, is that Anne Hardcastle at Tanagra's party had fallen in love with Brian Elme. The whole thing is so fantastic that I tell it to you more from a sense of duty than from any hope of being believed. This erotic, sensual woman was 'received' everywhere. In a single season she was accustomed to traverse at least three miles of red carpet, and her curtsies to royalty, if measured en masse, would have probably been found equivalent to the deepest coal mine. And she fell in love, after her fashion, with a comparatively unknown, rather shabby, excessively decorative young journalist.

Nothing new in that, you would say. One understands that all Argentine widows, for example, do the same thing. And one has read of many a pretty page who has drifted his long legs into the keen vision of many a naughty lady, of many a smiling knight who has thrown his trusted spear clattering into the limbo of past poverty to bask in the smiles of many hundred-percent women of the past. No. There is nothing new in the *fact*. The only thing that is new is the *attitude*. Anne's attitude in her *amours* was regarded as quite normal, and really rather amusing. All of which arouses the gloomiest thoughts about that district of Mayfair in which we all have our habitation.

'That's what I think is so wonderful about life,' she went on. 'One can make so many friends. I *never* know when I am going to make a new one.'

And, indeed, she never did. She might even make a new friend if her butcher happened to have a good taste in errand boys. But, of course, Brian did not know that.

Anne drew on her gloves, and said, 'Now we'll go and do a little shopping.' Brian had no desire to shop with her, but he failed to see a way out of the difficulty, because he was a polite young man.

And so, once more, he said that he would be delighted.

Now, Bond Street, whither Anne was whirling him, was in some senses sacred to Brian. Its shops seemed to him like theatres in each of which a different scene was set for his delectation. On winter evenings, when the curving thoroughfare was glittering with lights, he would stand before window after window, peopling these miniature stages with many and various puppets. Against a backcloth of flaming silks he brought from his mind black figures who gesticulated with the passion of unearthly creatures. He caused dim and tiny sprites to dance over trays of diamonds, to balance the great emeralds in their frail fingers, to roll helter-skelter in a bowl of pearls. Out of ancient Chinese vases he evoked the ghostly heads of mandarins, and, so acute were his senses, that he seemed to see rising from a burner of twisted brass the tenuous snaky coils of smoke long-forgotten, to savour the scent of an incense which had drifted, an infinity ago, over the borders of the world.

Thus, when Anne Hardcastle proposed a visit to Bond Street, instinctively he rebelled against the idea. Bond Street was his own street. He could share it with nobody. But it was too late to protest now. They were already in it.

Anne's plans were perfectly clear. There was, in fact, no reason why they should not be, for she had successfully operated them on many previous occasions. She would give him a gold cigarette-case, and then she would ask him down to Hardcastle. That usually worked, but occasionally she had to add a visit to the tailors as well. Most young men were content with the cigarette-case, but since the increased popularity of London with the Argentine brotherhood, or rather sisterhood, her visits to the tailors were becoming rather more frequent. Still, she did not mind. She was a nice, generous woman.

They stopped outside a jeweller's. Brian knew the shop well. It contained all those stones which have been used with such effect to brighten the pages of Dorian Gray, and the later work of Mr. Carl van Vechten. Round those stones he had sketched many delicate fancies. In dreams he had hung pearls about the necks of ideal maidens, and, if truth be told, had decked himself in the crown of an Indian rajah (made in Amsterdam). To enter the shop was therefore an adventure.

They went inside. 'Good afternoon, m'lady. Good afternoon, m'lady.' Forests of black-coated young men were bowing round them. Brian little knew that they had done this many times before, that they had participated at the propitiation of many a sleek young man, had recommended cigarette-cases to so many dozens of 'nephews' that they were beginning to wonder when Lady Hardcastle would invent some other form of relationship.

'I want to see some gold cigarette-cases, please.' She paused, mentally undressing the suave attendant, and having done so, dismissing him from her mind. 'For my nephew.'

'Yes, m'lady.'

A tray was produced. Why are cigarette-cases so 'suspicious'? Is it because they so often seem to contain, nowadays, curious and partially incriminating inscriptions? Or is it because they have been so largely *repandus* by Anne Hardcastle? One wonders.

'Which do you like best?'

'Well . . .' He paused. 'I really don't know if my opinion's worth much.' (Poor child! He really did think it was for a real nephew.)

'Don't be silly,' she crooned. 'Say which *you* like.'

Dutifully he pointed to a delicately chased object with platinum bands. 'That's rather a beauty.'

'Yes – isn't it?' She took it. 'Of course, I always think the great thing about . . .' (Brian was sure she was going to say 'Life,' but she went on . . .) 'about cigarette-cases is, that they should open easily.' She turned to the attendant. 'How many does this hold?'

'Ten, m'lady.'

'That means twelve in stinkers,' said Brian.

'How delicious you are!' said Anne, with large eyes.

Why a reference to 'stinkers' should qualify the speaker as 'delicious' Brian did not for the moment grasp. But he strongly objected to being called delicious in front of a blue-chinned dago who was smirking at him with a look of damnable condescension.

'Very well,' said Anne. 'I'll take that. And if you'll give me a pencil, I'll just write down the address.'

Brian discreetly looked away. Oh, to get rid of this woman. One would have to be fumigated if one went about with her much longer. He glanced at his watch. Two thirty-five. He would stay with her till three, and then go.

'By the way,' said Anne, as soon as she had written down the address, 'could you come down to Hardcastle the week-end after next?'

A few months ago Brian would have jumped at the suggestion. He knew all about Hardcastle, with its moats, and its mazes, and its minstrel galleries. He even remembered a paragraph which he had written about it, long before he ever met Anne. It was headed, 'PICASSO IN THE BATHROOM,' and it read:

'Few of us realize the difficulties with which owners of old houses have to contend when they desire to make a collection of modern paint-ings. Thus, the lovely Lady Hardcastle, who has just brought back from Paris a superb Picasso, found that the walls of Hardcastle were so filled with Romneys, Gainsboroughs, Reynolds, Opies and Lawrences, that she has been forced to hang her treasure in one of the many bathrooms. "What a tonic for the beginning of the day," whimsically remarked the Prince of Wales, as he emerged from the bathroom, clad in a pale blue

dressing-gown, having just been splashing in the shadow of the modern masterpiece.'

He did not, however, narrate this piece of information to her ladyship. Nor did he tell her that he was quite determined never to be lured between those fatal walls. He merely said that he was terribly sorry, but he was engaged.

Anne sighed. This meant a visit to the tailor's. And what with the price of young men's clothes to-day, and the super-tax, as well . . . Still, she was a nice generous woman. She had a momentary impulse to remind him, in case he had not realized it, that the cigarette-case was intended for him. But she quelled it, as not being in the best of taste. For she was nothing if not well-bred.

'I'm so sorry,' she said, more to herself than to him. 'That means we shall have to go to the tailor's now, doesn't it?'

Brian stared at her in open astonishment. Were the bats already winging their way through her belfry? He had said, 'I can't come to Hardcastle.' She had replied, 'Then we must go to the tailor's.' Where in the name of Heaven was the connection?

'If you like,' he answered, hoping that at least she would not become violent.

Her face had the look of one who is resigned to heavy expenditure. As a matter of fact, she adored extravagant young men. But it did not do to let them know it.

'Clothes are so terribly expensive now, aren't they?'

'Awful,' said Brian, who at one time had been used to paying five guineas for ready-mades, and had grudged it.

'Still, one must keep up appearances. I think that's really the great thing to do in life, to keep up appearances.'

'*One* of the greatest, certainly,' he remarked. It was one of the ninety-ninth greatest things since lunch.

They arrived at the shop. Anne had decided that she would go to two lounge suits. 'Further than that,' she said to herself, 'no *decent* woman would go.'

There is nothing quite like the atmosphere of a really first-class English tailor's shop. Even film stars who are in the habit of ordering suits of clothes in Hanover Square with a carelessness which the average man would reserve for his cigarettes or his handkerchiefs, are slightly quelled, a little hushed by the austerity, the rich discretion of it all. In these surroundings, beneath an Adam ceiling, among a few sober rolls of perfect tweed, in the shadow of that yellowing notice over the mantelpiece, informing customers of the dates of Courts and Levees, clothes partake of something of the sanctity of state robes. One feels a little ashamed if one is not going to the levee, and as for one's under-garments – but there are some subjects which are too painful for discussion.

When, therefore, Brian entered this establishment with Anne, he instinctively braced himself to meet the scrutiny of the suave attendants, who were drooping in the shadows with the air of weary diplomats who knew how much more important was the cut of a waistcoat than the boundary of a country. All his past, his present, and indeed his future seemed sordid before the gaze of these gentlemen.

However, he had no time for reflection. A second edition of the forest of young men was once more swaying round Anne, who said:

'I want to see some patterns for lounge suits. For my nephew.'

'Certainly, m'lady.' And here the foreman, who was Scotch, cast a gloomy and suspicious eye at Brian.

Suddenly, he understood. Oh yes, he was very dense, if you like. He should have understood at the beginning of the chapter. But when you are comparatively new to London, and are still in the stage when you regard presents as part of the disappointments of birthdays and Christmas, when, in fact, you are still a fairly decent young man, you may be excused for a little lack of comprehension. The realization that Anne intended to give him some suits, coupled with the realization that her interest in him was not that of a mother, or a sister, or indeed of any of the list of female relatives so tantalizingly railed off from matrimony in the end of the Prayer Book, made him shy like a young colt. He could think of nothing but escape.

Over his crimson face a look of much agitation passed as he glanced at his wrist-watch.

'Good Lord! Lady Hardcastle. I must fly!'

Her mouth drooped, and her eyes opened wide.

'But the suits?'

'I'm sure your nephew will be able to trust to your judgment.'

'Oh – how silly you are. You're the nephew!'

She beamed at him. Now, surely, he would come to Hardcastle. But the beam soon faded, for an expression which nobody could have called encouraging came over his face.

'I see. It's very kind of you. But I'm afraid I couldn't possibly accept a present like that.'

'But I *want* to give you some suits,' she pleaded.

'I'm awfully sorry.' He looked completely dogged.

She seemed baffled. Really this boy was impossible.

'The great thing about life,' she began, 'is never to . . .'

'Never to miss an experience,' said Brian. 'I know. But this is an experience which I'd really much rather miss. So, if you don't mind, I think we'll go.'

He turned, went to the door, and waited. He was trembling with shame and indignation. She was trembling with thwarted plans and stagnant desires. She came to the door.

'Won't you change your mind?'

His voice was hoarse. 'You really shouldn't have done that,' he said.

'But I *wanted* to do it. . . .' Her voice trailed off like that of a child who has been denied an extra sweetmeat. She looked dangerously near to tears.

'I wouldn't let anybody give me things like that.'

'Like what? I wasn't patronizing, was I?'

He felt acutely uncomfortable. 'No, of course not. But . . .'

'There aren't any "buts." Why can't you look upon me as a friend?'

'That's what I hope I may do.'

And he was gone. She thought that it was a curious thing for a young man to say.

Of course, he *would* come. She had never failed yet. But how? That was the question.

She clambered into the car alone, and whirled away into the shadows. As she applied the nineteenth coat of powder to her nose, she wondered, in her slow, obvious way, what this strange young man *did* want. He was really quite different from the rest. When she had taken that divine young dancer from the ballet to be fitted for a new suit he had chosen not one but a dozen. He had run amok among tweeds and broadcloths and merinos, choosing costumes that would have equipped him for a world-tour. And not only 'would' but *did* so equip him, for he had sailed for America on the very first day that the suits had arrived, without even giving her a kiss.

Well, here she was at Madame Vadaire's, and really she almost shuddered to think of all the things they would have to do to her face to conceal the ravages which her very emotional afternoon had traced on it. They would have to cover it with towels, and smooth it with creams, and rub it with ice and – oh, dear, why *was* Love so tiring?

She climbed up the stairs, entered the rose-lighted *salon*, and followed her own attendant to a little white room filled with bottles and lotions and strange electrical appliance. Around her rose the babble of voices from the ladies of Mayfair – tired voices, harsh voices, greedy voices. She recognized among them the tones of several of her friends. Pretty ladies! Charming ladies! They were all sitting back, like her, being hurt, being bored, being twisted and torn and slapped, in order that their faces might smile bravely through another season. The feeling that she was surrounded by kindred spirits encouraged her. For though she did not realize it, the peculiar attitude of Brian had quite troubled her turgid spirit. Really – such an odd young man. But so terribly attractive.

'The usual treatment, m'lady?'

She glanced up, and cast a look of acute envy and malice at the uncannily smooth face of the masseuse who bent over her.

'Yes. The usual.'

She closed her eyes, and the first application of cream stung her face. It hurt – ooh – how it hurt! But it was worth it.

And that evening, when Brian returned to the flat, there was a little parcel for him, with red sealing-wax and blue ribbons. When he discovered the cigarette-case inside it, he had a spasm of moral indignation which lasted for quite ten minutes. But he kept the case.

Which shows that he was not such a fool as you may be beginning to think.

CHAPTER TWENTY

THE observant reader, who has followed Brian's passage through London, ticking off the various vices, plain and coloured, with which he has come in contact, will doubtless be puzzled by a curious omission. Where are the drug fiends? No single whiff of cocaine has blown across these pages, nor have we heard the rattle of even a miniature hypodermic syringe.

That omission will now be rectified, not, it must be confessed, in order to please the reader, nor even to round off Brian's experiences, which are still far from complete, but as a sober record of fact. There is nothing particularly exciting about, say, the taking of cocaine as a mere physiological phenomenon. Its action on the body is coarser and far less exquisitely balanced than the action of a common pill, and its effect on the mind is, after a regrettably short period, less stimulating than a dramatic criticism by Mr. George J. Nathan.

No. The interest is in its reaction on the spectators. Take a young man like Brian, to whom the very idea of cocaine suggests the Evil One. Take Lord William Motley, the subtle reference to whose little gold box, a few chapters back, will not have passed unnoticed. Bring these two characters together, produce the gold box, describe the deed. What happens? Something not without interest.

But why did Lord William choose, at this particular period, to lay his cards on the table? For the simple reason that the desire to spoil is among the keenest desires of the human race. Few of us can resist scrabbling with our walking-sticks on a stretch of virgin sand. There is something almost damnably irritating about a field of untrodden snow. And though Brian could not possibly be described as either virgin or snow-like, he was still deliciously innocent of the more advanced stages of unmoral amusement.

In any case, whatever the motive, and whether it is boring or amusing, it happened, and that should be enough for us, for it accelerated the whole action of Brian's life. For the first time that one sees a drug addict 'at work,' as it were, is as shocking as the first time one sees the face of the dead.

There are dining, in a private room at a celebrated little restaurant, Lord William, Brian, Gloria – the æsthetic young woman who figured briefly at Hayseed – and Gloria's sister, Avril, who is a slightly pathetic, and smaller, imitation of Gloria herself. Lord William had arranged the dinner at a moment's notice, feeling the itch for a sensation upon him, undecided how he would obtain that sensation, but choosing the least sophisticated of his friends, in order to heighten the effect.

It is a painful dinner. Lord William is drunk. He is irritated, at times moody, at times riotous. The two women are obviously alarmed. Brian is puzzled and a little disgusted, not only for himself or for the women, but for the charming old head-waiter, who hovers round with a crimson, beaming face, like an ancient Pirate King, drawing attention to the vintage of the wines, which he has preserved for many years with the care of a father.

The scene which now occurs may be described with the greatest simplicity. It will always remain in Brian's mind as one of the most hideous of all his life's experiences. Lord William had been comparatively tranquil during the last ten minutes. He had merely sat with his head leaning on one hand, gazing vacuously before him, while his fingers drummed monotonously on the tablecloth. True, if examined closely, he was a repulsive sight, with his white skin, and his drooping eyes, but there was no need to examine him closely. He could just be treated as an accessory.

Brian was talking to Gloria. Suddenly the white figure became animated.

'Let's have some brandy.' The words were gargled like water coursing out of a bottle.

Gloria looked at Brian with a mute appeal. 'I don't want any,' said Brian at once.

Avril was silent, petrified.

Lord William took no notice.

'Patron,' he shouted.

The pirate king appeared.

'Brandy.'

The pirate king beamed. In a moment there were four glasses before Lord William. In another moment those four glasses were filled with brandy – exquisite, golden liquor, whose very smell was intoxication. The pirate king's face, as he regarded those four glasses, was paternal.

Lord William took a glass in each hand. And he tossed the brandy on to the floor.

That sounds a simple, sordid, and unexciting act. To Brian it was certainly sordid, and sufficiently simple, but it was also horrible. He saw Lord William's twisted smile. He saw the black cloud over the pirate king's face. He saw the twittering fear of Avril, and the unsophisticated shame of Gloria. He saw the glint of the shattered glasses on the stone floor, smelt the perfume of the outraged vintage. It was a very nasty moment. But not so nasty as was to come.

'You damned fool.'

Quickly Brian took the remaining two glasses out of his reach. He became heroic, semi-hysterical.

'If you were a gentleman you'd ask these ladies' pardon and drink their health.'

'Not a gentleman.'

There was silence. Lord William breathed heavily. His eyes glared in front of him, glazed. And then:

'Want some cocaine.'

'Don!' Gloria's voice broke in. He took no notice. Already his hand was searching in his pocket.

'I've not got much, but it's enough.'

It all happened in a second. A little packet of blue paper was in his hand. It was opened and his fingers dipped into the white powder. With a clumsy gesture he stuffed the powder into his nostrils and sniffed – once, twice.

Brian felt desolatingly sick. Why, he could not tell. It was not as though the action were unfamiliar, because it had frequently been described to him. Rather was it the fact that as Lord William took it, his whole being seemed charged with the melancholy of the damned. It was not done with a smile, nor even with a gesture of defiance. It was done in the manner of some mournful and inevitable rite. The corners of the mouth drooped, the head drooped, the eyes drooped. The fingers themselves were weary, seeming to realize the futility of their task.

He gazed, fascinated. Lord William seemed not in the least ashamed. His features were still set in a mask of idiotic depression. Slowly his fingers closed round the packet, pressing it very tightly.

Then gradually the transformation took place. It was as though a corpse were being generated into activity by the application of electricity. The muscles of the face twitched, contracted again, and then seemed to be pushed together by a powerful agent. He began to sit up. He breathed less heavily, though more quickly. His eyes began to sparkle, became very bright, dilated. He actually smiled. And he pushed the packet to Brian with a smile.

'Have a bit?'

Brian turned to the women.

'I expect you'd like to go.'

'Please. Please.'

As though fleeing from a madman they stretched out their hands for their cloaks. For a taker of cocaine, to those who see him for the first time, is a madman. He is animated by a devil. He is a horrible sort of Robot. One feels that nothing he says or does is human. One cannot speak to him. One can only speak at him, beyond him.

They did not speak to him. They flew out, through the door, along the vestibule and into the windy street. Brian hailed a taxi. They got in, and whirled away.

He went back to the little room. Lord William was sitting up in his chair, talking volubly to himself.

Brian watched. He was experiencing a purely primitive sensation. It was not Lord William nor his loathsomeness that was shocking him. It was not even an under-surge of inherited Puritanism that filled him with nausea. It was life itself, or rather, the distortion of life with which he had allowed himself to drift. As he listened to the babble of meaningless talk, studied the clawing of the fingers on the tablecloth, he said to himself, 'Brilliance has come to this. Youth has come to this, and gaiety. All things eventually come to this. I shall be like it one of these days.'

Gradually, the figure became calm, comparatively sane. Taking a large white handkerchief from his pocket, Lord William wiped his forehead.

'My dear child,' he said, in a fairly clear voice, 'you are inimitable. You always play up. Nobody could have simulated a more heavenly expression of outraged innocence. It was worthy of Eric, or Little by Little . . . such an attractive young man. And the way you hurried off those cow-like women was masterly.'

'I wasn't pretending, thank you.'

Lord William smiled broadly. 'And you can even keep it up now. It is quite brilliant of you. As a reward . . .'

He put his hand in his pocket and produced the little gold case. He pushed it across to Brian. 'This is what I call true friendship.'

Brian put out his hand, and seized the case and threw it on the floor.

'You damned swine!' he cried. 'You damned swine!' He felt breathless, filled with a bubbling, childish hatred. 'I didn't know anybody could be so foul. Oh – God!' He turned away. He told himself he was behaving like a melodramatic fool. He tried, even for a second, to see the thing calmly, to treat it as an amiable eccentricity, but he could not. His whole being was nauseated. His very fingers seemed to burn where they had touched the box. His heart beat very quickly, and he had to swallow to prevent himself from actually being sick.

There was the sound of a scraping chair, a few shuffling footsteps, the slamming of a door. Lord William had gone. Out of his life, for ever. That was all he knew at the moment. He did not realize the complications which such an exit implied. He did not begin to ponder the reactions which such a breach would entail among his circle of acquaintances. He only knew that never would he speak to him, see him, again.

He took a deep breath, and gulped some water. He went to the glass, and smoothed his hair with trembling fingers, and laid his head on his hands.

Reflected in the glass he saw the door open slowly, and the crimson face of the patron peeped through. Slowly that gentleman tiptoed into the room, cast a look at Brian, cast another eye upon the floor, observed a little gold box. He picked up the little box, put it into his pocket, cast another look at Brian, and tiptoed from the room, a smile on his lips.

The little ceiling light in the inner sanctum at Queen Anne's Gate was swinging backwards and forwards in the wind from the open window, casting the strangest shadows down the long black room, seeming to make the masks on the wall alternately to smile and frown. Bending over his table was the bulky silhouette of Lord William. He was working feverishly at a mask which lay almost finished before him. It represented the face of a young man of remarkable beauty, but it was the face of a fool. The lips of sodden clay hung slightly apart, the cheeks were the faintest degree too rounded, the eyelids drooped as though with the hint of sleep, and there was something foolish even in the way he had caused a curl to brush carelessly over the forehead.

He ceased modelling, and stepped back, wiping his hands, regarding his handiwork. Very soon the mask would be dry. It was one of his best efforts.

Up and down, up and down the room he walked, muttering to himself. Still the lamp swung, still the shadows caused the masks to smile and frown. To his highly stimulated brain, working at top pressure, the room seemed to stretch into infinity, the ceiling was lost in distant spaces, and the little shadows were like vast ghostly arms, sweeping round him with titanic gestures. He had the impression that he was a prince who walked down a medieval hall, and that the mimic faces on the wall were his obsequious courtiers, lined up to do him sycophantic homage.

He paused, and stretched out his arm before the mask of Lady Hardcastle, which stared at him with blank, narrowed eyes. A phantom Lady Hardcastle, in a gown of faded silk, rustled from the wall, and stood by him. He escorted her to the other side, where, already glimmering in the shadows, could be discerned the form of Tanagra Guest. She, too, drifted out, luminous and whispering, and took her position on his other side. Near the doorway, at the other end of the room, there was a stirring in the shadows, and Maurice, slim and wraith-like, clad in translucent doublet and moonlit hose, glided over to do his homage.

Then in all corners of the room, there were sighings and whisperings, a wreathing as of smoke, which curled snake-like from the corners, and gradually in the half-light assumed human shape. He waited till they were all ready, lined behind him in a vast serpentine procession. The echo of distant fifes drummed in his ears. Ready? He glanced behind him. Yes. They were all there, lined up. He gave the signal, and began to lead the procession down the hall.

Up and down, up and down, walked the bulky figure of Lord William. In the street outside there was the sound of passing taxis, but he heard them not. The early spring leaves lisped against the window, but they were not for him. He was far, far away, leading his strange creations – the only children which he would ever give to the world – down the corridors of the past.

Suddenly the solitary figure paused, the head drooped, the body seemed to crumple. His eyes opened, staring out, half glazed with an overpowering fatigue. His face was deathly white, and he shivered. He dragged his feet over to the table on which lay the mask which he had lately been modelling. He touched it with listless fingers. Of what interest was it now?

Then, so swiftly that he almost fell, he sank on to the couch by the table's side. In a moment he was asleep.

Still the light swung backwards and forwards. The shadows passed over the face of the inane and beautiful young man, which was now quite dry. And each time that they passed, they seemed to twitch it to a smile.

CHAPTER TWENTY-ONE

WHEN Brian woke up on the following morning, and saw Mrs. Pleat standing by his bed, holding out his eggs and bacon, he could have kissed her for being so 'ordinary.'

All night long he had tossed in the grip of a nightmare, in which he was chased by a gibbering Lord William through a snowstorm. Thicker and thicker fell the snow, and ever and anon Lord William would catch him up, trying to cram the snow down his throat. And at last he had been left desolate and alone on an immense plateau, in which the snow was trampled all round him by unseen, cloven feet.

But with Mrs. Pleat, and eggs and bacon, and inferior coffee, he returned to the world of normal human beings, the world of people who read *The Daily Mail*, and think twice before they spend ten shillings, and follow with real interest the private life of Gloria Swanson. He leant back in bed, and drank his coffee, listening eagerly to Mrs. Pleat's acid comments upon the woman who lived in the flat above.

'*She* says she never uses the bath,' Mrs. Pleat observed. Having made this statement, she retreated to the door, as though the matter were closed. At the door, however, she suddenly turned round, folded her arms, and regarded Brian more in sorrow than in anger. 'And you believes 'er.'

'Well – I've never seen her in it, but . . .' Brian began.

'There ain't no need to *see*,' Mrs. Pleat interrupted. 'It's the traces.'

'How do you mean?'

Mrs. Pleat again advanced. 'You pay five shillings a week for that there bath, don't you?'

'Yes.'

She snorted. '*Some* people would call it robbery. Still. You *pays* it. And she isn't supposed to 'ave nothing to do with it, is she?'

'No.'

'Well, then.' Here she lifted her finger triumphantly. ''Ow is it that this morning the linoneum is drippin', 'ow is it that the water is cold, and 'ow is it that she's 'anging wet towels out of the window, and walkin' up and down the stairs with 'er 'air 'anging down 'er back, looking so comical that I could 'ave laughed in 'er face if I didn't know what she'd been a-doin' of.'

To this elaborate injunction Brian could frame no adequate reply. He was only aware of the existence of the woman upstairs

by occasional swift meetings in the hall, and by the sound of
hymns, delivered in a guttural voice (she was of Swiss extraction)
which penetrated through the matchboard during his morning
splashings.

But to Mrs. Pleat, the woman upstairs was an active, hostile
entity. She was a malicious schemer, who spent her life popping
in and out of forbidden baths, littering the staircase with hairpins
(merely to annoy Mrs. Pleat) and doubtless leading an immoral
life. For it must be understood that after Mrs. Pleat's unfortunate
matrimonial experience, all women were hateful. There was no
good in any of them. They were her natural enemies.

Brian propitiated her by promising to complain to the landlord,
finished his eggs and bacon, had a cold bath, and came down, feeling considerably refreshed.

The telephone bell rang.

'Is that you, Brian? It's Maurice. I want to see you dreadfully. It's
about Don. What? No. I can't explain over the 'phone. Could you
come along straight away?'

Brian paused for a moment. What had happened? Had Lord
William . . . However. It was no use trying to speculate. Better
learn the truth and face it.

'All right. I'll come.'

'Angel.'

Brian put down the receiver and began to prowl round the
room. He wanted to saturate himself in his own, personal atmosphere before setting out. He wanted to feel his feet grounded
firmly on something which could be called *himself.*

He turned to the mantelpiece. It was a treasure-house of absurd
but homely associations. There was the egg-shaped ornament of
glass, containing water, which produced a snowstorm when you
shook it, and covered with white flakes the tiny green enamel
house which was fastened to the bottom. There was an old colour
engraving of the Countess of Suffolk, painted on black glass, which
Walter had picked up for sixpence. It was supposed to be worth the
enormous sum of three pounds. There were the four miniature
china flower-trees, which had come from Vienna almost smashed
to pieces. They had been carefully gummed together again, and

would last intact until the warm weather. After that they would come unstuck, and would be put away in a drawer until another winter.

From the mantelpiece to the piano. Dust lay thick over the scattered, ragged music. Mrs. Pleat really was awful. He would begin to play the piano again soon. Some *études* of Couperin, 'Poor Little Rich Girl,' George Gershwin's 'Rhapsody in Blue' (first pages missing), a very vulgar transcription of 'La Bohème,' a Stravinsky waltz which nobody had ever been able to play, glaring unconquered behind a barbed-wire fence of double sharps and unsuspected flats.

Over to the three book-shelves, which Mrs. Pleat insisted on calling The Library. The poems of Henri de Regnier; *Beasts and Superbeasts*, by Saki; Trollope's *Barchester Towers*; *La Feerie Cinghalaise*, by Francis de Croisset; a poor translation of Pirandello's *Naked*; Theodore Dreiser's *The Financier* (unreadable); Sacheverell Sitwell's *Southern Baroque Art*; a rather rude volume entitled *Madame ne Veut pas d'Enfants* (120th *Mille*); *Cranford* – his favourite book. He took down this last and glanced once again at that immortal description of the Hon. Mrs. Jamieson's tea-party, with the wafer bread-and-butter, and Miss Pole's aristocratic conversation for the benefit of 'her ladyship,' and the firelight shining on the little table where frail old maids played spadrille. Oh – this was ripping. Every word was a step back on the road to sanity. He felt that if only he had read a little *Cranford* every morning he would not have strayed into the hopeless morass in which he now found himself.

He must be getting on. As, on the top of a bus whirling towards Chelsea, he thought of his approaching interview, the very idea of Maurice seemed grotesque. Even more grotesque when he stood in his studio, faintly scented with yesterday's odours, before a figure in a dressing-gown of chocolate satin, splashed with huge yellow sunflowers – a figure that held its face away from the light as though it had been a woman dreading the relentless tale of wrinkles.

'What have you been saying about me to Don?'

'What?'

He repeated the question. 'I know. I know.' He was hysterical already. 'And not only to Don, but to heaps of other people.'

Brian stared at him in genuine amazement.

'What the hell are you talking about?'

Maurice sat down at the piano, and wiped his lips nervously with a yellow handkerchief.

'He rang me up this morning,' he went on. 'He told me you'd been going round London saying I ought to be shot. Saying – monstrous things.' In feminine irritation he tapped E flat quickly, six times, with his right forefinger.

Brian understood. Lord William had not lost much time. He must have decided to queer his pitch. Well – there would be a fight. No. It wasn't worth it. Lord William could keep his futile friends. Yet – Julia? Oh, Lord! – it was ghastly.

'Lord William's a blasted liar.'

Again those maddening six taps on E flat.

'And what's more . . .' he began the story of last night. He spared not the smallest detail. And as he went on, he watched Maurice. He expected him at least to be moved, or ashamed, or frightened. To Brian's utter astonishment, he merely appeared irritated. At the end of it, he said:

'Well? What on earth d'you tell me that for?'

Brian paused. . . . 'But – isn't it enough?' Tap, tap, tap, tap, tap, tap. 'For Christ's sake stop that row!'

He stopped. 'As if you didn't know before.'

'I didn't. I swear I didn't.'

'In any case, it's no reason why you should blackguard me.'

Brian looked at him almost in pity. 'So you still believe I've said – whatever I'm supposed to have said?' It was hopeless trying to argue with such a fool.

The atmosphere seemed suddenly different – colder, calmer, but more malicious. Maurice stroked E flat again without sounding it.

'You do your tricks very well,' he said.

'Tricks?'

He played a few chords with his left hand. 'This wide-eyed innocence. Terribly attractive.'

'You sound slightly bitter.'

Maurice gave a shrill laugh. 'Oh, my *dear*! You *have* come on. Answering me in my own language.'

'It's the only language you understand.'

'And still keeping your lovely moral qualities.'

'That must infuriate you.'

For answer he rose quickly from the piano and came up to Brian. His face was contorted. 'Yes. It does infuriate me. Hypocrisy always infuriated me and always will.'

'Aren't you being a little intense?'

Maurice did not answer the question. 'You're setting all my friends against me.'

'Don't be childish.'

'You think I'm a freak, effeminate, something that ought to have been strangled at birth. Don't you? Don't you?'

'Oh, shut up.'

'I shan't shut up. I shan't. You haven't a right to say those things.'

'I tell you I've said nothing.'

'I'm as natural as you are. I can't help – I can't help . . .' Suddenly, grotesquely, he began to sob, silently, with a tight-shut mouth, and dry eyes.

Brian looked away. He felt acutely uncomfortable.

'I can't help how I'm made.' Maurice was walking up and down the room, biting his lips mechanically, rubbing his hands with a restless movement against his thighs. 'I've never liked things that other people liked. I've never fallen in love, or wanted to marry, or longed for children. I've tried and tried till I'm almost insane. But I can't.'

He opened his cigarette-case, found it empty, threw it on the table. Then, speaking more slowly: 'I'm frightened. Hideously frightened of life.' He came up and put his hand on Brian's arm. 'Sometimes I come back from a party and I turn on all the lights and I play the gramophone, and I stand in the middle of the room, just waiting, till I could scream. The room is bright and noisy, but I feel it's full of people, looking at me, condemning me. They crowd round me, out of every door, they climb in at the window, they grin down from the ceiling, and oh, God! . . .' he put his hand over his eyes, 'they all accuse me. Accuse me. Why should I be accused? Tell me that.'

'Look here. Nobody's accusing you.'

'Did I make myself? Did I go to God and say, please make me a freak? Please take away from me all power to love anybody? Please put me into this world with desires that I mustn't satisfy and longings for something I can never get? Did I? Did I?'

'I'm fearfully sorry for you.'

Maurice looked at him, almost calmly, for a moment. Then his face again twisted. 'I might have been so happy. Other people are happy. There are other people who are made like I am, and they make friends, wonderful friends, that stick to them all their life. I haven't got a single friend.'

'You've got Don – if that's any satisfaction.'

'Don! He encourages me in everything. If he sees me doing something I ought to cut out, he encourages me, just for his own amusement. If I wear absurd clothes, he approves of them. If I drink too much he persuades me to drink more. He knows I'm a freak. He loves it. It's only freaks he does love. Until *you* came along, with a better trick. A much better trick. And now he hates you, too. Oh – I wish I could die.'

He fell on to the sofa and buried his head in the cushion. Brian sat on the edge, placing his hand on his shoulder, trying to think. The accumulated traditions of his sturdy upbringing were impelling him to condemn this youth who had just spread before him the tattered garments of a tortured spirit. Yet his own sympathy urged him to tolerate even so grotesque a fantasy of nature as Maurice. It was typical of him that at this moment he should recall the old-fashioned remedies for cases of mental stress. A long walk, a cup of steaming milk and cinnamon, and to bed with the windows open wide. But for this product of 1926 such treatments seemed feebly inadequate. Maurice was suffering from a malady which had twisted him in his very cradle, a malady, moreover, which the entire resources of modern Society seemed designed to intensify.

'If only . . .' he began.

Maurice paid no heed to him. 'The worst part of it is that I'm so terribly fond of him.'

'Don?'

'Yes. I can't help it. One day he'll get tired of me. And then –'

'It'd be a damned good thing if he did. . . .'

'Oh, you fool! You fool!' Maurice shook his shoulder irritably from the contact of Brian's hand. 'Don't you *see*?'

'No.'

Maurice looked at him curiously. 'Well, it's no use trying to explain that. I might try to explain something else, though. You think I'm mean and grasping, don't you?'

'If you must know – yes.'

'Well, you're right. But why *am* I like that?'

'I suppose it's constitutional.'

'Well, you suppose wrong. I'm mean because I'm saving up for my old age. I shall want every penny. Every penny, I tell you. I'm young now, and people still like me. But one day they won't like me any more. They'll leave me alone in this room, with the lights on and the gramophone playing. And if I hadn't any money I should stay in it, lonelier and lonelier, till I went mad. . . .'

He suddenly swept out of the room. The door slammed and Brian was left alone.

Oh, this crazy merry-go-round of fools! What was it all about? Why was everybody gesticulating so wildly for nothing? Why were they torturing themselves when there was no need to be tortured, cursing when there was no need to curse, making a sorrow even of youth itself? The whole thing was beyond him; he could not hope to grapple with it. He would rather starve on the Embankment, pick stones in the road, sleep in a doss-house, than take even a small part in so distorted a problem-play as this.

Maurice's Italian servant appeared in the doorway, bearing a note. Brian opened it. He read:

'*Please go away now. I don't think we'd better meet again for some time.*'

So Maurice too had departed from his life. Once more he felt a sense of overwhelming relief. He crumpled up the piece of paper, took his hat and walked from the studio, whistling with an energy which he had not displayed for many months.

CHAPTER TWENTY-TWO

Two or three days had passed by, but it was still too early for Brian to discover the results of his breach with Lord William and Maurice. However, Julia was back in London, he was to see her that very evening, and if there were any awkward questions he would stifle them with a kiss. In any case the atmosphere seemed to him to be much clearer. It usually is, when thunder is in the air.

So light-hearted did he feel that his gossip page almost wrote itself. Sir Thomas and Lady Turf-Moore were still obligingly exploring the Amazon, and as long as they remained well out of the way of the newspapers he determined to regale the readers of *The Lady's Mail* with an account of their heroic exploits.

'Wonderful, isn't it, the way that the British character asserts itself under the most trying conditions? A friend who has just returned from the Amazon tells me that Sir Thomas and Lady Turf-Moore, the intrepid explorers, insisted on dressing for dinner even when they were hundreds of miles from civilization, with nothing to eat but a little corned beef, and some coarse native wine. Sir Thomas, indeed, declared that he was more perturbed by having to wear a grimy dress-shirt than by having to sleep without a mosquito net.'

That was enough about the Turf-Moores. He turned his attention to Lord Agincourt, who was unlikely to cause any trouble since he was permanently exiled at Monte Carlo, owing to a misunderstanding with his creditors.

'In gambling there are systems and systems,' he continued, *'but surely that which Lord Agincourt (who, for reasons of health, is obliged to remain at Monte Carlo for the season) has invented must be the most ingenuous. He tells me that he counts the number of people gambling at a table, multiplies them by three, divides by two, and then backs the dozen into which the number falls. There was quite a friendly little squabble the*

other day when, having calculated that he should back the first dozen, the pretty Folly Sisters suddenly arrived at the table, making him change his stakes to the second dozen. And the FIRST *won! However, as Lord Agincourt gallantly remarked, the presence of two such charming beauties at any table more than compensated for the loss of fifty pounds.'*

Faster than his pen could transcribe these revelations, he went on: *'Unless I am very much mistaken, there will be quite a vogue for Indian music in London next winter when the popular Lady Gallstone brings back her collection of Indian native songs, which she has collected at considerable risk to herself. On one occasion, the story runs, Lady Gallstone was wandering on the outskirts of the jungle in the heat of the afternoon – (a time when most Anglo-Indians are sound asleep). Suddenly she heard the wail of an exquisitely mournful melody. Stepping forward, that she might catch it more clearly, she observed in her path a poisonous asp. Most women would have flown screaming, but Lady Gallstone, passionately determined to capture the melody, seized a stick and with a single blow broke the reptile's back. She then proceeded on her way, and found an ancient native, who played the tune to her over and over again until it was for ever registered in her mind. Lady Gallstone has whimsically christened it "the Song of the Asp."'*

There is no excuse for lingering longer over these frivolities. Brian must be taken from the stage, the curtain must descend, and after a decent interval it must rise again, on the same day, in the early afternoon, at the house of Lady Hardcastle in Mount Street.

Anne – as we will continue to call her – had not been idle during the few weeks which had ensued after her fruitless lunch with Brian. Many things had been passing in her mind, many plans had been laid, countermanded, re-set, scrapped. She had considered the open appeal, the indirect approach, the powers of money, greed, pride and shame.

And then – fate had shown her a way. There had been a chance encounter with Grist – Lady Julia's maid. A few words had suggested a plan of campaign. One morning Anne had gone to the bank and cashed a cheque for a hundred pounds. On the same evening, in her exotic boudoir, she had received Grist, and had accepted from her, in return for the hundred pounds, a certain package. It may sound crude and mysterious, but that is only because there is no particular interest in describing the mixture of coincidence, intrigue and bribery by which there came into the possession of Lady Hardcastle certain letters which . . . But it is best to allow the characters to speak for themselves.

Anne was wearing a green Lanvin frock, which was in itself one of the most cynical commentaries upon womanhood which even a French *modiste* has delivered. Julia was dressed in black.

'I expect you know, darling, why I have asked you here.'

It was after lunch, and Julia was sitting, slightly bored, in Anne's music room. Even music, where Anne was concerned, seemed to be given an amatory significance, for the lid of the piano was decorated with Cupids and across the ceiling were painted the wings of an immense swan, poised in the act of descending upon a Leda, who bore a singular resemblance to Anne herself.

'No, Anne, I haven't the faintest idea.'

Anne raised her eyebrows. 'Really? Well, it's terribly simple. I only want you to bring your nice Mr. Elme down to Hardcastle next week-end.'

Julia repressed a smile. 'Why don't you ask him yourself?'

'I wanted to be quite *sure*.'

'I see.' This time she smiled openly. 'Well, darling, I'm afraid it's no use.'

'Why?'

'Because he wouldn't come.'

Anne flushed slightly. 'You seem very sure of that.'

'Positive.' Julia stretched out her hand for a cigarette. 'Match, darling.'

'Don't smoke for a minute.' Anne's voice was suddenly harsh. 'I hate to appear insistent, but . . .'

'Oh, Anne, really! Is this quite dignified?'

'Not in the least. I never have been dignified, and I never wish to be. All I want, at the moment, is that you should bring your charming young man down for the week-end. You tell me it's impossible. I fail to see why. He'd do anything that you told him.'

Julia was genuinely surprised. Hints she had expected, and possibly an overt request, but not this determined onslaught.

'But why should I tell him?' she said calmly.

'Oh, I see. You're still in love. . . .'

'Darling!' Julia's light laugh echoed through the room. 'I've never been in love.'

'Never?'

'Certainly not. I like people to be in love with *me* – in fact, it's rather necessary to me. But love. . . . Really, I think we'd better talk about something else.'

'Not yet.'

Julia moved impatiently. 'I tell you, Anne, I shall not do it. You're being a perfect fool. Besides, even if you did get him down to Hardcastle, it wouldn't be the faintest use.'

'Oh yes, it would – with your help.'

Julia was bewildered. Did Anne seriously imagine that she was going to help her, for no conceivable reason, to give Brian away, to throw him into her arms?

'I'm completely astounded,' she said to her. 'It's the most extraordinary proposition I've ever heard. Would you mind saying quite clearly what you *do* want?'

'I want Brian Elme. I've fallen in love with him.' Her voice sounded a little thick but entirely sincere.

Julia tapped her foot on the floor. 'Do let's keep this discussion on its proper level,' she said.

'I am doing so. I have fallen in love with him; and I'm quite determined to get him.'

'Don't be childish. He's in love with me. It's a bore, but he is.'

'Therefore he'd do anything you wanted.'

'Anne! You horrible old woman!' Even Julia was shocked.

'It's my turn to tell you not to be childish.'

'Childish! I've got some sort of decency left.'

'All the same – you're going to help me.'

'On the contrary, I'm leaving you.'

'Just a minute.' There was something in Anne's tone that made her pause. 'I have a little thing to tell you first.'

'I'm tired of your little things.'

'It's only a short recitation.'

'Oh, Anne – you're insufferable!' Julia hurried towards the door. Anne was standing with her back to the wall, her head tilted back, her eyes half-closed. She began to intone . . .

Darling, I can't help myself. I've been such a rotter all my life, and foolishly, I had tried to persuade myself that I did not wish to be any-thing else. But you have stirred me as nothing else has stirred me. You have made me want to begin again. Darling, will you always be by my side? Will you always . . .

The voice stopped abruptly.

'My letter! My own letter!'

Julia's hand was on Anne's wrist. She was breathing quickly, passionately, staring into Anne's face.

'Yes, darling.'

'How dare you? How dare you?'

'It's a beautiful letter.'

'How dare you? Where did you get it?'

'If you would leave my wrists alone . . .'

Julia dropped them. Anne walked to the fireplace. 'I have them all,' she said.

'Oh, God!'

Julia felt sick and faint. She did not doubt Anne's word. How Anne had obtained her letters, what she was going to do with them, to whom she had already shown them – those were minor ques-tions. The fearful fact was that she herself was revealed, naked, stripped. Her whole heart had been bared before this vulgar, sen-sual woman. The one beautiful thing in her life had been made cheap and obscene. Fool that she had been. Fool! To imagine that one could ever keep anything beautiful; to imagine that there were any corners of one's heart which might always remain uncorrupt. Almost, had she not been so angry, she might have laughed.

Anne interrupted her meditations. 'I shall never tell you how I got your letters, darling.'

Julia was silent. She was thinking furiously. Already she sus-pected Grist. Still – what did it matter?

Anne went on: 'The point is that I *have* got them. All of them. They are written on your notepaper, in your own extremely individual hand. They are privately locked up in the bank, with the exception of a few of the more highly-flavoured ones, which are in my own safe in this house.'

'I see. So it's blackmail.'

'Yes. Isn't it fun?'

'Only a half-crazy woman like you could think of anything so disgustingly fantastic.'

Anne purred. 'Disgusting, yes. And fantastic too. But perfectly plausible. I want you to help me to get something that I want. You don't want it any more. You can easily say that if he's – er – amenable he will be saving you from a terrible scandal.'

'There's nothing scandalous in those letters.'

'That's the whole point, darling. That's why they're so valuable. They're everything that you would hate to be thought. They're sincere, and true, and unaffected, and deeply, tremendously passionate.'

'D'you think that my friends would even condescend to look at them?' said Julia contemptuously.

Anne laughed, her hot deep laugh.

'You really are delicious. This sudden defence of human nature. Oh no, your friends wouldn't look at them. Not at all. Lord William would *hate* the idea. Maurice would run away if I began to talk about it. And as for Tanagra! She'd faint, my dear, at the very thought of it. She's such a good friend of yours, isn't she?'

Julia felt trapped. Anne was perfectly right. They would all gloat over them; they would repeat her phrases to each other behind her back. They would shout them out in chorus at parties. They would set them to music. They would even make covert allusions to them before her face. Oh – it would be insufferable, insufferable!

'Your sarcasm is a little heavy, Anne.'

'But, darling, so is your style. That's what makes it so interesting. If you'd written nice, witty, cynical things nobody would be in the least amused at you. But these are – really – well – is it Ethel M. Dell who does it so well? They're the sort of things that a really nice plain schoolgirl would write – a sweet, wholehearted schoolgirl who plays hockey and worships the German instructress.'

'And what of it?' said Julia angrily. 'I've only to say that I wrote them with my tongue in my cheek. . . .'

'But, darling – to keep one's tongue in one's cheek so brilliantly for over twenty thousand words. . . .'

'I don't care,' Julia answered.

'Oh yes, you do. Bitterly. It's the only thing you do care about. It's the only thing that *anybody like you* would care about.'

There was unconcealed hostility in her voice.

'Anybody like me?'

'Yes.' Anne rose to her feet. 'Anybody like you. Anybody who's terrified of people finding out that one has a heart. Anybody who's posed and posed as bitter and hard and unsentimental. Anybody whose whole life is made up of little smart things. Anybody who boasts before a dinner table that she never intends to have a baby because it's too much of a bore, that the only possible reason for marrying is for money, and that love is merely a chemical illusion. You've *got* to say those things, you've got to go on saying them; you've got to continue in this attitude because any other attitude would be ridiculous, and because the humiliation of becoming a real person in front of your rotten friends would be more than you could bear . . .'

She paused breathlessly, her face deeply flushed at her sudden outburst.

'You! To say those things to me!' Julia's face was contorted with anger. 'You – who have an affair with every single man you meet, from lift-boys to Italian jugglers . . .'

'Oh yes.' Anne held up her hand. 'I know. I have affairs and affairs and affairs. But then I've never pretended *not* to have a heart. It's a very large heart, and a very practised one. I can't help that.

'But at least,' she went on, her voice rising shrilly, 'when I have an affair I feel it. I *believe* I'm in love. I don't go about behind my lover's back saying that it's all a pose simply because I'm afraid of looking ridiculous. I don't mind looking ridiculous because I know I *am* ridiculous. So is everybody who loves.'

'Love!'

'Yes. But even if I didn't, even if it was only physical (and in nine of my cases out of ten I know it is) it's genuine. That's the difference between you and me. You think that my friends are rotten because they're more actively immoral than yours, but they're nothing to William and Tanagra and Maurice and all those precious fools. They're sterile, sterile! A lot of barren, poisonous sticks. A lot of . . .'

She paused. She was going too far. She checked herself and fumbled nervously for a cigarette. 'I don't know why I'm getting so excited.'

'No?'

She lit her cigarette with trembling fingers. 'After all, it doesn't do any good to lose one's temper.'

'So I always imagined.'

'Oh, do come down to brass tacks.'

There was acute irritation and impatience in Anne's voice.

'Very well, then. I don't want the things.'

There was a forced note of challenge in Julia's voice which did not deceive Anne.

'You mean – you don't care who sees them?'

'No.' She was frowning, and her hands were tightly pressed against the mantelpiece.

'You mean – I may show them to whom I like?'

'If you are sufficiently contemptible.'

'Even to . . .' Anne paused, to give greater effect to her remark.

'Well?'

'Even to Brian?'

Julia turned round quickly. 'Oh – you beast. You utter beast. Give me those letters.'

'Ah!' Anne was smiling again now.

'Give them to me. I'll get them somehow. . . . I'll . . .' She had raised her arms over her head; they fell down hopelessly. 'Oh, God. What do I care? What does it matter?'

'I see.' Anne was almost purring again. 'So you wouldn't like *him* to see them.' Julia was silent. 'It almost sounds as if you were still in love with him.'

Julia forced a smile. 'You needn't worry yourself about that.'

'Are you sure?'

'Quite,' she answered.

'I asked the question,' Anne said coldly, 'because the word "eternity" is so frequent in this correspondence. But since you assure me that you aren't, I presume you want to get rid of him.'

'He'll be easy enough to get rid of.'

'On the contrary, nothing would be more difficult if he had once read those letters. He'd stick to you like a leech for the rest of his life. Any man would. After all these purple passages. . . .' She began to read . . . '*I may fail, I may falter, there may be months, even years, in which we shall drift apart, but always, darling, even though my every word and my every action may seem to tell you that I have forgotten, I shall remember, and I shall still belong to you.*'

She folded away the letter again with a smile and dabbed her lips with a small pink handkerchief. 'Really, Julia, your epistolatory smile makes one feel quite warm.'

Julia was not looking at her. 'I wonder if that sort of thing would really encourage him to go on,' she said, almost to herself.

Anne drummed on the table irritably. 'You don't wonder at all. You know. Brian's a ridiculous sentimentalist. He believes that if one loves once one never loves again. Why people ever get such ideas into their heads, I don't know. Still, they do. And if he sees that you've ever felt for him like that, even if it was only for a minute, or for a second, nothing would ever stop him thinking it. . . .'

Julia was silent. Anne studied her face closely. She read in it no longer anger, but a deep distress, the sort of distress which comes to those who are forced to give pain to a child. She saw that she was gaining her point. Her voice softened. When she spoke again she almost crooned.

'It would be a pity,' she said, 'for such a very charming boy to remain permanently attached, don't you think? Permanently – er – sterile? After all, he *is* charming, even if you no longer particularly want him. And one would hate to see him hoping and hoping for years to come just because of these letters.' She closed her eyes and repeated by heart the phrase from the letter which she had read before. . . . '*There may be months, even years, in which we shall drift apart, but always, darling . . .*'

Julia interrupted her. 'You needn't go on. Please stop talking for a minute, I want to think.'

CHAPTER TWENTY-THREE

A NNE's last argument had moved her more than all the rest put together. The ridicule of her friends she felt she could bear. After all, it would be something quite new – a nine days' wonder. Disagreeable, of course. She could see the sneers which would greet her – the sort of sneers which greet all apostates from any faith. And she, after all, had shown herself an apostate from the faith of infidelity. True, it was a brief secession, but a tell-tale one.

However, she might have borne that. What she felt she could not bear was the effect that the reading of these letters would have upon Brian. She no longer loved him; of that she was convinced. But deep in her heart there was an instinctive reverence for this one episode which, in her own strange way, she had kept beautiful. The memory of the many hours when, late at night, alone in her bedroom, she had sat down and allowed herself, for the first time in her life, to be a real woman, even if her reality was only a dream – that memory must never be taken from her. She clung to it feverishly, passionately. The thought of its surrender, its efface-ment, was as bitter as the sacrifice of a child.

And then there was Brian himself. She had never minded hurt-ing anybody before; it had usually amused her. But Brian was different. He would have to be hurt in any case – terribly hurt. That was going to be painful enough – boring enough, one might almost say. But if he too were allowed to share her secret – her secret that was past, yet still living – his agony would be indefi-nitely prolonged. Had she not averred a hundred times in those letters that he must not believe her if she told him that her love was dead? Were there not a hundred passages in which she swore the perpetuity of her passion? Had she deliberately designed the letters for Anne's purpose, had she racked her brains to set a trap for herself – a trap that no hands could ever set free – she could not better have done it. She thought of the beginning of the letter which she had written at Hayseed, when the tempest had been at its height . . .

'Darling, I am frightened. Not of the storm, but of all that the storm seems to typify in my life. Outside, the whole world seems as though it would be blown away. Leaves flying against my window, clouds being swirled over the greeny moon, even the big oak tree bending. So bitterly cold. And I feel it is like my life – so much storm, so great an unrest, so little warmth.

'But here, in this room, I feel as though I were with you. I feel sheltered and secure. I can stand aside and watch the turmoil and not be frightened by it, and listen to the racket and not be deafened by it. Isn't it strange that you should have that effect on me? Nobody else has ever had. Nobody will ever have it again.

'I kiss your photograph. You will never know that, Brian darling. I never want you to know it, because I am so poor a lover than even when I long to be possessed I cannot utterly surrender. If I were a great lover I should surrender everything and come to you. But I'm not a great lover. Only in dreams, Brian. Somehow, I have lived too intensely, have been selfish for too long, have built my life on too false a theory of values. But in my dreams I am as great a lover as Heloise. If you knew how happy that made me . . .'

In a flood the memories came back to her, poignant, alluring. She must keep those memories. What did it matter if her love were now dead? What did it matter if Brian were now merely a bore – something to be placed gently on one side and forgotten? The memories remained – not so much memories of him, but memories of herself, of a unique emotional beauty through which she had passed – an experience which at all costs she must keep intact.

'Well?'

She started. She had forgotten Anne. How absurd she looked, standing there with her plump figure and her sewn-up face and her great antelope eyes. The sight of this actress in the drama which was playing itself out made the whole thing seem more fantastic than ever.

But not disgusting. It had ceased to be disgusting. Brian had become so unreal to her that she could no longer visualize all that Anne's proposition implied. He was merely a pawn in the game – to be treated with more reverence than most – but still a pawn. For now Julia realized that she herself was fighting for a memory only. That was all that mattered.

And so one had better surrender with a certain amount of *chic*. She achieved a smile. 'Anne, you should really have been a Borgia.'

Anne sighed with relief. 'I knew you wouldn't force one to be tiresome. Julia, darling, do have some Cointreau.'

'No, thanks. I'd rather have the letters.'

'But, angel – I think, first . . .'

Julia saw what she meant. 'I understand.' There was an awkward pause. 'Then the arrangement is that we both come down to Hardcastle on Saturday week.'

'Yes. That will be divine. I'll send the car.' She spoke eagerly, like a child that has been promised a trip to the seaside.

'Is there anybody else you'd like?' she said. 'William, for instance?'

Julia laughed, very coldly. 'You think he'd prevent me from being lonely?'

'Don't be so ridiculous, darling.' She was portentously girlish. 'I was only thinking of bridge. Or should we have Maurice?'

'Oh, anybody. I do know a *few* other people, Anne.'

'But, my dear, you know everybody in London. That's why it's so difficult to find anybody new.'

'There's one thing, Anne.' Julia looked her straight in the face. 'I have not the faintest intention of allowing myself to be bullied. I'll do what you want because I choose to do it. It doesn't hurt me, and it seems the simplest way out of the situation. But please don't – don't forget yourself in front of *me*.'

'Darling, as if I *could*!'

'Very well, then. That's all.'

Anne rang the bell. The two women stood looking at each other in silence. A strange look came over Anne's face.

'You're sure that – that you don't love him any more?' Her voice was almost affectionate.

'Quite, thank you. You needn't waste any sympathy in that direction. I'm in love with – with something else.'

'Oh, I'm *so* glad.'

The door opened and Julia went out. As she walked down the stairs she noticed the decorative profile of the footman who preceded her. She remembered that there had been rumours about that footman.

CHAPTER TWENTY-FOUR

A T eleven o'clock that same night Brian walked into Julia's sitting-room in Berkeley Square, to be told by the maid Grist that her ladyship was expected to return at any moment.

'I'll wait,' he said, and sank into a chair with a little sigh, for his limbs were weary. Through the open door he watched the black, impersonal figure of Grist.

She was bending over the bed, arranging and rearranging a heap of dresses that shone gold and rose and purple under the lamplight. They were far more alive than she, those dresses. They were smiling and colourful, whereas she was blank and expressionless. They rustled and whispered as she folded them away, but she was silent always. They suggested grace and pride, while she suggested nothing but a machine.

'Grist,' called out Brian in a sudden curiosity, 'don't you ever want to wear any of those pretty things yourself?'

The figure paused, quite motionless – strange caricature of humanity, with stiff sombre arms and a face etched in harsh shadows.

'You called me, sir?' (How could she speak like that without moving her lips? How could so monotonous a sound come from any living throat?)

Brian repeated his question, blushing a little. It was as though he were speaking to himself, or addressing a waxwork.

'I have never thought of it, sir.'

'That's funny, isn't it?'

His voice echoed away into silence, the inane remark repeating itself and repeating itself through his drowsy brain. Still, it *was* funny that God should create so radiant and wonderful a thing as Julia with one hand and so purposeless and dried-up a creature as Grist with the other. In fancy he set himself wondering what sort of life Grist led: if she ever ate, if her wooden head was capable of such a thing as an ache, if she ever was tired, what appearance she presented in her bath – even more intimate details, in this sensuous, shadowed state between sleeping and waking, suggested themselves.

Grist in bed, Grist out walking, Grist's parents – what on earth could they be like? Out of what stony womb could she silently have emerged? From what iron breasts could her first impersonal nourishment have been taken? With what grave toys could her mechanical fingers have played? And what fruitless prayers could her thin, childish treble have delivered to the Deity who in irony had created her?

Whether or no he dozed during these reflections, he could not tell, but he suddenly found himself very much awake again, with Grist standing in front of him. She stood there, her arms extended ever so slightly, like some clockwork thing that is about to move. So odd, so unexpected, did she appear that Brian, for an instant, felt that he must laugh, until he saw her face. That was tragic – with the tragedy of a mask, the pathos of a dumb thing, or, even worse, of something that is dead and is called to life again by extreme peril or agony.

There was no mistaking Grist's humanity now. Fire burned in her eyes, like embers blown to warmth in a long-deserted grate – fire that spread until it brought a faint flush to the emaciated cheeks; and the smooth surface of her forehead was suddenly wrinkled with suffering, and from the white lips there came, in no uncertain voice, these words:

'Sir. Her ladyship will be back now at any minute. I ask you to go before she comes.'

Brian gazed at her almost in alarm. At first he did not realize the meaning of her words. He only knew that she had suddenly melted into flesh, and that she had spoken with a voice of human feeling. But when the first shock was over he rose quickly to his feet.

'What do you mean?'

'I can't say.'

'Why should I go?'

'Don't ask me.'

'Are you mad?'

'Perhaps I am.'

Snap, snap, went this dialogue, like steel and rock striking sparks. Out of nothing at all a tense, terrifying moment had been born, and equally suddenly it died. And Brian, as he searched her face, saw it gradually fade back into insignificance, saw the light die from the eyes, the cheeks pale, the furrows fade from the forehead, the hands fall back to her sides. An uncanny metamorphosis.

'I beg your pardon, sir.'

Should he ask her what damnable impertinence had prompted her to make this extraordinary suggestion? The point was solved for him by Grist herself, who turned and left the room without a word.

Brian remained staring at the door for a moment. Then with a shrug of his shoulders he sank back into the chair. What the devil did it matter what Grist thought now that he was here, and now that Julia was coming back to him? Julia! He found himself looking into the laughing eyes of the bronze Cupid by his side. He laughed too, happy – absurdly, utterly happy.

But tired. Distinctly tired. Dare he doze for a few minutes? No. Certainly not. But there was no reason why he should not let his mind wander at random. What fun that was! He stretched his legs, closed his eyes, and gave himself up to making dreams. He always made the same dreams for himself, and they always vastly entertained him. Here are some of them:

(1) *Scene, Piccadilly, late at night.* The Prince of Wales is returning from a ball, defying royal convention by walking alone and on foot. By some lucky chance Brian happens to be walking behind him, for as the Prince passes a dark side street, a dozen anarchists dart out, seize the Prince, and are about to throttle him. With a sudden leap Brian rushes forward, knocks down anarchist after anarchist, who fall with thuds on the pavement. He then bows to the astonished Prince, clicks his heels, turns and walks away.

In this dream virtue had its reward. (Brian was most careful about *that*.) In fact, he sometimes hurried forward the first part of the dream in order to reach the reward, which consisted in knighthood, special interviews in all the morning newspapers, and apparent affluence – though how this latter blessing occurred he was not quite sure.

Dream number One faded imperceptibly into *Dream number Two*. This featured as its main characters himself and Julia. The scene was usually set on a vast and gloomy mountain over which rose a sallow moon. Upon the peak of this mountain Julia was perishing in white satin (white, because it showed up so well against the black rocks of his imagination, satin because it gleamed so deliciously in the moonlight). Somewhere in the background of his mind was the baying of wolves, somewhere in the foreground the clatter of hoofs – the hoofs of the horse which snortingly transported him to her rescue. A charming picture to dwell upon, which always ended in the same way – by his climbing to the perilous summit and dispersing the wolves by clouts with an immense stick. He usually made this part of the dream a little dim, because the wolves of his desire had a faintly kittenish appearance, and the idea of hitting them too hard was repulsive to him. However, the kiss was often prolonged indefinitely, and a very beautiful, satiny kiss it was.

Brian turned in his chair with an entranced, though increasingly sleepy, smile, and allowed his mind to play with *Dream number Three*, which might be termed the Political Dream. In this he played the part of a very youthful Prime Minister suddenly called upon to save the nation from the clutches of a universal strike. This dream had for its first tableau Brian standing in front of a crackling fire in his study at Number 10, Downing Street, reading with a calm smile a scathing leading article in the *Daily Mail* commenting on the madness of the electorate in entrusting its destiny to a 'callow schoolboy.' This part of the dream was very delectable, giving him all the sensation of a William Pitt without any of the disadvantages of the eighteenth century (one of which was that there would then have been no *Daily Mail* to attack him).

Scene two of the dream shifted to the north of England. Under

ashen skies, and before an immense and hostile crowd, Brian
poured his golden eloquence into the hearts of grim and brutish
men. It must be admitted that the substance of his remarks, when
analysed in cold daylight, always struck him as being somewhat
thin and not altogether original; but in the dream they shone with
uncanny brilliance, and always affected the miners so deeply that
he was soon able to pass to:

Scene three, which consisted in his being carried on the shoulders of the miners (no longer grim or brutish), who cheered him
to the echo, and finally departed to their holes in the earth, fully
satisfied that it was best for all and sundry that they should do so.

Scene four of this drama was brief, but superb. It was laid in
the Conference Room at 10, Downing Street, where all the Cabinet ministers (whom Brian provided with beards and white hair
to heighten the contrast) were assembled, waiting in an agony of
suspense for his return.

Brian entered the room humming a tune. A man with a particularly long beard – probably the Chancellor of the Exchequer
– rushed forward.

'Sir – your Excellency – Prime Minister – tell us – what has
happened?'

With marvellous detachment Brian looked at him. 'Your meaning, Chancellor?'

'The strike?'

'Oh – *that*.' (Here came a phantom laugh.) '*That's* all over. I just
suggested to the men that they should go back to work. And they
went.'

Collapse of the old men, leaving Brian standing alone and triumphant above a sea of beards.

Brian sleepily opened his eyes. No Julia yet? No Julia? He made a
motion to get up, but fell back again. God! How tired he was. She
would not be in yet. He would make a few more dreams.

This time, inevitably, his thoughts turned to cats.

He pictured a long empty street, down which, in superb and
adorable procession, twenty black cats stalked, tails erect, eyes
gleaming in the moonlight. From over the roofs of the city came
the sound of music, and the cats started to sway, kept step, and

finally danced. How they danced! Tails waved in the wind, soft paws were daintily pointed, satiny backs arched, pink tongues protruded in excitement. Through street after street they danced, swifter and swifter, till the streets were left behind and the moonlight had faded. Out into the open country they fled, the ghostly music following after them, up into a bare and desolate land of mountains where their black backs gleamed against the grey rocks. Suddenly the black cats all leapt, in one straight line, over an inky precipice, and he awoke.

Julia was standing before him. Across her forehead was a thick band of diamonds that glittered in the shadows. One hand was on her hip, trailing an immense feather fan that shaded from the palest pink to a bright crimson. He drew in his breath at her beauty.

'Darling,' she said coolly, 'it's nearly two o'clock.'

'Is it?' He was not in the least ashamed. Had he not possessed her? Was she not entirely his? The relationship was no longer that of the Princess and the Peasant. She belonged to him. Boldly he took her hand and kissed it.

'Come and sit down.'

She raised her eyebrows and smiled. 'You're very sure of yourself to-night, aren't you?'

He nodded. 'Completely.'

'I'm so glad. All the same, I think it's a little odd of you to come and call at this time of night.'

He frowned, puzzled. 'Darling, don't make fun of me.'

She moved impatiently. 'I'm not making fun of you. I'm merely saying what I'd say to anybody.'

'Am I – anybody – then?'

She turned away. Oh – it was abominable to be pestered like this. She would like to have said, 'Yes. You *are* anybody. You bore me to tears.' But she was silent.

Brian's lip was trembling. What had he done? All his exaltation, his excitement, had suddenly died down.

'You asked me to come,' he said sullenly.

'Don't be ridiculous.'

'You did.'

'I said you might come in for a moment after dinner, that's all. I didn't ask you to wait here till the small hours of the morning.'

He bit his lip and tried to fumble in his pocket for a cigarette. At all costs he must not show her how deeply she was hurting him. 'Sorry, Julia.' He tried to smile. 'I was tired, I expect. I fell asleep.'

'So I observed.'

He looked at her curiously, then with a quick movement he stepped forward, put his arm roughly round her shoulder and kissed her mouth.

She said nothing.

'I had to do that,' he said breathlessly.

Still she said nothing.

'I had to do that,' he went on. 'I don't know what's the matter with you. I haven't seen you for a whole month. But you seem all cold and hateful. Why? I've done nothing, have I? I haven't changed, have I? So why should you?'

She was not even looking at him.

'I'm not going to let you change,' he went on, his voice almost breaking. 'You can't ignore love like mine. Life isn't big enough to let you. The whole world isn't big enough for you to escape from my love. I don't care whether you want it or not. No. That's a lie.' His voice trailed off hopelessly. 'You do want it, don't you, Julia?'

While he had been speaking, she had suddenly remembered Anne and her promise. She frowned. The whole situation was maddening. Still, she had to go through with it; and till she had gone through with it there could be no open breach. Brian must be conciliated in some way or other.

She threw down her fan, went over to him, and put her cool lips on his hot forehead. 'Darling, I'm sorry. I've got a terrible headache.'

He swallowed something in his throat and looked down at the carpet.

'It's the weather I think.' She went to the window. 'So hot and peculiar. I'm sure it's going to thunder.' She looked at him over her shoulder. 'That's why I felt I couldn't stand anything very *emotioné* to-night. Do you understand, darling?'

He smiled at her bravely. 'Of course.' Oh yes! He understood.

Women, he supposed, were like that. It was hell, absolutely hell, but it couldn't be helped. He'd have to wait till her mood had altered. As if there could be any moods in love!

'Would you like me to go?'

'Darling! Please don't. I'm terribly happy now you've come. But I just want to be – calm, that's all. D'you see?'

He kissed her hand very gently and placed it back on her lap. Then he got up and stood by the mantelpiece.

'Right you are. I'll have a cigarette, and then I'll be wandering.'

'Give me one, please.'

'You oughtn't to smoke so late at night.'

She smiled again. 'That means I shall have two.'

He shook his fist at her. 'Aren't you a devil?'

'Yes.'

She pursed her lips and puffed out the smoke in a thin blue stream. She had better broach this wretched subject now.

As she glanced at him she felt an urgent desire to turn aside from the whole business; not because it was distasteful to her, but because some deeply possessive instinct rebelled at the self-imposed sacrifice. Brian was hers, in soul and body, and she was about to throw him away. To-day he meant little in her life. But to-morrow, having lost him, what might he not again mean? She was an example of the eternal truth that the secession of but a single lover leaves an ache in the heart of even the most worshipped goddess.

Then she hardened her heart.

'I saw Anne Hardcastle this afternoon.'

'That sweet thing.'

'I think we're all a little hard on poor Anne.'

'Darling! Are you feeling quite yourself?'

'Oh, don't be silly. You're so credulous. You believe everything you hear about her.'

'I believe *you*, at any rate.'

'But my stories about Anne were fearfully exaggerated.'

'Even if they'd been a hundredth part true . . .'

'Yes?'

'There'd still be enough left to produce twelve quite hearty nymphomaniacs.'

She walked to the window and leant her head against the curtain. 'I'm rather trying to see people in a kinder light nowadays.' (God! How hard this attitude was!)

'Well, I should let the darkness close about Anne. She works marvels then. As soon as the electricity failed at Tanagra's party the other day she leapt over two hundred chairs and was almost sitting in my lap in fifteen seconds.'

She raised her eyebrows and looked at him a little contemptuously. 'I suppose it's only a rumour that you're getting impossibly conceited?'

'I should find it extraordinarily difficult to be made conceited by Anne Hardcastle.'

'Why are you always harping on sex?'

'Sex! Mention Anne, and all the other motives of human conduct wilt away.'

'I think you're being dreadfully hard.'

'Julia darling, what *is* the matter?'

'You never used to say such foul things about people.'

'I'm sorry. Oh, damn it all, why are we talking about Anne at all?'

She fingered the beads round her neck. With lowered eyes she said:

'She's asked us both down for the week-end together.'

Brian stared at her for a moment, and then laughed out loud. 'Phew! what cheek!'

'Cheek?'

'Well, isn't it?'

'I fail to see why. . . .'

'You don't mean to say you weren't furious?'

'I told her we'd be delighted.'

Brian's brain was in a whirl. . . .

'Look here, Julia. You're not pulling my leg?'

'Not to my knowledge.'

'But . . . But . . .'

She got up and stood in front of him in sudden anger.

'Oh, I'm tired of this virtue – this very easy virtue. Anybody would think you were made of cotton-wool – a little plaster saint. Aren't you capable of taking care of yourself?'

'It isn't a question of that.' His voice was very cold. 'It's the fact that I don't care for the rôle of Joseph with such a particularly powerful Potiphar's wife.'

'It wouldn't kill you, would it?'

'No. It would only make me feel sick.'

'You seem very sure of your attractions.'

'Well, perhaps I am. In this case, at any rate.' He too got up, and they stood facing one another. 'If you'd seen some of the letters that woman wrote to me you'd understand. She's entirely unscrupulous, and she's determined to get *me*. There. Have I said enough now?'

'I fail to see that it much matters.'

'Julia!'

She was frightened. She had gone too far. She put her hand on his arm. 'Silly Brian. Brian darling, look at me.'

He turned his head away, not answering.

'I didn't mean anything like that. I meant . . .'

He still did not answer. But he took her hand.

She went on: 'You see. Oh, I don't know. But I love you so much that I forget what I'm saying sometimes.'

He pressed her hand.

'I forget, and then I hurt you.'

He turned and kissed her impulsively. 'You could never hurt me for long.'

'I think we're both nervy.'

'You're certainly right there.'

'That made me angry. And it made you silly about Anne, too.'

Trying to control himself, he said, 'Darling, must we talk about that woman all night?'

Instantly she flared up again. 'Oh, really. This is the *height* of conciliation.'

'You can't have conciliation with that type.'

'That type? What type? What do you know about her?'

'I've told you what I know.'

'Nothing. A silly love-letter. If you can't cope with that . . .'

'No, I can't.'

'And haven't any intention of trying.'

'Why should I try?'

'Because I ask you to.'

'Why?'

'Because I do.'

'Why?'

'Because . . .' She turned away in angry confusion. 'Why do you cross-examine me like this?'

'There's some other reason.'

'Really?'

'What is it?'

'How should I know?'

'You've got to tell me.' He took her by the arm. 'I've got to know.'

'Leave my arm alone.'

'I *will* know. You pretend to love me, and then you throw me into the arms of a woman who's notorious all over England. Why? Why? Why?'

'Oh, God.' She was very pale. He let her arm fall. 'Please go away.'

'I'm not going till I know what all this is about. She's asked you to bring me down, has she? And you want to take me, do you? And why? Why? Is it blackmail. Is it money? Is it . . .'

'Go away. Go away.' Suddenly, without warning, her head fell back on the sofa, white as paper.

In a second the flood of Brian's anger was stemmed. He felt sick with an appalling fear. He knelt down by her side, rubbing her hands, kissing them, babbling broken words which she could not hear.

'Julia – Julia – I didn't mean . . .'

He sprang to his feet. There was some brandy in a decanter on her desk. He poured out some, and cared not that as he gave it her it trickled on to her dress. Still she made no sign.

'Julia! Julia!'

He took her in his arms. She was as something dead. He pressed his face to hers, keeping his warm lips against her cold mouth, breathing quickly, as though his life were passing into her body. For an age he seemed to hold her thus, more and more tightly, with the sense that only by some physical incorporation could he bring her back to consciousness.

Gradually he was rewarded. A touch of colour came back to her cheeks and the lips beneath his trembled. She made a movement to release herself.

Still he held her.

'Thank God! I thought you were dead.'

She opened her eyes and looked at him.

'What's the matter?'

'You fainted.'

'Oh yes.' She closed her eyes again and sighed. 'I'm so tired.'

'Darling. Have some more brandy.'

'No.'

'You must.'

Mechanically she drank it. 'We were angry, weren't we?'

'Yes. I was an absolute brute.'

'Oh – I remember. Anne!' She laughed, with the stormy feebleness of hysteria.

'I know. It was all about nothing.'

Her brain was working again keenly. This was a moment which might make or mar her plans. Instinctively she knew that she would conquer by a retreat.

'I give in,' she said. 'I won't ask you ever to see her again.'

'I'm going to.'

'No, Brian darling.'

'I'm going down with you for the week-end.'

He hardly knew what he was saying; he only felt an overwhelming desire to make up for the wrong he had done.

She smiled and held out her arms. Once again they kissed, and once again the white arm was stretched above him.

It was only when, an hour later, he stepped out into the empty square and made his way home in the faltering light that Brian began to realize the full implications of his promise. To bring

Anne Hardcastle so definitely into his life would mean yet another struggle. He told himself it was only a question of being rather rude, and that there was nothing in the least to worry about. But it was the sort of strife which he bitterly detested.

However, as he walked up Park Lane the grey and ragged loveliness of London caught him by the heart, and he forgot all else. At this heavy-lidded hour of dawn the pavements were without stain or shadow. The long grey façade of houses stood steeped in quiet, nor was there any wandering wind to stir the trees from their stiff repose. There was a strange mingling of scents in the cool air – the scent of streets from the east, subtle and civilized, the scent of grass from the west, dew-drenched and sweet. And above all that scent which can only be called the scent of dawn, which flies when the curtains are drawn in silent rooms or when the sun scatters the lingering dusk of empty squares.

CHAPTER TWENTY-FIVE

WELL – here he was at Hardcastle. And at last he realized, as he had never realized before, that he was 'up against it.'

In the old days, when he had found himself in a difficult position, he was in the habit of going away to a quiet room, where he would sit down, close his eyes, and face each problem one at a time, deciding on its solution and scribbling down an obscure plan of action on a sheet of notepaper. And now he was trying to do the same thing, but the problems seemed so vast that they were insoluble.

Sitting at a tiny yellow escritoire in his absurdly luxurious bedroom, he played with the head of the inevitable Cupid which surmounted his inkpot, and tackled the first problem . . . Julia. She loves me, she loves me not, she loves me, she loves me not – not – not? And even if she loved him, where was he then? The idea of marriage was fantastic. He had been a crazy, drunken fool not to face it all before. A thousand problems seemed to flutter round him, filling the air with omens.

What were his assets? Nothing. Absolutely nothing. He supposed that he could go on for a year or two, dining, and accepting cigarette cases from women like his hostess, being invited to weekends – and then? When he began to show signs of wear? When a new generation of pink-faced young men appeared? He shuddered at the degradation of it all.

He stared at the pouting Cupid. How he hated Cupids! They had the faces of babies and the paunches of old men. They were damnably intrusive and impertinent. Their arrows were tipped with poison. If he ever had any money he would bar anything that looked like a Cupid from his house.

He went to his dressing-table to brush his hair before dinner. The sight of his face alarmed him; it had a deeper pallor than was warranted by the heat and the thunder which lay hiding in the stiff clouds outside. He tried to whistle, but the whistle died on his dry lips, for he felt hunted and ashamed. He was sickened with the same sort of distaste which had overwhelmed him when, at school, he had first heard, from casual lips, the revolting chronicle of sex. Once again, in the midst of this highly-developed eroticism which surged round him like a heavy perfume, he became a boy, timid and shrinking from a battle which he felt to be hopeless, his arms beating against the empty air.

Pathetically he endeavoured to joke about it to himself. 'Nasty old woman,' he muttered. 'Ought to be turned up and spanked and sent back to her husband. Ought to have three weeks on an island with a few Bolsheviks. Ought to . . .'

But the thing was beyond a joke. He was in the midst of it all. The spell was thick around him. Probably, had he been fitter, had he not been weary with late nights, mentally emasculated by constant drinking, to which he was not accustomed, corrupted by a universal example of licentiousness, enervated by an unwonted luxury, he might have treated it all as a vastly entertaining procedure, allowed Lady Hardcastle to come to his room, tickled her playfully under the chin, and dismissed her unsatisfied, telling her to be a good girl. That was what a healthy young man would have done – unless he had packed his trunks and departed by the next train.

But Brian was no longer a healthy young man. He was spoiled

in body and soul. He still possessed his exceptional good looks, but that was about all. His courage in the face of difficulties had gone, for the simple reason that his belief in the essential value of life had been taken from him. He believed in nothing – nothing. He loved nothing, except Julia, and even that love was a form of agony more bitter than the rest.

Dinner was over, and they were together in a long room lined with mirrors. Julia had gone outside. The night seemed hotter than ever.

Brian lay on the sofa and listened to Anne's singing. Her voice was like herself: it was infinitely suggestive. It was an entirely animal voice, deep-rooted in the body. One felt that, had a photograph been taken of her at that moment, the voice itself would actually have appeared on the negative, after the fashion of those psychic photographs which show a thread of protoplasm emerging from the mediums. It seemed to curve round him, stretching out tentacles of sound, exploring his mind, penetrating his body.

She sang, too, the type of song that one would expect her to sing:

> 'Te souviens-tu, o Romeo, te souviens-tu
> Des beaux soirs en sang sur Verone
> Et de l'Adige vert et jaune?
> Te souviens-tu
> Du jardin frais
> Et des fontaines
> Et des Cypres
> Et des palais rivaux et verrouilles de paines
> Avec leurs herses et leurs chaines?'

Never before had he realized how appalling a woman can be. Appalling, because desire, to a woman of this type, was a drug. She allowed it to saturate her. She welcomed its advances, she moved lazily and luxuriantly in the swell of its tide. No man had ever been so possessed. A man's passion might cut like a sword, or burn in a sudden destructive flame, but it could never attain to the proportions of a disease.

'Do come over here.'

He tried to smile. 'I'm so terribly comfortable on the sofa.'

'Shall I join you?'

He rose to his feet quickly. At any other moment he would have felt the situation to be extremely ludicrous.

'No. You've got to go on singing.'

He stood by her at the piano. She struck a chord, then paused.

'Damn,' she whispered. 'My bracelet's come undone. Be an angel.'

She lifted her arm. The coolness of the coarse emeralds was refreshing to his finger-tips. He fumbled with the clasp, thinking, 'This is an old trick.'

'Clumsy.'

Her head was close to his, and as he raised his eyes their lips almost met. He looked at her with an expression that seemed to plead dumbly to be left alone. She found it intensely attractive.

The clasp was fastened; he released her hand. 'Please go on singing.'

'I'm tired of songs about love,' with the accent on the 'songs.' 'The great thing about life is to love – not to waste time singing about it.'

'Well, sing about hate.'

'It's funny you should say that.'

'Is it? Why?'

'Because you hate me so much.'

Her hand was stretched out towards his. He shifted his fingers and laughed nervously.

'That's absurd.'

'Is it?'

Neck back, eyes drooping, lips half-parted. 'Oh, I want to tell you you're foul,' thought Brian to himself. 'I want to tell you that you're undignified, and contemptible, and that I hate you.' But he only said:

'Lady Hardcastle. It's terribly rude of me, but I'm going to leave you now. I've got a nasty headache.'

'Poor darling.' She was smiling and her eyes were glistening. 'It'll be better soon.'

'If you go and lie down, I'll bring you some eau-de-Cologne.'

'Please don't bother.'

'It isn't any bother.'

She struck a chord. And he escaped.

He had been in his room half an hour, leaning out of the window, listening. He heard the voices of Anne and Julia raised as though in some fierce argument. A few words drifted up, which seemed to have a sinister, horrible meaning. For a moment he listened in wide-eyed fright; then he shut the window.

The acuteness of his senses almost frightened him. The thin rustle of the leaves outside was a clap of thunder. The scent of the roses was overpowering. He hated the moonlight for bathing the gardens in so glaring a radiance; and he hated the voices below.

The voices below. Julia and Anne, Anne and Julia. Julia and Anne. Angry voices. Arguing about him. Was ever situation more contemptible?

The voices ceased. There was a long pause. He waited for a knock at the door. It came.

Here was Julia. She stood there in the doorway, the light shining behind her, outlining the smooth surface of her arms and shoulders, giving them a ghostly radiance.

'Can I come in?'

'Darling. Of course.'

His heart was thumping, thumping against his shirt. Why had she come? Had she come because . . . Had she come from Anne? From Anne? Was she still playing that woman's game?

He did not go towards her. He walked to the mantelpiece and poured himself out a drink.

'Julia. There's something I want to say.'

For a fraction of a second she frowned. Then: 'Do give me a cigarette first.'

'There are some in the box by your side.'

With a shrug of her shoulders, she stretched out her arm and took one.

'Would it be troubling you too much to ask for a match?'

Impatiently he struck one and put it between her fingers. He did not wish her to see how his hand was shaking.

Almost he felt inclined to laugh. One tries to talk seriously, and – lo, a cigarette must be lit first. Always these cigarettes. Could one never escape from them? They burned away one's life; they stifled one with their smoke. He had a cigarette between his own fingers at the moment. Irritably he threw it away.

'You seem *distrait*.'

'I am.'

'Why?'

He looked at her and smiled. There was a quality in the smile which did not please her, for she turned away.

'Anyway,' she said, 'you're a crashing success with our hostess.'

He made no reply. He was waiting for her next remark. His fists were tightly clenched.

'Did you hear me, darling?'

'Yes. I heard.'

'Well?' She raised her eyebrows. 'Why don't you answer?'

'What do you expect me to say? That I'd been a crashing failure? Or a crashing bore? Or a crashing angel?'

She laughed. 'Oh, don't be silly. You've got a headache. Run along to Anne and she'll take it away for you.'

There was a long pause before he said: 'Do you mind repeating that?'

'Darling, you're getting deaf. I said, "Run along to Anne and she'll take it away for you."'

He leant back his head and closed his eyes. Instinctively he felt this was the knock-out blow. This was the thing he had been waiting for – his *coup de grâce*. Misery and anger fought in his heart, and misery being the child of slower step, anger won. He turned and brought his fist down with a crash on the table.

'So it *was* true!'

'What was true?'

'What I heard in the library.'

Instantly she, too, threw off the mask.

'So you've been listening, have you?'

'Yes, I have. It seems to me the most honourable occupation anybody has in this house.'

'And what did you hear?'

'If I heard right . . .' He could not finish the sentence.

'If! If! So there's an if in it, is there?'

'No. I'm damned afraid there isn't.'

'Oh – swearing? That's hardly the little innocent, is it?'

He took a step towards her. Frightened, she withdrew.

'Now, once and for all, we're going to talk.'

'There's nothing to talk about.'

'There's everything to talk about. Put down that cigarette. We'll get some fresh air.'

Insolently she puffed the smoke in his face. Without a word, he seized her wrists, took the cigarette from her fingers and threw it into the fireplace.

'Now.'

'Yes, now.' She was breathing quickly. There was hatred in her eyes.

'You want me to go to Anne Hardcastle's room, don't you?'

'Yes.'

'Why?'

'That's none of your business.'

'Why, I ask you.'

Again he was a step nearer.

'Why? Why? Why?' she cried. 'Oh, stop this ridiculous scene. It's getting on my nerves.'

'It'll have to. For once in a way you're going to forget your nerves. You're going to face facts.'

'This piffling melodrama,' she muttered.

'Melodrama? Yes. It is a melodrama. A pretty dirty one too.'

'I see.'

Ridiculously, as in all human arguments, there came a pause, stemming the flow of passion, bringing them back again to the status of normal human beings. But the atmosphere was too electric for this to be more than a few seconds' grace. Once more they drew their swords, all the more highly wrought because of this instant's return to the normal.

'You haven't answered my question.'

'I'm not going to.'

'Shall I answer it for you?'

'If you please. It doesn't interest me.'

'You want me to go to Anne Hardcastle's room' – he spoke very slowly and deliberately – 'because you want me to . . . to make . . . love. . . .'

Each word was like a blow which he was striking against his own heart. But she merely regarded him with unabated calm.

'How amazingly intelligent you're getting.'

'So it's true.'

'Perfectly true.'

He gazed at her, his hands raised above his head, feebly, in desperation. Misery filled him like a poison, contorting his face, his limbs, stabbing his heart with pain.

'But, Julia – Julia . . .'

'Oh, for heaven's sake, *what*?'

'Julia!'

'Are we always to be so utterly virtuous?'

'But it's filthy,' he cried, his voice rising with hysteria. 'It's nauseating. I wouldn't believe that any human being . . .'

'No human being is any more nauseating than any other. I fail to see what the fuss is about. If you can't take a little trouble to help me out of rather an unpleasant situation . . .'

He looked at her dumbly. Anger was slowly lighting up her face, painting a deep glow on her cheeks, a flush round her neck.

He tried to say, 'You used to love me,' but the words stuck in his throat. He could only whisper them. Yet she heard.

'I used to love you? Why, I can't imagine.'

She turned to go.

'Julia,' he whispered again.

'Oh – what is it? What have we got to say to one another now? The first thing I ask you in my life you refuse. Well, it's the last time I shall ask.'

'But anything – anything in the world . . . but –'

'But the one thing one happens to ask.'

'You don't know me. You don't know one little thing about me. And I thought I'd told you everything.'

'What *are* you?' she laughed hysterically. 'A pretty boy. Not quite so pretty as he was, but still pretty enough. And rather spoilt, too, isn't he? Thinks because he's been asked to dine a few times, and has bought a new suit or two that he's everything that's most *chic*. Thinks he's irresistible. Thinks he's – oh, God knows what!'

'Go on.'

'Yes.' Her voice was almost screaming now. 'Well, let me tell you that you're merely rather a vulgar second-rate reporter. That and nothing more. Why the devil any of us took the faintest notice of you I don't know. You're merely one of hundreds of young men who occasionally amuse us. Where they come from, where they go to, I don't care. Nobody cares. They disappear after a time. That's all. Well, you've had a long run for your money. You can disappear. And the sooner you disappear the better. Good night.'

CHAPTER TWENTY-SIX

T HE season was ended, and the vulgar month of August was everywhere in evidence. Blinds were being drawn, one by one, in the windows of Grosvenor Square, like lids lowered over eyes that had grown glassy with sparkling too late into the night. Once more the few remaining members of White's Club glared suspiciously at their fellow-members in the St. James's and Boodles' who, for reasons best known to themselves, had not departed to Scotland or the Lido. Once more the restaurants were deserted save for a few Americans, wandering like lost sheep among a surfeit of stale *hors d'œuvres*.

London, in fact, was empty – quite empty. You might have felt inclined to doubt the fact, seeing the black throngs of pedestrians in the Strand, the buses roaring down that dear little valley in Piccadilly, the wagons, and lorries and taxis cavorting dizzily about the merry-go-round of Hyde Park Corner. You might have felt inclined to say, 'London is as full as ever.' But how sadly would you be lacking in taste!

These are not *real* creatures, these creatures of the bus and the pavement. They are ghosts. They have no moral or physical reason for existence. They are Robots, phantoms, ideas – what you will, but they are not *real*. Occasionally, through the crowded solitude, a Rolls-Royce glides disdainfully, and inside it, perhaps, you may see a real person, with real paint on her face and real pearls round her neck. But, oh! how lonely she is! as lonely as though she were in the desert.

And somewhere amid this crowd of ghosts, in his little office in Fleet Street, Brian was working. You know enough about his state of mind to excuse me from further elaborating it. It may be remarked, however, that in his passage between the first and last chapters of this book he has grown considerably older in appearance. His face is thinner, there is a droop about his mouth, and his eyes seem darker and more deeply set.

He was back at his old job, writing paragraphs. A suitable occupation indeed, for a tragic comedian. To fawn and smirk and lie and prate about the great ones whose littleness he knew so well! To write sycophantic nonsense, in a vulgar news-sheet, around a name which he had lately breathed to the stars! To pretend a lackeyed respect for those whom he knew to be contemptible and obscene! Oh, God! – if he could but tell the truth! If instead of his specious platitudes he could take up his pen and dip it in bitter aloes, and give to the world a few of the facts which seemed to have shrivelled his own heart. That would be worth while indeed! The idea dominated him. He laughed out loud, startling the grimy office boy, and wrote, so quickly that the words flowed together as though they were molten with anger:

'Amusing, isn't it, quite terribly amusing, the affair which Lady Julia Cressey has just had with that strange young man, Brian Elme? Who Mr. Elme was, nobody seems to have known or cared, but he was one of those people that one meets positively everywhere nowadays, who seem to imagine that they can know anybody merely because of their appearance.

'It really was delicious to see the way she managed him. They tell me that he actually used to cry at her feet. And all the time, of course, she was merely amused by him, because he was so charmingly gauche, and did the wrong thing at the right moment with quite exceptional regularity. Eh bien! It's over. And Lady Julia is in Scotland, looking too lovely in all sorts of tweeds. They say she has found dozens of new lovers, who are more than compensating her for the loss of dear Brian . . .

He threw the paper on the floor and began another. It seemed to be a way of working off a great deal of perilous energy.

'*How pretty the Hon. Maurice Cheyne looked when he went to Mrs. Grindhaven's Ball dressed as a woman! Really, I think it a most admirable idea, don't you, dearest? I could not conceive what that little group of old-fashioned people on the stairs meant when they said that they thought he ought to be shot! Fancy being shot for wearing a quite lovely Molyneux dress, with an exquisite phallic design in diamante round the waist! After all, he is a deliciously girlish creature, and in these days of self-expression one knows how dangerous it is to repress one's natural instincts. I only hope that lots of charming young men will soon be following his example . . .*'

The scene of a month ago, in the café, flashed through his mind, and again he wrote:

'*That fine example of the British aristocracy, Lord William Motley, has a charming scheme for carrying the cocaine which is so necessary to his existence. He keeps it in the top of a long walking-stick, in a tiny phial of onyx and platinum, and after each little sniff his epigrams become more brilliant than ever. I expect we shall all be copying him soon, shan't we, darling? After all, life is too exhausting to allow us to carry on without just a little stimulant, even if the doctors do say it is naughty of us.*'

'*I was really shocked the other day to read in some horrid Bolshevik paper a suggestion that it really did not matter whether "we" carried on or not. How amazing those Labour people are! What would all the darling little night clubs do without us? And the poor sturgeons? And Mr. Cartier? All nature would be upset if it weren't for "us." Roses would be forced to bloom in season, and diamonds would lie all cold and dirty in the clay, without any of those sweet black men to dig them up and bring them to us. The dear geese would be bored to death if nobody wanted any more foie-gras, and really, one knows that the footmen would quite go to the dogs. . . .*'

He stopped writing, suddenly realizing that he could not put even his bitterness on to paper. His little paragraphs, instead of being the searing, vitriolic things which he intended, still remained 'gossip' paragraphs. The power of expression was denied him.

He covered his eyes with a hand that shook and sweated. He would never be a writer, he told himself. Not for him the bright balance of words, the stabbing sentence, the phrase that rolled with the echo of thunders from infinite skies. 'At least,' he thought, 'my experience might have given me that. At least sorrow might have made me articulate.' But no.

He bit his lip, and laid down his pen.

The door opened, and through it Mrs. Gossett peeped her head. She was in fine fettle this afternoon, and had been cooing over the telephone to such an extent that she could seldom obtain the right number until after repeated applications. However, conversations with 'wrong numbers' were among Mrs. Gossett's most ardent delights, especially when the wrong numbers proved to be men. She would blush, and grip the receiver with feverish fingers, murmuring, 'Oh, I'm *so* sorry. Did I? Yes, *aren't* they?' And sometimes, if she were feeling very daring, and there was any audience to hear her, she would say, to her unseen friend, with wide-open eyes, 'What do you *mean*?' After which she would replace the receiver, and make breathless remarks about 'men.'

This time, she tiptoed up to Brian, and suddenly tapped at his desk. He started violently.

'Oh, Mr. Elme! Nervy – nervy!'

He put his hand over what he had been writing, and tried to smile.

'You startled me.'

She held out a reproachful finger. 'Too many late nights,' she cried. '*I* know.'

'That's not it,' he said, shaking his head.

'Well, what *is* it?'

'You wouldn't understand.'

This was her favourite sort of talk. 'What do you *mean*?'

'Nothing.'

Her eyes were like goggles. She scented violent improprieties.

'Have you been – I mean – that is to say – Oh, really, I *do* think, Mr. Elme . . .' She looked away, achieving a very healthy blush.

Not receiving any answer, she turned her neck slightly and looked at him out of the corner of her eye. Had he been watching her she would again have turned her head, and might even have buried her head in her hands, or flown timidly from the room. But he was staring straight in front of him, with eyes that saw nothing. So, with a sigh at so much wasted opportunity, she allowed herself to cool down a little, turned towards him, and said sweetly:

'Is your copy done?'

Again he started. His hand closed over the top sheet, crumpling it, holding it tightly.

'No. I'm afraid not yet.'

'But what are you writing?' Her curiosity was strongly aroused.

'Nothing.'

'They *look* like paragraphs.'

'They are. But they're not for publication.'

'Not for publication?'

Brian looked at her, and thought how easily one could have placed one's whole fist in her mouth.

He shook his head.

'But why not?'

'They're a little too frank.'

She gasped. She was so used to creating naughtinesses out of nothing that this open admission on his part was like a plum which was too large for her to swallow.

'Too frank! B-b-b-but . . .' Oh, the appalling ingenuousness of that stutter!

'You don't *mean* . . .' she hissed.

'Yes. I do.'

She giggled nervously. 'But really, I might have *seen*. And I do think it's terribly odd to – to write – indeed, I don't know what you've written, but if it's what I think – n-n-not that I'm thinking at all, really . . .' She paused, out of breath. 'Oh, why do you look at me like *that*?'

'Like what?'

'Oh, Mr. Elme, really! I don't know what I ought to say. It's most difficult. I really think you might remember . . . I mean . . . I'm not shocked, oh no, but after all . . .' It was too much for her. It was really unkind of anybody to give her so large and delicious a plum to swallow all at once. One could not possibly manage it. And so, with a toss of her head, and a look that was meant to express outraged innocence, dark knowledge, enticement and discouragement simultaneously, she darted from the room.

As Brian left his office, at about seven o'clock, he realized from a certain liveliness in the streets that it was an anniversary of something or other. A few people waved flags. Across the street a trio of young men were singing, a little sheepishly, 'It's a long, long way to Tipperary.' Of course. August 4th. The war. The *great* war.

There is something faintly vulgar about anniversaries. Independence day is far from exclusive, and the only people commemorating Guy Fawkes (who, in case we have forgotten, conferred a somewhat dubious benefit upon mankind by failing to blow up the Houses of Parliament) are the lowest urchins of the gutter.

But Brian wanted vulgarity, wanted it passionately, the very stuff and smell of it. And after dinner, during which he drank far too much, he set out in a tram to the other side of the river, and got it.

Do you know Great Charlotte Street? It runs away from the Ring at Blackfriars, where so many burly noses are broken on Thursdays, and so much plebeian blood stains the sawdust. On every holiday night, the pavements of Great Charlotte Street are lined with booths, selling every conceivable object, and the marketing populace becomes a pandemonium lit by the crude flares of gas and naphtha.

Thither Brian a little unsteadily wended his way, guided by the memory that in the old days he and Walter had sometimes wandered there, exploring the pubs, buying absurd trophies from the more rickety barrows.

To-night, the chaos, the noise, the glare, the smell seemed intensified. Under a harsh white light, that turned every face to chalk, a gaunt man was crying in a fierce wail, '*Eels all alive, all alive. Any' ow you like. They're all alive.'* And then his red hand delved into a bucket, extracted a slimy wriggling horror, and, in one shuddering moment, cut off its living head, slitting its back with a single movement, while spurts of brownish blood stained his sleeve.

Brian watched, fascinated, and went to have another drink. When he came out, the crowd was denser than ever. He wandered up the stalls. There were doughnuts at two a penny – 'Something you *can* enjoy,' and barrows of jars containing vermilion pickled cabbage and gherkins. There were slabs on which reposed rabbits, with flesh like wet clay, decorated by pieces of desolate fur. There were bright tin kettles, and stalls of fluttering lace, and a great rushing and shouting where they were selling jellied eels in white bowls, at twopence a portion.

There was a sort of peace here, in this crowd. These people had not time to worry about the sort of things which had been worrying him. They were too busy wondering if they would be able to afford a Sunday dinner, or to pay for their next week's rent. He caught a little of their own clear spirit.

Besides, at every turn there was something new. A dwarf holding up his arm, from which hung many strings of white tape, barrels of 'Ice Gems,' biscuits with little hard sugar tops in arsenic green, a man flicking his macaroons with a brush of gay feathers, a tired girl trying to sell pots of aspidistras, frightened birds in their cages, shut-eyed and trembling, parrots, pink and gay, shabby, pathetic canaries.

There were quick bursts of colour – a load of tomatoes, glittering like enamelled balls, piles of soap, purple and jade and orange, and daisies in the gaudiest tints of summer. And always the barrel-organs pealed, and the crowd on the pavement grew thicker and the lights were more wildly distracting.

A sudden flare of red, and smell of blood, and he was before a butcher's shop. A raucous voice bawled out, 'Go on. Keep on keepin' on. That's all you got to do. You don't want to worry. I don't. 'Ullo, 'ullo, 'ullo. *There's* beef for yer.' And next door a rival merchant cried, 'Quality, quali*tee*. Abserlootly the prettiest bit of sirloin you ever see.'

The red turned to pink, and he was by a sweet stall. Here glittering masses of walnut cream chips, London rock, and coco-nut ice sparkled beneath the jets. By the side of the stall a bunch of ugly children protruded pink tongues, licking carmine ice-cream. Like an immense cornelian, a glass barrel of orangeade glittered against the gas.

Strange scraps of conversation came to his ears.

'Tied a bit o' string round 'is neck, I did. That's the last of 'im.'

'I wouldn't go to church with that woman if you paid me a dollar.'

'Don't believe 'e *can* work.'

'She 'ad a glass of bitter and I 'ad a glass of stout. Did us good, it did.'

And still the barrel-organs, throbbing on the air like tom-toms, and the cheap cracked gramophones making strident cries into the street.

Another drink. Oh – this was good – better far than the streets of the west with their smug brilliance and their careful costliness. For endless was the pageant which unrolled itself here beneath the aloof skies of night. There was a little man with a bowl in which floated twenty-four white ducks. There was a boy selling the champion fly-catcher – two a penny. A specimen, covered with greasy, grisly insects hung from his arm. There were 'men's strong pants and vests – 1*s*. 11½*d*.,' and masses of white china, coarsely splashed with the price in blue chalk. At one stall a woman was squeezing a steaming rag over a row of beetroots, at another a girl was trying on a pair of cheap shoes, balancing on the curb, waving a slim foot before the bright eyes of local youths.

He paused before a window bearing the strange legend, 'The lady in the window wishes you to know that she has obtained great benefit from Jones's hair lotion.' Beyond the legend sat a female with hair down to her knees, gazing with an expression of acute boredom at the gaping crowd.

He had a longing to buy everything. Who would not want these bright balloons, painted with a map of the world, with the British Empire splashed so generously in red that Canada, for example, almost infringed upon Mexico? And who could resist these rolling wagons of fruit and vegetables, with pomegranates at a halfpenny, sliced through the centre, ruby red? And luscious plums, warranted English, at threepence a pound? And these cabbages split in half, revealing a creamy, complex centre? And these round, sleek onions, 'sound Spanish,' whose praises the swarthy man with earrings was singing so lustily?

This was England. This would go on, triumphant, coarse, obscene, vital, long after Lord William, Maurice, Julia and the rest of them had retired to their futile tombs. He felt more than exhilarated. He felt tearful – seized with an absurd nationalism that made him sing out loud.

And – as you will have observed – a little drunk. More than a little. For here he was stumbling through the door of yet another bar, a bar which in the old days he had often visited with Walter, more in sorrow than in anger.

He found his way to the counter. But before he got there, his tired, confused legs seemed to give way. He found himself sitting on somebody's knee. Amiably he looked round. His heart stopped.

Yes. It was Walter.

'You never did know how to get drunk, did you?'

Angel of tact! He tried to get up. Walter steadied him.

'Can't sit here like this.'

He was guided to the seat. Utterly weary he buried his face in his fingers. The room was going round. The world was going round. He was hot and cold. It was the end and the beginning. He put out his hand. Another hand gripped it.

'Don't go.'

''Course I won't.'

'I want you – awfully.'

'Right-o.'

'Lots to say.'

'Yes.'

They remained there, without speaking. A cool wind blew through the window, making an ineffectual effort to dissipate the thick fog of smoke which hung round the room like a pall. The air was insufferable. A gramophone bawled:

'You'd better not
You're getting hot
Getting away with a terrible lot.'

A momentary pause.
Brian – thickly, 'What about getting along?'
Walter took his arm.

CHAPTER TWENTY-SEVEN

'OH last regret . . . regret shall die!'
As a matter of fact, it is a comparatively early regret. The old cling to their griefs, in a sort of desperate emotional loneliness, as though afraid of being left without even sorrow as a companion. The young can throw them off. And Brian, though we must bid him farewell, was still absurdly young. His regrets had died. He was, in fact, exactly as we first met him.

He lay in bed. The sunlight poured in on the sheets, golden and generous, but still gentle with the cool airs of morning. A slender finger of light lit upon the old green counterpane, which, on the other side of the room, covered the sleeping figure of Walter.

Brian stretched his limbs. Gee! It was good to be alive this morning. He took in a deep breath of the sweet air and felt the blood coursing through his lungs, down to the tips of his fingers, along his eager legs, up again to his funny excited brain. One oughtn't to be lying in bed like this. In a few minutes one would get up and put on some flannel trousers and scamper with Walter over the clean-swept streets, into the mists of Hyde Park, and splash with a whirl of white and silver into the Serpentine. The first bathe of the year. Lord! he would get up and give Walter a clout on the head for snoring like a sick elephant.

There was a noise outside the door. It was Mrs. Pleat. She'd get the shock of her life when she saw Walter was back. He lay very still, waiting.

The door opened softly, and she peeped in. In an instant her mournful but searching eye had noticed the familiar figure sleeping on the floor. She went up to it, bent over and sniffed. For a moment her underlip protruded itself, and then tightened back again, as though drawn by elastic.

'So 'e's come back.'

Brian nodded.

''Bout time, too, if you arsk me,' she said darkly, and again disappeared.

There was the sound of dishes being taken from racks, the gurgle of water being poured into a kettle, the sudden pop and sigh of a gas-jet.

Then, a shuffle of footsteps, and once more Mrs. Pleat appeared.

She stood in the door, and regarded the recumbent figure of Walter with infinite meaning, and profound melancholy.

'It's Toosday,' she said.

NEW AND FORTHCOMING TITLES FROM VALANCOURT BOOKS

R. C. ASHBY (RUBY FERGUSON)	He Arrived at Dusk
FRANK BAKER	The Birds
WALTER BAXTER	Look Down in Mercy
CHARLES BEAUMONT	The Hunger and Other Stories
DAVID BENEDICTUS	The Fourth of June
PAUL BINDING	Harmonica's Bridegroom
JOHN BLACKBURN	A Scent of New-Mown Hay
	Broken Boy
	Blue Octavo
	The Flame and the Wind
	Nothing But the Night
	Bury Him Darkly
	The Household Traitors
	Our Lady of Pain
	The Face of the Lion
	The Cyclops Goblet
	A Beastly Business
THOMAS BLACKBURN	The Feast of the Wolf
JOHN BRAINE	Room at the Top
	The Vodi
JACK CADY	The Well
BASIL COPPER	The Great White Space
	Necropolis
HUNTER DAVIES	Body Charge
JENNIFER DAWSON	The Ha-Ha
RONALD FRASER	Flower Phantoms
STEPHEN GILBERT	The Burnaby Experiments
MARTYN GOFF	The Plaster Fabric
	The Youngest Director
	Indecent Assault
STEPHEN GREGORY	The Cormorant
CLAUDE HOUGHTON	I Am Jonathan Scrivener
	This Was Ivor Trent
GERALD KERSH	Nightshade and Damnations
	Fowlers End
	Night and the City
	On an Odd Note

Selected Eighteenth and Nineteenth Century Classics

ANONYMOUS	Teleny
	The Sins of the Cities of the Plain
GRANT ALLEN	Miss Cayley's Adventures
JOANNA BAILLIE	Six Gothic Dramas
EATON STANNARD BARRETT	The Heroine
WILLIAM BECKFORD	Azemia
MARY ELIZABETH BRADDON	Thou Art the Man
JOHN BUCHAN	Sir Quixote of the Moors
HALL CAINE	The Manxman
MARIE CORELLI	The Sorrows of Satan
	Ziska
CAROLINE CLIVE	Paul Ferroll
BARON CORVO	Stories Toto Told Me
	Hubert's Arthur
GABRIELE D'ANNUNZIO	The Intruder (L'innocente)
JOHN DAVIDSON	Earl Lavender
THOMAS DE QUINCEY	Klosterheim
ARTHUR CONAN DOYLE	Round the Red Lamp
BARON DE LA MOTTE FOUQUÉ	The Magic Ring
H. RIDER HAGGARD	Nada the Lily
CHARLES JOHNSTONE	Chrysal (2 vols)
CAROLINE LAMB	Glenarvon
FRANCIS LATHOM	The Midnight Bell
SOPHIA LEE	The Two Emilys
SHERIDAN LE FANU	Carmilla
M. G. LEWIS	The Monk
EDWARD BULWER LYTTON	Eugene Aram
FLORENCE MARRYAT	The Blood of the Vampire
RICHARD MARSH	The Beetle
	The Goddess: A Demon
	The Complete Sam Briggs Stories
BERTRAM MITFORD	Renshaw Fanning's Quest
JOHN MOORE	Zeluco
OUIDA	Under Two Flags
ELIZA PARSONS	Castle of Wolfenbach
WALTER PATER	Marius the Epicurean
ROSA PRAED	Fugitive Anne
BRAM STOKER	The Lady of the Shroud

Lightning Source UK Ltd.
Milton Keynes UK
UKHW040613231219
355886UK00002B/459/P

9 781939 140357